I0760852

CADILLAC TRACKS

RON FISHER

Fisher, Ron. Cadillac Tracks (J.D. Bragg Series Book 1). Published by MysteryRow.

ISBN-13: 978-1-949073-02-7 (hard cover)
ISBN-13: 978-1-949073-03-4 (paperback)
ISBN-13: 978-1-949073-00-3 (Kindle)
ISBN-13: 978-1-949073-01-0 (epub)

"The battle line between good and evil runs
through the heart of every man."

Aleksandr Solzhenitsyn

This book is dedicated to Romie and Ruby.
Without them I wouldn't be here. Literally.

ACKNOWLEDGMENTS

This is my first novel, and I hope there will be many more to come. But just getting to this point took a lot of work—and a lot of help. So, I'd like to thank the people who so freely helped me with the journey: Hal Fisher, Wil Fisher, and Travis Fisher for their design and production skills and knowing about mysterious things like metadata and HTML. Michael Fisher, Mackenzie Squires, Jamie Squires, and Chip Fisher for their invaluable and talented help, love, and encouragement. I couldn't have done this without you.

PROLOGUE

Eastatoe Valley, Upstate South Carolina, February 2016.

The Bluetick hound came out of the woods behind Cecil Hood's farm and stood in the thin shadow of a leaf-bare sweet gum. She stabbed her pointed nose into the air several times and then followed the airborne scent she was tracking into the open pasture and toward a weathered old barn.

Back in the woods, a young voice called her name. The dog turned and looked, torn for a moment between the familiar call and primordial instinct. The urge to follow the hunt prevailed, and she moved on, the hair on her back bristling to an uneven ridge along her spine.

A small, sandy-haired boy came running out of the trees behind her.

"Damn you, Jody," the boy said, "you get back here right now."

He watched in dismay as the dog ignored him. They had strayed too far this time and were gone too long, even for a Saturday. But when Jody picked up the scent of a coon back in the woods and took off after it, the boy followed in a run without thought of place or time or what his dad would do to him if they weren't home by suppertime.

Jody finally treed the animal in a fork of a giant poplar. The boy stood and listened to the music of her baying while the old coon stared down at them. After a while, the boy managed to tear the dog away, and they made their way home. Along the way, Jody picked up a new scent and was off again. Now, there they were, on Mr. Hood's property, a mile from home, and the sun going down.

The boy watched as the dog began to stalk something near the barn. Some kind of old farm machinery sat on the ground beneath the open loft; something was draped over it—a sack of fertilizer or a cover perhaps, but it was too far away for the boy to tell. He wondered whether a cat was lying on it. Jody would chase a cat almost as quick as a coon.

"C'mon, Jody. C'mon girl, let's go!" the boy coaxed, trying to create an excitement in his voice that might lure her away. Killing Mr. Hood's cat—or worse, a chicken—would surely get his hide tanned if his daddy found out. He turned and ran back toward the trees, all the while looking over his shoulder, calling and whistling, hoping Jody would join the game. Finally, the dog gave in and bounded after him, the bond of a boy and his dog winning over older, wilder instincts. They ran into the woods, the dog on the boy's heels, leaping and barking, caught up in a newer, more light-hearted chase.

In the darkened door of the loft, the man standing in the shadows inched closer to the opening and watched them retreat into the forest. He stood and listened as the dog's excited yelps faded into distant echoes. Only then did he look down at the old man lying prostrate across the disc harrow on the ground below. *He probably would have died just from the fall,* the man thought, but the edges of the machine's circular blades sharpened to turn the hardest earth, made his death certain. One of the steel discs had cleaved Cecil Hood's skull from his eyebrow to his hairline, the pooling blood turning the Carolina clay underneath an even deeper shade of red.

CHAPTER ONE

Atlanta, Georgia, Monday, April 4th. 2016

"John David, Mr. Lowe would like to see you in his office."

It was Burt Lowe's secretary. "Now?" I asked.

"Yes, now."

I hung up the phone and took the stairs up to Lowe's office two at a time, not because I was that eager to see him, but because I couldn't stand the suspense of why the publisher of *SportsWord* magazine—and the man who signed my paychecks—wanted to see *me*.

A summons to Burt Lowe's office rarely bodes well. Rumors of layoffs were rife around the coffee machine, but they always were. Competition was stiff, and the ever-shrinking business of the printed word was always a concern. Were it not for our online version, the magazine would probably have gone under. But if I were getting chopped, I couldn't see Burt Lowe swinging that axe; he'd leave that to Joe Dennis, my editor and immediate boss. Burt Lowe dwelled in the managerial stratosphere where he could pay as little attention as possible to those who wrote for his national sports magazine, preferring to deal with issues he actually had a talent for, like bottom lines and sales figures. To him, writers were just entries in a column entitled "overhead expenses." Not that I was that much of an expense. Nobody ever got rich working at *SportsWord.*

However, despite the slightly above-poverty-level salary, I liked my job and didn't want to lose it. For one thing, I wasn't stuck on a single-sport beat as I had been in my previous positions. Covering one sport, day in and day out, took a professionalism I didn't seem to have. I was easily bored, and as history has proven, when I get bored, I get into trouble. Boredom was the breeding ground for most of my problems with ex-employers—the emphasis here on "ex."

At *SportsWord,* I was considered a general sports journalist. I followed the story, regardless of the sport, which gave me a broader, more news-rich field in which to work, and a chance to do honest investigative reporting, the one thing that kept my brain from atrophying.

I also liked Atlanta and didn't want to leave. Atlanta was almost hometown to me since I grew up just over the state line in South Carolina.

Lydia Wells, Lowe's elderly secretary, sat at her desk outside his door, watching me approach. She gave me the once-over with an expression that said my faded jeans, Vortex Bar and Grill T-shirt, and worn Chuck Taylor's were beneath any civilized standard of sartorial acceptance.

I couldn't help thinking how much she reminded me of Doris Mozingo, my grandfather's longtime secretary in South Carolina. They both shared the distinction of being the only women I knew whose mere presence could intimidate me into a condition just short of paralysis. On those rare occasions as a kid when my grandfather allowed my sister and me to visit the small-town newspaper he published, Doris Mozingo always made me feel like she could see right into my head and read any acts of mischief that lurked there as easily as she could read that week's paper. She made me want to confess to something, whether I was guilty or not. Lydia Wells wielded the same power. This morning she looked especially dour, her silver hair pulled back and pinned so tightly to her head that it gave her eyes an Asian tilt—a Chinese dowager in a pinstriped pants-suit. I wondered if she enjoyed turning a six-foot-three, two-hundred-and-twenty-pound man into an errant schoolboy.

She stabbed a red-tipped thumb toward the door behind her. "They're waiting for you."

I took a step and then stopped. "*They?*" I said. "Who else is in there?"

"The best way to find that out is to go in," she said, showing me the top of her head, already busy with something else.

I had been dismissed.

On the walls around her desk, framed covers of famous athletes from past issues of *SportsWord* looked down on me as if they knew something that I didn't, and it wasn't good. With that uncomforting thought, I tapped once on the door of Lowe's inner sanctum and entered.

Burt Lowe was behind his desk waiting for me, elbows on the arms of his chair, pencil-thin fingers forming a tent in front of his face. I tried to read his expression but couldn't tell if he was pleased as punch to see me or sorry as hell.

"Have a seat, John David," he said, gesturing to a chair in front of his desk.

Stan Gilmore, the magazine's portly lawyer, sat in a wingback chair to one side, his eyes fixed on a spot of carpet just beyond the tips of his highly polished shoes, his several chins resting upon each other like a layer cake gone askew. He wore the expression, as always, of a man who smelled something foul.

I sensed someone behind me and turned. Seated on the sofa against the back wall was Barry Beal, the world-famous tour golfer and the subject of my latest investigative efforts. He was glaring at me like he wanted to tee me up and drive me out of Burt's window. Next to him was a natty little man in a well-tailored suit, bowtie, and large, black-rimmed glasses. I didn't know him, but something told me Stan Gilmore wasn't the only lawyer in the room.

Barry Beal was once a star on the PGA tour, but now at the end of his career, he was missing more cuts than he was making. He missed the cut again at the Houston Open last Friday and flew to Atlanta over the weekend to work on his game before the Masters kicked off in Augusta this week. I was running down a tip that he assaulted—and maybe raped—a young woman at a local hotel last Saturday night.

Beal was, in my opinion, a disgrace to the game. He was long rumored to be a sexual deviant, but no one had ever been able to prove it. I planned to change that.

For a second time, Lowe asked me to sit. I gave him a raised eyebrow and sat down, angling the chair to one side so I could face them all.

"You obviously know Mr. Beal," Lowe said before gesturing to Mr. Bow Tie. "This is his attorney, Arthur Pitt."

I smiled a private smile. Could I spot them or what? Lawyer Pitt and I exchanged slight nods, Beal continued to glare, and nobody offered to shake hands. I turned back to Lowe.

"What's this all about, Burt?"

"Mr. Beal tells me you're doing a story on him. Is this true?"

"He knows I am," I said. "I tried to get an interview with him all day yesterday."

"Mr. Beal has given me his side of the story, now I'd like to hear yours," he said.

I glanced at Beal, then back at Lowe. This was beginning to feel like a poorly rehearsed play.

"Seems Mr. Beal likes to beat hell out of his dates—and who knows what else."

"That's a goddamned lie," Barry Beal said, lurching forward from the sofa.

Arthur Pitt placed a restraining hand on his arm and spoke to him in a voice too low for me to hear. Beal settled back down and resumed glowering at me.

"If you have substantiation for that accusation," his lawyer said, turning his attention to me, "you'd better produce it because you've just slandered my client."

"Oh, I have substantiation," I said, wondering if they could tell I was lying. The truth was, so far, I couldn't find the alleged victim. Without her verification, all I had to go on was a tip from a hotel bartender, who didn't witness the actual event, but he did see the woman before and after the attack.

Arthur Pitt wasted no time replying. "That is impossible, Mr. Bragg because there's simply no truth to these outrageous accusations."

"My sources say otherwise," I answered. "They say that Barry had a little after-hours match play with some chick at the Palace Hotel in Buckhead, and she lost."

"That is bloody preposterous," Beal said loudly, his words edged with the accent of his native South Africa.

"Don't dignify that with a comment, Barry," Arthur Pitt chimed in.

"Sweet young thing," I continued, looking at Beal. "Maybe half your age. One brown eye, one black. Ring a bell?"

"I'm not putting up with this," Beal said and started to get up, but again, Pitt kept him seated.

"This man tried to ruin me with his lies once before," Beal said, "and I will not allow him to do it again."

"Lies?" I said. "I witnessed that particular story with my own eyes and ears, and you know it."

"Then why did your newspaper fire you?" Beal said. "I should have sued you then. I won't make that mistake twice."

"I was fired because I worked for a chicken-shit outfit that was easily bluffed," I said. When I said that, Burt Lowe refused to meet my gaze, and I felt a sudden blast of déjà' vu.

"Gentlemen, this isn't getting us anywhere," Arthur Pitt said. "As unfortunate as that incident was, it's in the past, and the damage is done. We can only try to prevent the same thing from happening again. As you may know, this is Masters week, but Barry is so upset that he's considering withdrawing." He pointed at me. "The ridiculous accusations and insinuations this man has been making have destroyed his concentration and ability to play his best."

Beal could withdraw from any tournament he liked, but it wouldn't be because of anything I was doing. My guess was he was playing so poorly that he didn't want to face the embarrassment of failing to make the cut for the third tournament in a row.

"Will the woman in question substantiate the allegation?" Burt Lowe asked me.

"If her jaws aren't wired too tight to talk."

"A yes or no answer is what we want, John David," Stan Gilmore said.

"The story is a work in progress, for Christ's sake. I haven't been able to talk to her yet."

"And why is that?" Lowe asked.

I sighed, and I'm not a sigh'er. This was getting to me. "I can't find her," I said. "But I will."

"Do you even know her name?"

"Not yet," I said reluctantly. I saw the hint of a smile appear and then disappear on Barry Beal's face.

"So, you haven't talked to this alleged victim, you don't know her name, and you don't know where she is," Gilmore summed up. "What corroboration d*o* you have?"

It was getting hard to tell which lawyer in the room worked for *SportsWord* and which one worked for Beal. I directed my answer at Burt Lowe.

"I have a source who saw this woman with Beal in the hotel bar, all grins and giggles, then later, she's found in the parking lot with scrapes and cuts, a bloody lip, and one eye swollen shut. According to my source, Vitali Klitschko looked better after the Lenox Lewis fight."

Pitt interrupted. "The woman with Barry at the Palace bar on that particular evening was someone who simply joined him for a drink. Afterward, Barry retired to his room for the night. Alone. If something happened to her later, while she has our sympathy, Barry is in no way responsible."

"So, who is she?" I asked. "Let *her* tell me that. If she says he didn't do it, then that's the end of it." I looked over at Beal. "And pigs may fly into the Georgia Dome and crap all over the Falcons at kickoff—but hey, anything's possible."

Beal turned an even brighter shade of red and stood up. This time Pitt didn't try to stop him. "Do you see what I mean about him, Lowe?" Beal said. "You call this unbiased journalism?"

Beal looked at Lowe while pointing a stubby finger at me. "If this man represents the kind of people you have working for you, then this outfit is in serious trouble. You know where I stand; now I'd like an answer. Are you going to put a stop to this or not?"

Lowe picked up a stack of papers on his desk and moved them an infinitesimal distance, then re-stacked them neatly, his brow furrowed as if the task required his utmost concentration. He glanced at Stan Gilmore as if to draw from a friendly source of support before responding.

"Without this woman's affirming statement, or an eyewitness, we will not pursue this story any further," he finally said, never looking at me.

"This is bullshit," I began, with more on the way, but Stan Gilmore cut me off.

"We don't print rumors, John David," he said. "*SportsWord* is not a supermarket scandal sheet."

Barry Beal got up to leave and gave Lowe a hard look. "You'd better throw a rope around him," he said, gesturing toward me. "Because if I read one line about this anywhere—or hear one more word spoken about it—I'm going to assume it came from him. And I'm going to hold *all* of you responsible."

He glared at me one last time, wheeled, and stormed out the door. Arthur Pitt nodded to Lowe and Gilmore, ignored me, and followed him out.

I was the first to speak after they left. "Can you believe this guy?" I said, standing up and shoving my hands deep into my pockets. "I'm going to hold you all responsible?" Who does he think he is, the Don Corleone of golf?"

"He's won a dozen PGA tournaments, including three majors, John David," Stan Gilmore answered. That's who he is."

"Spare me the hero worship, Stan," I said. "The man's over the hill. He hasn't finished in the top ten in years. Besides that, he's a kinky son of a bitch who gets his rocks off by knocking women around."

Gilmore glared at me, probably miffed that the hired help would talk back to him in such a way. "We can't run the story based on what you've got," Gilmore said. "And that's a simple fact. You ought to know that John David."

"He's paid the girl off; I'd stake my life on it," I said. "I'll bet she's driving around right now in a new Mustang. I'm not giving up on this, guys. I've never backed off a story in my life."

"I'm well aware of that," Burt Lowe answered. "And it's that kind of attitude that's hurt you everywhere you've worked. We took a chance on you, John David. Everyone said you were trouble, but Joe Dennis stuck up for you. He said your talent far outweighed any difficulties you might present. Don't prove him wrong. Don't try to use this publication to settle an old score with Barry Beal. I won't allow it."

"I assure you I have no score to settle," I said. "Sure, Beal got me fired. But everyone who knows what an asshole he is also knows the story was true. Christ Burt, Beal hit a duck hook into the crowd at Pebble Beach and knocked a woman stone cold. When he came down the fairway to where she was lying, he asked his caddy if the cameras were on him. When he found out they weren't, he said, 'Fuck her then, find my ball.' I was standing right there. I heard him with my own ears."

"Unfortunately, none of the hundreds of spectators lining that part of the fairway heard it," Stan Gilmore broke in. "Beal claimed you made it up because you were angry that he'd snubbed you in a press conference earlier that week."

"That's not true."

"As I understand it," Gilmore continued, "you got fired because after the paper killed your story, you leaked it to a late-night TV host. He went on the air and joked about it in front of millions of people."

I had to smile at that. It was my one fond memory of the entire incident. The late show host did what my insignificant piece could never have done. He made the story famous. For weeks afterward, the phrase "fuck her then, find my ball" could be heard on golf courses across America, uttered by weekend golfers anytime an errant shot was hit, and guaranteed to get a laugh from all who heard it.

"I can find this woman, Burt," I said. "I just need a little time. He probably raped her. Her clothes were ripped, and her face was beaten and bruised. We can't let him get away with this."

Burt looked at me for a long moment, then said, "I'll give you 24 hours, John David. After that, I want you working on something else. Check out what our stringers are sending in. Somebody somewhere might be on to something you can pick up on. Or go check out the Braves tonight. The word is there's already trouble brewing between their front office and a certain highly-paid superstar who isn't pulling his weight. Go look into that."

He showed me what I guess was his most stern look and repeated, "24 hours, John David, and I mean it. Otherwise, you might no longer be employed here."

There was nothing left to say after that, so I departed. Thankfully Lydia Wells was away from her desk. I was taking this poorly, and the last thing I needed was another disapproving gaze from her. I was sure about one thing, though. I wasn't about to give up on this story, no matter how long it took.

CHAPTER TWO

Thirty minutes later, I pulled under the portico of the Palace Hotel on Peachtree Street in Buckhead, not far from the Ritz- Carleton and two of America's most exclusive shopping malls: Lenox Square, where the well-to-do shopped, and Phipps Plaza, where the even more well-to-do shopped. I tossed the keys for my aging Jeep Wrangler to a uniformed parking valet. He peered inside the car like he was considering brushing off the seat before climbing in. I was through the revolving doors and into the lobby when he finally climbed into the car.

The lobby was packed. Apparently, half of the traveling world was checking out of the posh hotel at once. A platoon of bellhops laden with luggage bore down on me, one of them striking my knee with the hard edge of a baggage cart. He didn't seem to notice and never broke stride as he sailed past. No one paid the slightest attention to my misfortune—as if tall blond men hopping around on one leg were a common sight at the Palace.

I put my foot down gently, tried some weight on it, then stood and rubbed the pain out. Eventually, I was able to limp my way through the crowd and into the hotel's cocktail lounge, where I saw Tommy Upshaw behind the bar plying his trade. After the Lowe meeting, I called the Palace to see if Upshaw was working tonight and found out he was on brunch duty today. Upshaw was my source for the Beal story; he had also been my source for a few other stories over the years. A consummate hustler and professional gossip, he seemed to end up behind the bar at hotspots frequented by people who made the news, including many famous athletes. Whether the job was at the latest chic watering hole or a hotel like the Palace, Tommy Upshaw always managed to get close to the action.

He had called me on Monday morning telling me he had something really prime that he was holding just for me. In Upshaw's parlance, that meant he wouldn't call anyone else about it if I came across with enough cash. Fifty bucks—that I could ill afford—got the story from him; now I was hoping he could add to it in a second telling.

A half-dozen people sat at the bar, all bearing the look of departing guests who needed a bit of liquid preparation before their flights to Boise, or Baton Rouge, or wherever they came from. I found a vacant stool at the end of the bar and got Upshaw's attention. He came right over.

"J.D., my man, how goes it?"

"Fine, Tommy, how are you?"

"If I was any better, they'd want a urine sample," he said.

"How 'bout a drink?" He shot a glance down the bar. "My Bloody Marys seem to be in demand this morning."

I followed his gaze. Tall red drinks were indeed lined up on the bar like fence posts. "Why not?" I said. It was early, but it had been a rough day already, and a drink sounded good.

Seconds later, a celery-festooned libation was sitting on the bar before me, with Upshaw behind it, studying me with his ferret-like eyes.

"So, you going to nail a certain golfer's ass to the wall?" he asked.

"I'm working on it. But I can't find the girl. I thought you might be able to remember something else about her."

A man down the bar thunked a fingernail against a glass to get Upshaw's attention. I waited as he prepared and served another Bloody Mary.

When Upshaw returned, he said, "I don't know, J.D., I think I told you everything."

"Tell me again," I said.

He shrugged his shoulders and said, "like I told you, Barry Beal and this chick showed up around 9:30 on Sunday night. They sat at the bar and ordered drinks."

"You said she was a looker."

"Oh yeah, a real trophy—a lot younger than him. I thought about carding her, but seeing as who she was with . . ."

"Describe her again."

Upshaw screwed up his face in thought. "Long dark hair, brown eyes.

Average height. Well-built. Went for the girly drinks. Had me slicing goddamn fruit and running the blender forever. In fact, I think she might have even bartended at one time. We got into this discussion about the right way to make a Banana Ivanov. You put both lemon *and* lime juice in it. Not too many people know that, but she did."

"What was Beal doing while you two were discussing the finer points of mixology?"

"He was working her as hard as he could. Touchy-feely, you know. Kept the drinks stacked up in front of her. He was trying to play a little grab-ass below the bar, and she was fending him off pretty well. But I guess the booze finally got to her because she ended up leaving with him."

"Did you see them get into the elevator?"

"Naw, man. But Beal was attached to her like a pilot fish when they left."

"You never caught her name?"

Upshaw shook his head. "He always called her 'love' or 'sweetheart' in that phony British accent of his."

"South African." I offered.

Upshaw gave me a puzzled look.

"Beal is from South Africa."

Upshaw fanned his fingers as if to say "whatever" and continued. "I closed up a little after midnight, and that's when I saw her in the parking lot. She'd spilled her purse all over the pavement and was looking for her car keys. I helped her gather everything up and opened her door for her. Like I told you, she looked like a plane crash survivor. She was sort of bent over, holding her ribs. One eye was swollen closed, her lip was busted, and her blouse was practically torn off. Nice tits, I might add." Upshaw seemed to lose himself in the vision.

"Then what happened?" I asked, trying to drag him back to the moment.

Upshaw shrugged and gave me a blank look. "First thing Monday morning, I called you about it. And that's it."

"I mean in the parking lot. Did she say anything to suggest she'd been raped?"

"She didn't say that, but she could've been. She certainly looked it. I asked her if she needed help, and she refused. She jumped into her car and drove off."

"What kind of car?"

"Something red and small. Not too fancy. Japanese, I think."

"Did you get a look at the license plate?"

"Hell, J.D., I didn't notice that."

"Could she have been a hooker?"

"I'd say no. I think I know them all, and I've never seen her before. Besides, she didn't look or act like a pro. She was a little too naïve."

A customer at the other end of the bar called out, and Upshaw left to attend to him. He returned just as I drained the last of the Bloody Mary. The final swallow took my breath away as a generous shot of Tabasco waiting at the bottom of the glass blazed a flaming trail down my esophagus.

"Ready for another?" Upshaw asked.

It was a moment before I could speak. "Better not," I said, "I might need my stomach for later on."

Upshaw looked hurt. "Did either she or Beal talk to anyone else here?" I asked. I was running out of questions.

"Not that I saw," Upshaw said, turning his head sideways and looking at me. "There might be something . . ."

I knew the look. He'd thought of something new to sell me. I picked up the tab and studied it briefly, then brought out a twenty and threw it down, waving off the change as if I left tips like that every day.

Upshaw deftly palmed the twenty and leaned in closer.

"Beal and this chick may work together," he said. "When they first came in, they talked about real estate and some golf development or resort he's planning to build. She seemed involved somehow. That was before Beal started hitting on her so hard." Upshaw made a face. "The man needs to work on his lines. He was downright embarrassing—totally lame repertoire."

That Beal was into the golf course design and development business wasn't exactly big news. A lot of pros were, so why not Barry Beal? However, hearing that the two might be working together *was* something.

"Did you happen to hear where he's building this place?" I asked.

Upshaw grinned. "Hearing shit is my life, bro. Someplace in South Carolina. East toe or something. I didn't quite understand that part."

"Eastatoe?" I asked, surprised. "Are you sure?"

"Would I make up a name like East toe?"

"Eas-ta-toey," I pronounced phonetically. Was that it?"

"Probably. It was something weird like that."

"It's a Cherokee name for a trout stream and the small valley it flows through in the northwestern tip of South Carolina. I grew up around there."

"No shit. Small world, huh," Upshaw said, holding up a finger to a woman waving an empty glass at him.

Before he moved off to attend to her, he added, "Come to think of it, she may even live there. She had a pretty strong hillbilly accent. I used to have a girlfriend from up that way that talked just like her. Sort of twang rather than drawl."

It was my first real lead to finding the victim of Beal's assault, and unexpectedly, it was taking me home.

CHAPTER THREE

As I left the Palace, I considered my options. I could go to South Carolina to look for Beal's assault victim—which might turn out to be a wild goose chase—and would certainly eat up the 24 hours Burt Lowe gave me, or I could call my grandfather, the one person who could probably find her easier than I could. But could I swallow my pride and set aside my bitterness to call him? The last time I asked for his help was a dozen years ago, and the stringent old man with his unyielding principles turned his back on me. Since then, we have barely spoken to each other. But if asking for his help again for the sake of expediency proved me more selfish than proud, so be it. He already thought worse things of me anyway.

I listened as the rings summoned the offices of the *Clarion*, the small weekly newspaper in Upstate South Carolina that my grandfather, the almighty Garnet Quincy Bragg, had published for all of his adult life. I fought the urge to hang up before anyone answered by telling myself this wasn't a personal call. It was business. Any path the conversation took would likely be away from the troubles that lay like a minefield between us.

Besides, once my grandfather learned that a developer was planning to skin the top off hundreds of acres of pristine countryside in his backyard, family problems would take a back seat.

As the self-proclaimed guardian of the environment in all of Upstate South Carolina, Grandfather would have a keen interest in anyone intent on uglifying the landscape. Since Eastatoe Valley was one of the loveliest spots in the county, still untouched by the developer's blade as far as I knew, he would jump into the fray with fangs and claws bared—and I hoped— locate my missing woman in the process.

Doris Mozingo, my grandfather's elderly secretary, answered after the first ring and failed to hide her surprise at hearing my voice. We exchanged brief but awkward pleasantries, then she put me on hold to break the news to Grandfather about who was on the line.

He picked up and after some hesitation, said, "This is Garnet."

He sounded tired. Or maybe just old. He was in his eighties now, but it was hard to think of him as that old. I guess I would always see him through ten-year-old eyes, the age I was when my sister Eloise and I went to live with him after both our parents were killed.

"Hello, Grandfather," I said.

"What's wrong?" he asked.

"Does something have to be wrong for me to call?"

He didn't answer; he didn't have to. He seemed to always expect the worst from me. "Relax," I said. "I haven't been arrested in a month, and I've got the coke habit down to a c-note a day."

I heard him sigh and felt a slight pang of something like regret for being a smartass. But he always brought that out in me. Or maybe I waited for him to bring it out.

"What should I think?" he said. "I never hear from you, and suddenly you call? I worry about you."

The conversation was becoming too personal. As I was more comfortable with small talk, I said, "I've never been better. How are you?"

"Fine," he answered, a question in his voice as if he were still waiting for me to deliver bad news.

"How are things at the paper?"

"Same as always."

"That old Cadillac still purring along?"

I pictured Grandfather's vintage 1959 Cadillac Eldorado, black as a hearse with tailfins like the Batmobile. It was his toy, his hobby, and his great love, and he took better care of it than he did of himself. Or anyone else, I thought, with some bitterness.

Having spanned the entire universe of small talk, I decided it was time to get to the point. "A story I'm working on has led me to your neck of the woods, and I need to talk to a young woman who I think lives there. I can't get away right now, or I'd come up there myself. I was hoping you could help me out."

It was a moment before he spoke, stunned, I supposed, that I was actually seeking his help. "What's this story about?" he asked. "Are you still working for that sports tabloid?"

He pronounced *"tabloid"* as if it were a dirty word. Garnet Bragg, the quintessential serious journalist.

"Yes, I am," I said. "The story involves a professional golfer."

"I don't know much about golf."

He said it as if he was proud of the fact—and I knew he was.

My grandfather believed that the attention given to sports in America was a monumental waste of time and intellect. I'd learned that firsthand. He never missed a school science fair, parent's day, or speech club debate, but it was a rare event when he came to one of my football games.

The sports section of the *Clarion* only covered local events, such as school sports and church softball leagues, and was written by someone with other duties that probably came first. I suspected that the only reason Grandfather ever read his sports page was to check the quality of the writing. The *Clarion's* hard news was mostly local, too, with a large portion of the paper devoted to human-interest pieces, family reunions, obituaries, and wedding announcements. The *Clarion* was about the community and for the community and had been since the day my grandfather bought it over sixty years ago. But I had to admit, when real news did come along, the *Clarion* would rise above any other dull tome from Hicksville. Grandfather's tenacious reporting and barbed editorials were the stuff of journalistic legend—and he had the Pulitzer to prove it. As a publisher, he was everything Burt Lowe was not—I would give him that.

"You want me to interview this person?"

"I just need you to help me find her, Grandfather. I'll come up there to talk to her myself if you do."

"What is her name?"

"I don't know her name or where she lives. All I know is that she's young and pretty, sporting a black eye and busted lip. I think she works for this golfer named Barry Beal," I added and told him what I thought Beal did to her. "She may have met him up there."

"*The* Barry Beal? he said. "What's he doing here? Does he have one of those new homes over on the lake?"

"You know who he is?" I asked, surprised.

"Of course, I know who Barry Beal is, John David. "I may not know much about golf, but I don't live on the dark side of the moon."

"So, do you know he's about to build a golf course and mini-mansions in Eastatoe Valley?"

He didn't speak for a moment. Then he said, "I haven't heard anything about that."

I could tell by his voice that the hook was set. This news would guarantee his help, regardless of how little he had to go on. The prospect of someone carving such a place out of peaceful little Eastatoe Valley would be as horrifying to him as ethnic cleansing.

"I just got wind of it myself," I said, "and even if Beal hasn't started construction yet, he would have been up there looking things over and making plans, probably several times. Time enough to meet and hire this girl I'm looking for."

"I find this news particularly disturbing, John David, but not really surprising," he said. "They won't stop until every square foot is graded over, built on, and fenced off."

I knew he was referring to the shores of Lake Keowee, the vast man-made lake just west of Eastatoe Valley, where gates and guards now protected multi-million-dollar homes, closing off much of a spectacularly scenic and recreational area that was once accessible to everyone, rich or poor.

"Where is this Beal located?" Grandfather asked. "I want to talk to him."

"Maybe that's not such a good idea," I quickly said. "Firstly, I don't think Barry Beal would accept a call from anyone named Bragg. I'm not exactly on his favorite-people list. And secondly, the magazine is overly nervous about lawsuits, and if they were to find out that I've shared this story with—of all people—another newsman, I could lose my job."

"If you ask me," he said, "it sounds like a job that isn't worth having in the first place."

His tone suggested there was more he could say about the choices I'd made in my life.

"It won't help me if you stir this up, Grandfather. Can't you just help find the girl and leave Barry Beal to me?"

He was silent for so long that I thought he'd hung up on me.

Finally, he said, "I'll do what I can and get back to you." Then he did hang up.

I knew all too well that Grandfather's method of pursuing a story was to wage an all-out frontal attack, and it went against his grain to accept any restrictions, even if the outcome harmed his only grandson. But I had kindled this fire and would have to take whatever heat came from it.

CHAPTER FOUR

I spent several hours at my apartment licking my wounds and feeling sorry for myself. It wasn't the first time a publisher pulled me off a story, but that didn't make it easier to accept. My only hope was that my grandfather could work a miracle for me, and soon.

At about five o'clock, I pulled myself out of my funk and decided to take Burt Lowes' advice and cover the Braves. The Mets were in town for the season opener, and first pitch was scheduled for seven-ten. It was too late for a bit of locker-room time beforehand to jaw with the players and Manager Freddie Gonzales, but I'd try to catch them after the game. Not that I would learn anything. Freddie, like his predecessor Bobby Cox, kept team problems in-house. That made the job of guys like me more difficult, but I admired them for it. At worst, I'd get to relax a little and enjoy a bit of America's favorite pastime, which was a pretty good way to end a bad day. I climbed into the jeep, took 10th Street to Interstate 75-85 South, and merged into the usual bumper-to-bumper vehicular stream, moving at a sphincter-tightening pace.

"The Ted," as Turner Field is lovingly called in honor of the former Braves owner, lay several miles south; I began an early move toward the right-hand lanes for the exit, having on several occasions over-shot it, thanks to the inhospitable refusal of Atlanta drivers to let me through.

Lunch for me was the celery stalk in Upshaw's Bloody Mary, so I was famished. I found myself looking forward to a couple of hotdogs with child-like anticipation. A warm spring evening, a cheerful crowd, and the crack of a bat could make a ballpark hotdog taste like a porterhouse.

A Lexus SUV cut in front of me from two lanes over, forcing my attention back to the traffic out of pure self-preservation. Atlanta drivers have the reputation of being among the wildest in the country, and when the traffic allows it, some of the speediest. Cars zoomed by me, switching lanes and tailgating like NASCAR veterans. I gritted my teeth, clutched the wheel, and glued my eyes to the road.

The game started with a ceremony honoring the 40th anniversary of Hank Aaron's 715th home run and had the Braves fans amped for the home opener. However, the Met's Bartolo Colon pitched seven quietly effective innings, and some timely hitting and an overturned call lifted them to a 4-0 win. The Braves Jason Heyward ended the game by watching his potential game-tying grand slam fall into Juan Lagares' glove approximately 7 feet from the center-field wall.

My foray into the Braves locker room after the game was unexciting. I didn't pick up anything juicy or untoward—in other words, nothing piqued my sensationalistic interest. I wondered if management was spiking the player's Gatorade with Prozac. I never even heard a curse word. The Braves were a squeaky-clean bunch.

It was after midnight before I made it home to my solitary little apartment in Virginia Highlands, thanks to a stop along the way at a neighborhood pub for a couple of drinks. Two months ago, I would have passed up drinks at the pub. At that time, I didn't live alone. A fiery, pint-sized Latina named Rosita Perez, a dancer with an Atlanta Modern Dance group shared my apartment and my bed. But like most of my relationships, this one eventually ran its course. That thing that always seemed to happen happened. Something slowly changed between us almost imperceptibly, like shifting sands in the desert, until one day, we found ourselves in a relationship of unrecognizable shape.

Some things about her I did miss: those marvelously sculptured legs, the indecipherable Spanish she spoke when we made love, the passion on her face when she talked about dancing. But the stark truth was, whatever I felt about her leaving, I don't think it was heartbreak. This was the narrative of my love life.

As I went around switching off lamps, I noticed the message light on the phone blinking. I punched in the voicemail code, and the AT&T computer told me I had two messages. The first one was left at 6:37 PM; I played it and heard my grandfather say, "John David, this is your grandfather," as if I wouldn't recognize his voice. An old Jim Reeves song played in the background. He would not listen to that by choice; Chopin was more his taste. I also heard the angry-cat sound of a pneumatic wrench, the kind a garage uses on lug nuts or plugs on oil pans.

"I think I have a line on your young woman," he said. "But something here has me troubled, and I'd prefer not to talk to a recording machine about it. Call me at home tonight."

That was the extent of his message. He had wasted little time getting a line on the girl. The old man still had game. But what was it that troubled him? He sounded upset; his tone was more severe than usual, if possible. Or was he just being Garnet Bragg, seeing a dagger behind every cloak, as he had a penchant for doing?

The second message was from 11:51 PM. The message contained five seconds of air, the faint sound of what may have been breathing, and a disconnect. The caller ID showed this number was the same as the first one, meaning Grandfather had called again, but didn't leave a message this time.

It was too late to call him back, so I doused the rest of the lights and went to bed.

CHAPTER FIVE

The ringing phone by my bed woke me up. "John David?" a female voice said. It was my sister Eloise. I glanced at the clock on the nightstand. It wasn't quite 6 AM.

"What's wrong?" I asked before I realized that was my grandfather's exact response when I called *him*.

"Granddad didn't come home last night," she said. "I don't know where he is, and I'm worried sick. He would have called if he was okay," she added, the statement's implication clear in her voice.

There were probably many logical, harmless explanations as to his whereabouts, but I couldn't think of any at the moment.

"John David, are you there?"

"I'm here, Eloise."

"I keep wondering if he's had a heart attack or something. Or maybe he's piled up somewhere in that damned old Cadillac." Her voice suddenly broke. "What if he's hurt and can't get help?" I thought about the pneumatic wrench in the background of his message. Did he make the call from a garage or gas station? Maybe he had car trouble and couldn't get home. But as Eloise said, he would have called if that were the case. Although he didn't leave a message, he'd called me around midnight, so I knew there was nothing wrong with his cell phone then.

"When was the last time you talked to him?" I asked.

"I called him at the office yesterday afternoon. The electrical sockets in the upstairs hallway aren't working. I checked the fuse box, and that was okay, so I wanted to call an electrician, but I couldn't remember the name of the one we use. Granddad appeared busy and rather distracted and in a bad mood. My call was an obvious interruption, so I made it brief. If he planned on coming home late, he didn't mention it."

I wondered if his mood had anything to do with his "troubled" comment on his voicemail.

"Were you expecting him for dinner?" I asked.

"I always expect him, but I never know exactly when he'll arrive. You know him. He gets wrapped up in things and forgets about the time. So, I always cook for three, and if he's not home when Mackenzie and I are ready to eat, we go ahead without him, and I put his plate in the fridge, which is what I did last night. Mackenzie is sleeping over with a friend from school, so I ate alone and went to bed early to read. I fell asleep with the book open on my stomach. It didn't even cross my mind that something might have happened to him."

"And you still don't know that," I said, trying to believe it myself.

"Don't think I'm crazy, but when I woke up this morning, I had a weird feeling that something was wrong. A premonition, I guess. And when I went down to start breakfast and saw the leftovers from dinner still in the fridge, I knew it had. I checked his room, his bed wasn't slept in, and his toothbrush in the bathroom was dry."

"Have you called the hospitals?" I asked.

"Yes. They don't have him.

"What about the police?"

"I started to call them, but I thought I would sound like some silly, frightened woman. Men stay out all night, all the time. But they don't know Granddad like I do. They would just laugh at me for being such an alarmist."

She was probably right about how most cops would react, but maybe not in her case. "If Arlen Bagwell is still a sheriff's deputy," I said, "I'm sure he would take you seriously."

It was out of my mouth before I thought how inappropriate it was to tease my older sister at a time like this. Arlen Bagwell had been sweet on Eloise for years, but she refused to acknowledge it.

"John David, you know there's nothing between Arlen Bagwell and me. I wish you'd quit inferring that there is. And by the way, Arlen is the sheriff now."

"Maybe somebody at the *Clarion* knows something," I said, as much to change the subject as to offer a helpful suggestion.

"I called Doris Mozingo before I called you," Eloise said. "She said Granddad left the office at about six, but he didn't mention whether he was heading straight home or not."

I remembered he'd left his first message to me a half hour later. "What about the staff? Do you think they might know something?"

"Mrs. Mozingo volunteered to call them for me, but she doesn't think that will help. She said that if she doesn't know where he went, they won't either."

Eloise went quiet as if some new thought had entered her head. "Mrs. Mozingo said that you called Granddad yesterday." There was a hint of a question in the words.

"Yes, I did," I said.

"He didn't mention that when we talked. You two didn't get into it again, did you?"

"No, Eloise. I asked him for a favor, that's all."

"What kind of a favor?"

"I need his help to locate a person who lives in the area for a story I'm working on. Around six-thirty, he called back and left a message, asking me to call him at home last night. But I didn't check my voicemail until late. I was going to call him this morning."

I could almost hear her mind at work. "That means that at six-thirty, he was planning to be home. That scares me even more somehow," she said.

It didn't comfort me either.

"Did he sound okay? I mean, he didn't sound like he was sick or anything?" she asked.

"Not that I could notice," I said. "He did say that something was troubling him, but I didn't think he was referring to an illness."

I'd dismissed the comment from the message as typical Grandfather theatrics. *Was I right? Or was there trouble brewing about something?*

"Who is this person he was helping you to find?" Eloise asked. "Could they be together?"

"I don't think so, Eloise," I said. I would have smiled at the idea of Grandfather being out all night with an attractive young woman if it were not for the seriousness of the situation.

Eloise seemed to accept my reply and heaved a sigh in my ear. “I’ve gone out to the car to go searching for him several times,” she said, “but then I think he might call, and I’ll miss it, so I come back inside. I’ve just been sitting alone, staring at the phone and waiting. I don’t know what else to do.”

“Is Mackenzie still at her sleep-over?” I asked, thinking of my teenage niece, the only good thing to come out of my sister’s brief marriage to a wounded soul named Billy Gibson, a union that lasted only as long as it took him to drink and drug himself to death.

“Yes. I don’t want to worry her with this yet.”

“Eloise, I want you to call the sheriff’s office as soon as we hang up. I’m on my way. I should be there before noon.”

“No, John David. I’ll make the call, but you don’t need to come yet. I don’t know what you could do here that I can’t. There’s no reason for both of us to sit around wringing our hands; we’ll just depress each other. I’ll call you when I hear something.”

Her words held a familiar, steely ring that I recognized as her defense against unbearable heartbreak. This meant she was assuming the worst. She was already building a brave front, a survival mechanism she learned at a tender young age when a jack-knifing eighteen-wheeler swept our parents off a rain-slick highway like a giant mechanical broom, sending us to live with a grandfather we hardly knew, a man long past the patience it took to raise kids. What I heard from my sister was a combination of courage and common sense that said to heal, you first had to accept the unacceptable.

“I’m coming anyway,” I told her. I heard her sigh, either out of relief or at my stubbornness. “I just need to drop by the office first.” I hung up, and my thoughts went to the day long ago when Grandfather came to pick up my sister and me from the old lady who kept us while our parents were at work. He wasted no time telling us in his brusque manner what had happened to them and that we would be living with him from that moment on.

We had visited him at his big house in the country many times with our parents but never really got to know him. He paid little attention to us, and even at my young age, I had formed the opinion that he didn’t particularly like kids. That was okay. At the time, I didn’t like him either. I was determined not to let him see me cry as he and the woman who looked after us helped pack our bags. He later returned for the rest of our things.

I spent the first month holed up in an upstairs bedroom in his rambling old house, coming out only to go to our parents' funeral, eat, and attend church on Sunday—which he insisted on. Sometimes, women from the church would come over with cookies, cake, and even toys. Eloise would talk with them, but I said very little to them beyond a "thank you." Grandfather didn't seem to mind and mostly left me alone.

With Eloise's prodding, I eventually came out to join my new abbreviated family, and things gradually leveled out to a routine of sorts—if anything could ever be routine again after the sudden loss of both your parents.

I would eventually learn that Grandfather wasn't a mean man, just a serious one, without much use for small talk or children's games. I guess I had seen much of the same solemnity between my dad and Grandfather but had paid little attention. At least my dad didn't learn the same character traits. My dad would get down on the floor and play with my toys with me, as much a best friend as a dad. Grandfather treated me more like an adult than a kid, and when he spoke to me, it was usually to teach or lecture. I was scared of him and called him "grandfather" from the first, rather than a less formal "granddad" or "gramps," as Eloise called him. His aloofness and demeanor were more like a school principal than a parent, and "grandfather" seemed more appropriate. I had never called him anything else.

Maybe because she was older, Eloise ignored his gruffness and forced him to talk to her about mundane things, even joking around and making him laugh sometimes. They seemed to develop a warmer relationship than he and I shared. Grandfather and I remained distant, and as the years went by, nothing changed but my ever-growing resentment and rebelliousness.

I showered and shaved, noticing that the hit-and-run collision with the baggage cart from the Palace Hotel yesterday had left a nasty bruise on my knee. There was soreness, but it didn't feel as bad as the bruise looked. I quickly packed a bag with my usual attire of sports shirts, t-shirts, jeans, and sneakers, and then added a white shirt, tie, dress shoes, and a navy blazer. I stopped and thought for a moment about what I was packing. I had filled the bag with the clothes I usually took on a business trip—a suit and tie in case of an event such as a fancy dinner. But this wasn't a business trip.

Was my subconscious packing for a funeral?

CHAPTER SIX

As the *SportsWord* offices are located on Spring Street in Atlanta's busy midtown, I was surprised when I found a parking space on the curb right in front of the building. Usually, I parked in the bowels of the multi-storied parking garage next door. But then again, I was never in this early.

Using a key that I almost forgot I had, I entered the unremarkable two-story building and made my way down the darkened hallway, flipping on lights as I went. With my packed bag sitting in the back of the Jeep, my plan was to be there only long enough to do a couple of things to make my absence easier for my editor, Joe Dennis, to accept.

Joe didn't care when his writers came or went as long as they met their deadlines. But the only story I was working on was likely to be as dead as Osama soon, and if I were going away, I would need something to hold Dennis over until I could begin earning my meager salary again. Fortunately, I had a sneaky remedy for that. Filed away in my computer were a couple of stories I wrote as emergency backups—and if this wasn't an emergency, I didn't know what was.

I went to my cubicle ad sat down at my desk. A quick search of my computer files turned up the two stories I was looking for. The first dealt with major league baseball players who charged money for autographs. The money they made from it was insignificant compared to their stratospheric salaries. In my opinion, it was a petty and classless thing to do to fans, especially the kids. The other piece dealt with the college recruitment of star high-school athletes and the perks and expenses accrued while touring prospective colleges. One father and son racked up over five hundred dollars in hotel mini-bar charges alone.

Polishing the two stories took longer than I intended because my mind drifted to my grandfather. I had images of him crushed beneath four thousand pounds of vintage Detroit metal. Eventually, I wrapped up the stories, reread everything one last time, made a final nip or tuck here or there, and emailed the files to Joe Dennis. Just as I did, he stepped into the doorway of my cubicle.

"John David," he said, apparently as surprised to see me as I was to see him. "You're in early. I was going to leave you a note to come see me."

"Were you going to explain why you weren't at the meeting with Burt Lowe yesterday?" I asked.

He gave me a pained look. "I wanted to be there. But Burt felt that it wasn't a good idea."

I was sure that was true. Burt wanted me to be the lone punching bag in the room. There was no reason to add Joe Dennis or anyone else from *SportsWord* to Barry Beal's hit list.

"Then I guess you've got nothing to apologize for," I said.

He glanced at me sharply. "I didn't come here to apologize, but I will if you need it."

"Do what you feel like, Joe," I said.

"Burt gave you 24 hours to find this woman Beal allegedly assaulted. Is that going to happen?"

"I doubt it," I said. I didn't feel like saying anything more about Beal, the girl, or my missing grandfather.

"Then you'll drop this thing?" he said.

"I told him I would."

"He didn't believe you. Maybe I don't, either. Remember, J.D., I stuck my neck out to get you here. Don't let me down."

"I heard. And you have my undying gratitude. And I hope I haven't broken a rung on your corporate ladder."

Joe shook his head slowly. "I don't deserve that."

Maybe he was right. Joe Dennis was my only friend at the magazine.

"I'm going to be away for a few days on a family matter," I said. "I've got vacation time coming, so I thought I'd take it. I emailed you a couple of stories to get you through next week."

"Actually, a short vacation could be a good idea," Dennis said. "Take a few days off. Go see your family. Cool down." He tried to smile and almost succeeded. "I'll tell Burt you've shelved the story," he said before leaving.

I sat listening to his footsteps recede. I'd just told my boss, a man who was my friend, a bald-faced lie. The truth was, I wasn't going to shelve anything. I would find the girl, expose Beal for what he was, and let the story be my apology to Joe Dennis for lying to him.

My cell phone rang in my pocket. It was my sister. "Eloise?" I said.

"He's dead, John David."

I tried to wrap my mind around her words. "What happened?" I finally asked.

"Somebody shot him last night up on Highway 178."

She began to cry, and it was a moment before she spoke again. When she did, she said, "It was a robbery. Sheriff Bagwell and one of his deputies just told me. They just left. It happened at one of those roadside rest areas, or turnouts, or whatever you call them. They took his watch, wallet, and his camera. "Why was he even there?" she asked," more to herself than to me.

"Do they know who did it?" I asked.

"Sheriff Bagwell thinks it was probably some meth head looking to feed a habit, but he doesn't have anyone in mind yet."

"Is Mackenzie still at her friend's house?"

"Yes. She doesn't even know he was missing."

I could sense her focusing all her will and strength on the matter, like white cells rushing to an infection.

"I'm going over to pick her up now," she said. "I don't want her hearing about this from anyone else."

"I'll be there as soon as I can," I said. Experience had taught me that the best way to go was to drive. It was cheaper, easier, and just about as quick as flying. Actual flight time was only an hour, and driving time was about three, but by the time I drove to Hartsfield-Jackson Airport, parked in one of the long-term lots, and went through the tedious security check, I could be halfway there by car. Also, flying would still leave me forty-five miles from my final destination, depositing me at the Greenville-Spartanburg Airport, which would mean scrambling to arrange transportation for the last leg of the journey. So, I found the freeway and headed north.

CHAPTER SEVEN

Ninety-five miles north of Atlanta on I-85, I crossed the Lake Hartwell Bridge and left Georgia for South Carolina. I took the first exit onto State Highway 11, a rolling two-lane blacktop called the Cherokee Scenic Highway, which cut a northeastern semi-circle through a serene landscape of pine thicket, hardwoods, and hilly pastureland. To the north, the Blue Ridge Mountains climbed one above the other in progressively faded blues to merge with the sky. My destination lay at the foot of the mountains, still about forty miles away. The picturesque view almost made me forget the tragic circumstances taking me home. Almost.

Thirty-eight miles later, I passed over Eastatoe Creek, with Dug Mountain and the western entrance to Eastatoe Valley a half-mile to the north. I thought of the young woman I was trying to find and Barry Beal and wondered if he had begun construction on the golf course. Under different circumstances, I would have taken a short detour into the valley and checked it out. However, more important matters were waiting for me. Five miles on, I turned left at the intersection with U.S. Highway 178, just north of Holly Springs Baptist church. In the rear-view mirror, I could see the tombstones in the church graveyard rising up a hill in neat rows like marble and granite dominoes.

Among them I knew were the graves of several generations of Braggs: my great-grandmother and great-grandfather, deceased since the fifties; my grandmother, who died of breast cancer before I was born; four great-uncles who were all killed in action in World War II, (Grandfather was the only one of the five Bragg brothers too young to enlist); and buried next to them, my mother and father.

I tried to picture my parents, and as always, I saw them in black and white, my mom smiling prettily under the dark locks of a seventy's hairstyle and my dad with a devilish smile and a kiss-curl, the kind of guy who would carry a pocket comb and never be without a fresh stick of gum. It was a memory created by a photograph on a mantle and, over time, had replaced any other mental picture I had of them. Grandfather would soon join them on that hill; the Bragg clan had been reduced to Eloise, Mackenzie, and me.

A small private lane appeared ahead on the left, and I slowed down and took it. On either side of the narrow gravel driveway, Dogwoods bloomed in clusters of small white crosses against a backdrop of dark green foliage. Honeysuckle vines covered the banks along the driveway and wound around a stand of ancient cedars to reveal the house. It stood like an aging sentinel over an acre of perpetually well-kept lawn, two stories of neat, white clapboard, with stacked-stone chimneys rising above the gables on either end. The windows, upstairs and down, were braced by green-painted shutters, and a wide porch surrounded the house on three sides. I was impressed again by the beauty and peacefulness of the place. Every time I came home on one of my infrequent visits, it was as if I'd never been there before. When I was younger, I guess I'd taken the place so much for granted that I never really saw it. It's strange how time and distance can sharpen your vision.

The house sat on land in our family since the late 1700s; the property, still the original two hundred acres acquired by a bounty land grant—the grantee, a discharged colonial soldier named William Bragg, who ended his military service in the Carolinas, and with no family, prospects, or reasons to return to his native Maryland, he stayed.

Locals knew the Bragg home-place as "Still Hollow," but not because of the peaceful and serene setting—which *was* a fitting description—but because several generations of Braggs were notorious bootleggers, with a moonshine still always working in some remote hollow.

The infamous family business ended with the death of my great-grandfather, whom I never knew, but from all I heard, was truly a rascal. A gambler, hell-raiser, and staunch combatant of revenuers, he was said to be a man quick to put birdshot in a rear-end if someone got on his wrong side. My grandfather inherited the place when he passed away and set out to cleanse the Bragg reputation. But a history of scalawags lay only one generation back, and it seemed like the specter of that reputation made Grandfather try to raise my father, his only son, and then my sister and me like novices for the seminary. It didn't work, at least not in my case.

The driveway made a circle in front of the house, and I stopped by the steps and killed the engine. Eloise came out and down the steps to meet me with a silent hug, her tears warming my neck.

"Oh, John David," she said, "I feel so misplaced. It's like the whole world turned upside down and dumped me out." We held each other tightly. "I know, sis, I know." It was all I could think of to say.

"What did we do to deserve this?" she asked, defeat in her eyes.

I knew she was talking about all of it, not just Grandfather but the accumulated sadness of her life: the devastating loss of our mother and father that made us sudden orphans as children; the addiction that overwhelmed her husband, Billy, and threatened to destroy both of them; and finally, the tragedy of Billy's premature death. I knew of no answer that would console her.

I threw my bag over a shoulder and led her inside. I asked about Mackenzie, wondering how Eloise's 15-year-old daughter took the news.

"When I picked her up from her sleep-over," Eloise said, "she was so cheerful and happy. She was still giggling about something silly her friend did. It was hard to watch her go from such a high to absolute rock bottom in seconds."

"Where is she now?"

"Holed up in her bedroom with the phone unplugged. The calls have been too much. Most of them have been from people who just want to express their sympathy—but the Greenville newspaper and the TV stations have been simply ghoulish in their curiosity."

I wondered if Eloise realized that had it been some other prominent man murdered and someone else's grieving family answering the calls, Grandfather likely would have been one of the ghoulish callers.

"Mackenzie was too young to remember Billy dying," Eloise said, "so this is really her first experience with the death of someone she loves." My sister looked at me, her eyes searching mine. "But we know it doesn't get any easier no matter how many we go through, don't we?" she said.

"No, it doesn't," I said, knowing that was a lie. The death of our parents was by far the toughest for me. Billy, I never liked, and while his death was tragic, it may have been a blessing for Eloise and Mackenzie. And Grandfather? Beyond the anger I felt at whoever killed him, I wasn't sure how I was taking his death yet. Everything was happening so fast that I subconsciously placed that on a shelf to be dealt with at a later time.

"Let's go sit on the porch," I said to Eloise. "It's nice out, and we can talk without disturbing Mackenzie."

We went back out and sat on the porch swing.

"Are there any new developments?" I asked.

"I don't know any more than I did earlier," she said. "When I heard a car coming up the drive, I ran out, thinking it was Granddad. But it was Sheriff Arlen Bagwell. When he got out of the car, I could tell by the look on his face what kind of news he was bringing."

A small gray rabbit emerged from the row of junipers at the yard's edge and froze in place as it sensed our presence on the porch. We both stopped and watched it decide whether to advance or retreat. After a moment, it made a leisurely hop back into the shrubbery.

Eloise continued, "Arlen said it happened sometime last night. I guess they'll know a more exact time when the coroner makes his report. They found Granddad up on Highway 178 early this morning, not far from here, at that turnout just this side of the intersection with Cleo Chapman highway."

The turnout she was referring to was one of a number of short loops of tarmac and gravel built at intervals along the shoulder of the two-lane mountainous highway as it wound like a drunken snake into North Carolina. These turnouts allowed slower vehicles to pull over, so faster ones could pass. Some had a picnic table and garbage barrel for roadside picnics.

"His camera was the most valuable thing they took," Eloise was saying. "He never carried much cash money on him, his cell phone was old and outdated, and his watch was inexpensive. But you know how he was about photography. Only the best equipment was good enough. This camera was a fancy digital model and was almost new."

I thought of my Grandfather's photography, his hobby for many years. Beyond the shots he took for work, he liked to photograph the beauty of the local landscape. One whole wall of the den was covered with his photos, and while not quite Ansel Adams, they weren't bad.

"He kept the camera in a shoulder bag filled with lenses, filters, and stuff," Eloise continued. "They took all of it. I gave Arlen serial numbers in case any of it turns up. Her eyes misted up again, and she said, "How could those things be worth a man's life, John David?"

Out on the lawn, a couple of yellow butterflies wobbled aimlessly in and out of the tree-shaped shadows. It was far too idyllic a backdrop for contemplating such an unanswerable question.

"What was he doing up there?" she asked again. "He had to pass right by here to get there, so why didn't he just come home?"

"Is there a garage or service station nearby where he takes the Cadillac for service?" I asked.

"Yes," she said, with some curiosity. "Grady Morton's Garage. On Highway 178, just this side of where they found him. Why do you ask?"

I told her about the pneumatic wrench sound I heard in the background of Grandfather's voicemail and how I thought he might have called from a garage or service station.

"Maybe someone followed him from there—and what do they call it—carjacked him?" Shouldn't we tell the sheriff about this, John David?"

"Yes," I said. "I'll do it."

She had another question. "You said Granddad was helping you locate some woman for a story you're working on. Could she be the reason he was up there?"

"It's a possibility," I said. "In Grandfather's voicemail, he said he had a line on her."

"Why were you trying to find her?"

I told her what I thought Barry Beal did to the woman. "I need to get her to attest to the assault," I said, "or I don't have a story, and Beal gets away with it."

"What an awful man," Eloise responded.

She would get no argument from me on that.

"This happened in Atlanta?" she asked. "How did you know to look for this woman in Pickens County?"

"Following a lead," I said. "She may live here and work with Barry Beal on a golf course community he's planning for Eastatoe Valley."

"They're going to build a golf course in Eastatoe Valley? And you told Granddad this?"

"Yes, I did."

"I'll bet that lit his burners," she said.

"It's probably the only reason he agreed to help me. An environmental menace to the local landscape would attract him more than any plea for help from his only grandson."

I regretted saying that the moment it came out; the hurt in Eloise's eyes was unmistakable. "I'm sorry, Eloise," I said, even though I'd spoken the truth as I saw it. "I shouldn't have said that."

"John David, this trouble between you and Granddad, shouldn't it finally be over?"

She started to say more but stopped. I was relieved, as I didn't know how to answer her. The rift between Grandfather and I was an old subject—years old—and one I'd never explained or even discussed with her—and I knew, neither had Grandfather. All I knew was that he was gone, but my bitterness remained. Unfortunately, any chance to ever resolve our problems face-to-face died with him. Both this and his death were tragedies that I needed to deal with, but until I did, I had no answers for anyone, me included.

"Maybe Grandfather took a trip over to Eastatoe Valley," I said, trying to get past the awkward moment I'd created. "That would explain his presence on Highway 178. As you said, the turnout where Grandfather was found is near the Cleo Chapman highway, the eastern entrance into the valley."

"Do you think that's where this woman lives?" Eloise asked.

"Or works," I said. "Maybe Beal has a sales or construction office there. When were you in Eastatoe Valley last?"

Her eyes widened a bit as she thought about it. "Several months ago, I guess. Mackenzie and I were loafing around one Sunday after church and drove over there. But I didn't see any construction offices or anything like that. The place was the same as always. Peaceful and quiet."

She put her head back and closed her eyes. She looked exhausted. I got up, took her hand, and led her to the sofa inside. "You need some sleep," I said, picking up her feet, stretching her legs out, and placing a cushion behind her head. A knitted comforter was folded over an arm of the sofa, and I spread it over her.

"I bet you're starving," she said, looking up at me with tired eyes. "There's food in the fridge. Women from church came by and dropped off some covered dishes. You know southern women; cooking is their way of expressing sympathy. I'll get you something," she said, starting to get up.

I gently pushed her back down. "I can manage Eloise. You get some rest."

"But we have so much to do. We have the funeral arrangements to make and . . ."

I stopped her. "That can wait. Close your eyes."

She placed a hand on my arm and kept it there. "I'm glad you're here, little brother," she said.

After a minute passed, her breathing became slow and regular, and she was asleep. Grief can be a strong sedative.

CHAPTER EIGHT

I was in the kitchen working on a plate of fried chicken, biscuits, and a glass of sweet tea when my niece Mackenzie came down the stairs.

"Hi, sweetheart," I said and walked over and hugged her. "Where's mom?" she said, hugging me back.

"Sleeping."

"Good. She needs it."

"How are you doing?" I asked her.

I'm as okay as I can be, I guess. I still can't believe it. It's like I'm in a bad dream and can't wake up."

I wished I knew what to tell her to make her feel better, but anything I could think of would sound sorely inadequate. I tried to convince her to eat a drumstick, but she didn't want it.

She hugged me a moment longer and said, "I'm going back to my room for a while if you don't mind."

"I don't mind at all." I kissed her on the forehead. She gave me one last squeeze, walked over to the fridge, dished out a bowl of banana pudding, and went upstairs. I watched her go. At fifteen, she was already an intelligent, beautiful young lady, mature beyond her age. She is my sister's daughter.

I heard the sound of tires crunching on the gravel out front and went outside. A white Ford Crown Victoria bearing the Pickens County Sheriff's Department insignia on the side was coming up the drive. Arlen Bagwell got out and made his way up the walk when it stopped. A second officer remained behind the wheel, the engine idling a throaty rumble beneath the occasional squawk of indecipherable radio traffic.

It was years since I'd seen him, but other than a brushstroke of gray at the temples, he looked unchanged: stick thin, with pale, piercing blue eyes and the deportment of a Marine Corps Drill Sergeant. I walked over to greet him.

"Mr. Bragg?" he said, obviously recognizing me, "You may not remember me, but I'm Sheriff Arlen Bagwell."

"Of course, I remember you, Sheriff," I said. But I think you were a deputy back then." What I remembered most was his soft voice and deliberate way of speaking, a manner that could easily mislead you into thinking he had a gentle nature. Many a miscreant had made that mistake as the stories went, only to end up sitting on a cell bunk with a large knot behind an ear. Bagwell had the reputation of being a fair man but one with zero tolerance.

He took off his hat and came up the steps, a faint odor of Juicy Fruit gum and hair tonic following him.

"I'm truly sorry about your loss," he said.

He offered his hand, and I took it. His grip was firm and dry. "I want you to know we're doing everything we can to find whoever did this."

Are you making any progress?" I asked.

"Some," he said. "But you have to understand we just got started." He looked over my shoulder at the front door. "Is Eloise at home?" he asked.

"She's taking a nap," I said. "She is absolutely worn out."

With a flicker of disappointment that he couldn't hide, he said, "Well, don't disturb her. I was by this way and just wanted to see if she was okay. That was some hard news I had to bring her this morning."

He put his hat on and adjusted the flat brim ramrod straight across his brow. I wondered if he would have been so concerned if not for his fondness for Eloise. His interest in her was no secret. But I was unaware if she ever showed reciprocal feelings or encouragement. Eloise seemed to have lost interest in men after her husband Billy died, and with the way Billy Gibson abused alcohol, drugs, *and* my sister, maybe she had good reason to do so. As to Sheriff Arlen Bagwell, there were rumors of an unfaithful wife and a divorce in his distant past, but I didn't know the details.

"Well, tell her that if there's anything that either I or the department can do, she just needs to ask."

"Thank you, Sheriff," I said. "There *are* a couple of things I'd like to ask. We need to plan the funeral, but we can't until we know when the body will be released. Do you know when that will be?"

"Tomorrow afternoon, the coroner tells me," he said. "Who's your funeral home?"

"Dillard in Pickens."

"I suggest you call them and tell them we'll notify them of the exact time they can come and pick him up."

"Thank you," I said. "One more thing. I'd like to hear more about my grandfather's murder. All I know is what I heard from my sister, and that's somewhat sketchy."

"What would you like to know?" he said, a crease forming between his eyebrows.

"Everything. The details."

He gave me a grim look. "Maybe we should wait until you've got the initial shock of this thing behind you," he said.

"I appreciate your concern for my feelings, Sheriff, but I'd like to hear about it now."

He took a long breath and widened his eyes as if looking for a starting point.

"After your sister called," he began, "I had all units keeping an eye out for him. He really wasn't gone long enough to file an official missing persons report— but being who he was . . .

And who Eloise was . . . I thought.

"I'd no sooner put it on the radio," he said, "and we found him. One of my Deputies was doing a routine up Highway 178 to the state line and saw an old Cadillac parked in a turnout. He knew right away whose it was. Only one man in the county drove a car like that. He pulled in to investigate and found Garnet's body on the ground on the far side of the car, determined him dead on the scene, and called it in. I was there within thirty minutes, with the crime scene unit and the coroner not far behind."

Bagwell paused and searched my face for a moment. "You sure you want to hear this?" he said.

I probably didn't, but I said yes anyway.

"He was shot in the head with a large caliber weapon," Bagwell went on. "A

.357 magnum or better. Struck him right about here," he added, touching a finger to a spot over his left eye.

"He was shot at close range, as there were powder burns on his face. He was probably looking right at whoever did it. The slug exited from the right rear of his head and most likely spun out over the mountainside. We haven't found it yet and probably won't. No brass was found at the scene, so they either picked it up or used a revolver. It left a large exit wound, a lot of blood, and uh . . . particulate body matter on the ground."

I felt bile rise at the back of my throat. I'd asked for it, and Bagwell gave it to me.

"Which way was the car headed?" I asked, swallowing hard.

"South. Like he was on his way home. We don't know where he'd been, and evidently, neither did your sister, but we're looking into that. We believe he stopped at the turnout to relieve himself. There was a damp spot in the dirt at the tree line near his body. Although the lab is testing it, we don't need them to tell us it was urine. We could smell it."

The thought of Grandfather pissing by the side of the road didn't fit my image of him, but I guess an eighty-year-old bladder sometimes supersedes decorum.

"He was outside the car when he was shot, probably just moments after he'd relieved himself," Bagwell continued. "They robbed him as he lay dying or dead on the ground. We think it was a crime of opportunity: someone came by and saw him there, pulled in, and shot and robbed him. Probably some meth-head looking to feed a habit. They stripped him of his watch, which skinned his wrist a bit, took his wallet, cell phone, and whatever cash he had. With your sister's input, we also determined that a shoulder bag containing a camera and photographic accessories was taken from the car. Time of death was between eight and eleven o'clock PM."

Something was off here, I thought. "Are you sure about the time of death?" I asked.

Bagwell gave me a curious look. "The coroner's convinced of it. Why do you ask?"

"Because Grandfather called me in Atlanta at about midnight. You have him dead then."

"You spoke to him?" Bagwell asked, the curious look morphing into one of surprise.

"No, I was out when he called. Actually, he called twice. He called earlier that evening at about six-thirty and, as I said, later that night. He left a message with the first call but not the second one. But the call showed up on caller I.D."

"You're certain about the time?" Bagwell asked, more of a challenge than a question.

"Positive. The first call came in at 6:37, and the second one at 11:51, to be exact. Both calls were from his cell phone. I recognized the number. Also, I know the time on my phone was correct because I checked it. So, it stands to reason that the times of the calls were correct too."

"6:37 and 11:51," Bagwell repeated. "You have a good memory, Mr. Bragg," he said.

The compliment, if that's what it was, held a false ring, as if he couldn't help showing irritation at the wrinkle I'd exposed in his investigation.

After a moment of thought, he said, "Have you considered, Mr. Bragg, that since there was no message left with that second call, there's really no proof that your granddad actually made it? It could have been made by whoever stole the phone."

"That's a chilling thought," I said. "Why would they be calling me, for God's sake?"

"Maybe your granddad had you on speed dial, and they accidentally punched it," he offered.

"Believe me," I said, "my grandfather wouldn't have *me* on his speed dial."

"Or they could have mistakenly hit the redial button," he said.

That was more plausible, but I wondered if Bagwell had a problem admitting to an error in the coroner's stated time of death. However, I wasn't going to argue. He could believe what he wanted.

"What was the message he left?" Bagwell asked.

"Grandfather was helping me locate someone who lives in this area. A woman I need to talk to. I'm a writer for an Atlanta sports magazine and trying to find her for a story I'm working on. His message said he thought he'd found her. He also said he'd turned up something that troubled him."

"Troubled? Bagwell said. "What kind of trouble?"

"That, he didn't say, and I got home too late to call him back to ask. I planned to wait until morning, but obviously, it would have been too late by then. Also, I think he was calling from a garage or a service station. I heard one of those pneumatic wrenches in the background. Eloise told me he takes his car to a little garage near where he was found, so maybe he was calling from there."

Bagwell thought about that for a moment and said. "That's probably Grady Morton's garage. I'll stop by there and talk to him. "Did you erase the message?" he asked.

I told him I didn't, and he asked if I had the kind of voicemail I could get from out of town. I said yes, and he pulled a cell phone from a trouser pocket and handed it to me.

"Call it," he said.

I called the remote number, keyed in the code, let it play down to the message, and handed the phone back to him. He stood for a minute with the phone pressed to his ear, his face bearing no expression. I didn't know if he was recording it or not. Then he closed the phone and put it back in his pocket.

"That's definitely a pneumatic wrench in the background," he said. "But I think you can read anything you want into that part about him being troubled," he said.

I agreed with him but didn't say so.

"This woman you're looking for. What's her name?"

"I don't know her name or where she lives. Grandfather was helping me to find this out."

"What's the nature of this story?"

"It involves Barry Beal."

"Barry Beal, the golfer?"

"Yes," I said. "I think this woman has some damaging personal information about him. I think he assaulted her. Maybe raped her. Beal wouldn't want her found."

Bagwell stood for a moment as if digesting what I'd just said, his eyes never leaving my face. Then he said, "So Garnet leaves you this message saying he thinks he's found her, is troubled about something, and is killed."

"Exactly," I said.

Bagwell stuck out his chin, scratched underneath it with his fingertips, and looked at me as if, under less morose circumstances, he might laugh out loud. "Are you saying you think Barry Beal, the famous golfer, may have something to do with your granddad's death?"

I felt the temperature in my cheeks rise, realizing how ridiculous the thought sounded when it aired. Even I didn't believe Barry Beal did it, at least not directly, but Bagwell had raised my defensive hackles, and damned if I would give him the satisfaction of admitting it.

"I'm just telling you what I know," I said. "And until you find whoever did it, maybe you shouldn't disregard anything— no matter how farfetched it might seem."

Bagwell turned his gaze to the lawn and stood for a moment as if mesmerized by the bees making lazy circles over the jonquils in Eloise's flowerbed. Then he turned back to me.

"Mr. Bragg," he said, "I know it's hard to understand why someone thought they needed to kill your granddad for what little they got. It makes us want to look for a more complicated, meaningful reason. But most of the time, murder isn't all that complicated. In the case of your granddad, every shred of evidence we have says that this was a case of murder in the course of a simple robbery. I'm afraid Garnet pulled in there to relieve himself, and some bad characters happened to come upon him."

I let his words sit for a moment. Maybe he was right. Maybe Grandfather's death *was* just a matter of being in the wrong place at the wrong time. But even if that were the case, a nagging, grim voice in my head kept whispering that if not for me, Grandfather wouldn't have been in that place at that time. Wasn't it me who sent him on that journey? Didn't I set it all in motion by asking for his help finding Barry Beal's assault victim? Illogical thinking, perhaps, but so far, logic was doing damned little to chase these thoughts away. Also, I knew I would never get beyond them by standing on the sidelines. I had to be in the game. What did Grandfather find that so troubled him, and did it play a part in his death? Someone needed to look into all this, and if Sheriff Bagwell wasn't going to do it, then I would.

"Eloise told me you think it was some druggie," I said. "Do you have anyone in mind?"

"The usual suspects, a list of known users with troubled histories. But we've just begun checking them out. Right now, we don't even know how many suspects were involved. One person or a dozen. The turnout's paved, so there are no footprints or tire tracks. We've got prints from the car, but we don't know which are Garnets and which aren't yet.

"No one saw anything?"

"Nobody has come forward. But I'm not surprised. There are no houses nearby, and not much traffic along there after dark."

"So you're telling me you're nowhere on this."

"We've got our entire Criminal Investigations Department working on it, and we'll keep them on it 24-7. There's nothing significant to report yet, but the investigation is moving forward according to plan."

It sounded like a canned press release.

"What the hell does that mean, Sheriff?" I asked.

His eyes flashed with the look of a man unaccustomed to challenge, then calmed, but I could tell it took a great conscious effort.

"It means that we don't have a single suspect yet," he said, "and we'll probably need to catch a break to find one."

The sudden candor surprised me, revealing an unexpected human side to the usually officious nature of the man.

"Our best hope is that they'll make a mistake," he added. "Such as try to use a credit card or hock the watch or camera, and we'll find out about it. In my experience, this type of predator usually isn't too smart. Most of them steal to buy drugs, and sooner or later, they screw up."

He waited a beat to see if I had any more questions, and when I didn't, he gave me a nod, got into the car, and drove away, braking only for one of Eloise's free-range chickens that came out of the trees and half-flew half-ran across in front of him.

CHAPTER NINE

After Sheriff Bagwell left, I sat in the kitchen staring out the windows at nothing in particular. Grandfather got on the trail of my missing woman quickly. Whether that somehow led to his death, or he just ended up at the wrong place at the wrong time, as Bagwell suggested, it didn't change the fact that I still needed to find her. And the best way to do that, I decided, was to try to retrace Grandfather's footsteps on the last day of his life. I might not know where he began, but I did know where he ended. I would start there.

I climbed into the Jeep; at the end of the driveway, I turned north up Highway 178. After about a mile, Morton's Garage came into view. At the sight of it, I wondered if Eloise knew what she was talking about when she said this was where Grandfather took his car for service.

Morton's Garage didn't look like a place he would trust with his precious Caddy. It was a dump, literally. An unpainted, cinder block building with two service bays and a couple of aging gas pumps out front, surrounded by a plethora of vehicles in various states of disrepair, auto appendages long past any usefulness, rusty engine blocks, bent tailpipes, burnt-out mufflers, used tires, and battered car shells punched through with weeds and morning glory vines.

I pulled in next to the service bays, got out of my car, and looked around. The garage was an eyesore along what would otherwise be a picturesque stretch of mountain highway. Across the road, a rusty sign nailed to a tree read "Jesus Is Coming," adding a bit of down-south embellishment to the setting. It was still a pleasant view if you stood with your back to the garage.

A man was in one of the bays working under the hood of a car that straddled the grease pit. I walked inside, and he looked up, stopped what he was doing, and came lumbering over to me, wiping his greasy hands on an even greasier rag. He was the approximate size of a mature black bear and about as wooly, with a mop of shaggy dark hair and a full beard. He had the name Grady stitched over the left breast of his grimy coveralls.

"How can I help you?" he asked.

"You can tell me if Garnet Bragg stopped by here yesterday," I said.

His expression turned somber. "Garnet? Yeah, he was here. Who might you be?"

"I'm his grandson, John David."

"You live in Atlanta," he said. "Garnet talked about you."

I wished I had been a fly on the wall during those conversations.

"I'm Grady Morton," the man offered, thrusting out a large

greasy paw, then pulling it back and wiping it on his pants leg when he realized how filthy it was.

"I can't tell you how sorry I am about what happened to him," he said. "That's all they been talking about around here today. He was a damn good man. I hope they find the sum-bitch who did it and fry his ass 'til he's as crispy as a store-bought pork skin."

I nodded in appreciation for his colorful condolences and said, "I'd like to talk to you about his visit here if you're not too busy."

"Hell, I ain't busy," he said. "Be glad to."

He must have noticed my glance over his shoulder at the car with the hood up.

"That's my wife's car, and she ain't in no hurry for it," he said. "Can't drive worth a damn anyway. I'm doing everybody a favor keeping her off the road. What'd you want to talk to me about?"

"What was my grandfather's business here?"

"He wanted the oil changed in that old Cadillac of his."

"About what time was that?" I asked.

Morton stared at the grease pit for a moment as if he could still see the Caddy sitting there and said, "He came in about six-fifteen, six-thirty, I guess. It only took about thirty minutes, so he was in and out. Gone by seven at the latest. I closed up right after that."

That was about the time of my grandfather's first voicemail, I thought. "Was anyone else here? Any suspicious characters?"

He thought for a moment and then chuckled.

"My nephew Albert was in here changing a tire on his old pickup, borrowing my tools as usual, but I don't know if you'd call him suspicious. A pain in the ass and a mooch, maybe. I don't think I had any other customers the whole time your granddaddy was here. That place down at the Highway 11 intersection has taken most of my through business, so about the only people I get these days are local folks like your granddaddy."

"Did Grandfather make any phone calls while he was here?" Morton nodded. "Yeah. I remember it because Albert was making so much racket with the air wrench that Garnet had to go outside to hear."

Air wrench. One small mystery solved, I thought.

"He could have made another call when he went back out with his camera a few minutes later," Morton added, "but I was in the pit under the car and didn't see what he did. I don't know why he took his camera; ain't nothing out there to photograph but junk."

I thought about my grandfather's ability to find an artful composition in about anything. "Did he say where he planned to go when he left here?"

"Nope," Morton said. "All I know is he headed north, up toward where I heard they found him."

Morton seemed to lose himself inside a thought for a second and added, "If they found your grandfather where I heard they did, and he was killed later on last night like they say, then he had to go somewhere else first. It don't take two minutes to get there from here."

"Has anyone from the sheriff's office been by to see you yet?" I asked.

"They've been racing up and down the highway all day, but nobody's stopped."

"They will," I said. "When they do, tell them everything we've talked about here."

"You think it will help?" he asked, his face full of concern. "

Maybe. At the least, it will help them build a time frame leading up to his death."

I thought again of the Cleo Chapman Highway and Eastatoe Valley. Maybe he did go there and was on his way home when he stopped at the turnout. A box of blank oil-change stickers was attached to the wall near where I stood. I picked one up and held it out for Morton to see.

"Did you put one of these on the Caddy?" I asked.

"Always do," he said. "Inside the door-jamb on the driver's side."

I was more interested in the odometer reading that usually went on one of those stickers and if the difference between that and the current mileage on the Caddy would explain where Grandfather went after leaving the garage. "Do you keep a record of the odometer reading at the time of the oil change?" I asked.

"I don't keep a record," he said, but I do add three thousand miles to the current reading and put that on the sticker. It's supposed to remind the customer when he's due for another oil change, but these days with them synthetic oils, most people are waiting a lot longer than that."

I wondered if they had removed the car from the crime scene by now. Surely they had.

"Where would the police take Grandfather's car?" I asked Morton. "Is there a county impound lot or someplace like that?"

He thought about it for a minute. "Usually, cars involved in accidents, traffic violations, and such are taken to one of a couple of private-owned lots. I buy parts from them sometimes. But something like your granddaddy's Cadillac, involved in a murder and all, they would probably keep in the lot out back of the sheriff's office in Pickens—at least while the investigation is ongoing. Then, they'll either move it to one of the private lots or let you come and get it."

I thought about that last thing he said for a minute. Bringing Grandfather's Cadillac home would be a cheerless task. He never allowed me to drive it growing up, and I didn't want to drive it now. I couldn't see Eloise wanting it either. For me, it would be like wearing his clothes—too personal and too much of a constant reminder of him. Maybe I could talk her into selling it straight from the impound lot.

I thanked Grady Morton for his help and headed north again. A strip of yellow police tape came into view along the left-hand side of the road, vivid against a green background of trees. If he had pulled in there, it meant he was headed home, probably. I crossed over the double line, parked, and got out of the car. Grandfather's old Caddy was obviously gone, and no one was around. However, police tape was still strung from a tree at one end of the short strip of tarmac to a tree at the other. A weathered picnic table and a rusted open-ended oil drum sat just inside the barrier, the drum for picnic refuse—paper cups and plates, soda cans, and watermelon rinds. There was no sign of human habitation along this stretch of highway in either direction. I wondered again what caused Grandfather to end up here. Was it really to take a leak, as Sheriff Bagwell suggested?

Maybe so. I didn't think it was for a picnic. Whatever it was, the thought remained that I had set it all in motion when I'd asked him for his help. Guilt trips suck.

I ducked under the tape and made my way toward the picnic table, the mountainside beyond dropping away into a forest of thick verdant hardwoods. I could smell the fecund odor of the forest floor, covered with ages of rotting leaves. Somewhere below, a crow cackled and cawed.

At first, I thought that the band of police tape was the only sign that a tragedy had occurred here, but a few feet from the tree line, I noticed a patch of white sand on the ground, starkly bright against the black asphalt. No one had to tell me what purpose it served. They had spread it there to cover up my grandfather's blood and whatever else had spilled from his body.

I looked at the fluffy white clouds that dotted the perfect blue sky above, thinking that if I stared at them long enough, they would replace the vision of that patch of sand.

It didn't work.

CHAPTER TEN

When I returned to Still Hollow, Eloise was still asleep on the sofa, and Mackenzie was still in her room. I made a fresh pot of coffee and quietly wandered about the house with a cup, reacquainting myself with the old place. A copy of the *Clarion* lay on a side table, and I saw from the date that it must be Grandfather's final edition. I took it into the kitchen, spread it out on the table, and sat down to read it.

The paper looked unchanged, still heavily weighted toward local news and events with little coverage of anything that didn't happen in Pickens County. I was thinking that Grandfather wasn't a man to be driven from a course once set when I saw something new. And surprising. The paper's editorial wasn't written by Grandfather—but by someone named Kelly Mayfield. That was definitely a change. Editorials were Grandfather's soapbox, his weapon to bludgeon readers with the truth as he saw it, and I never thought he'd give that up or share it with anyone. I read it, finding it a poignant observance on the indifferent treatment of the elderly in some nursing homes in the county.

Whoever this Kelly Mayfield was, she was good. The piece was thoughtful, gutsy, and well-written. I found the block listing the paper's staff, titles, and job functions and received my second surprise. Kelly Mayfield was listed as the *Clarion's* Editor. Nobody but my grandfather had *ever* held that title. He had been both publisher and editor of the paper from the beginning, and for him to relinquish either of those titles to anyone with less stature than a Horace Greeley was astounding. I found other examples of her work and saw she wasn't a bad hand at straight news, either. I had to ask Eloise about this. It was so unlike Grandfather.

I put the paper down and let my mind drift to the next couple of days, wishing I could fast-forward past them. I dreaded the funeral. Funerals were ceremonies that made mourning a public thing, while to me, grief, unlike joy, was an emotion best dealt with in private.

Suddenly the phone rang, and I hurried to answer it before it woke Eloise.

"Is this the Bragg residence?" a female voice asked.

I heard a slight southern accent but with a trace of something else—perhaps the effects of an up-east education.

"Yes, it is," I answered.

"This is Kelly Mayfield," the voice said.

Speak of the devil. I was just reading about her, and now here she was.

"Is it an appropriate time to speak to Eloise?" she said. "I wanted to check if there's anything I could do for her."

"She's asleep right now," I said. "But I'll tell her you called." A moment passed before she spoke again. "Is this John David?" She asked.

I detected a slight change in her tone, an almost imperceptible chill.

"Yes, it is," I answered. "I was just reading something you wrote. You're pretty good."

"That would probably be more of a compliment if you didn't sound so surprised."

Now, there was no mistaking the chill. An icicle hung from each word. "I didn't mean anything by that," I said.

"Please tell Eloise I called," she said and hung up.

My instincts are finely tuned when recognizing women who don't like me, probably because there have been so many of them. This woman definitely did not like me, but I had no idea why. As far as I knew, we were total strangers. I replaced the phone and tried to envision what Kelly Mayfield would look like. She was probably a thin, bookish woman with short hair, sensible shoes, sharp features, no makeup, and eyeglasses on a chain. Someone who would prefer attending a library lecture on Elizabethan literature to a night on the town. I knew the type.

From the other room, I heard Eloise call my name. The phone must have awakened her after all. I walked to the doorway and looked in on her. She was still on the sofa, the comforter up around her chin.

"Was that the phone?" she asked.

"It was Kelly Mayfield. She offered her help if you need it."

"Kelly," Eloise said sleepily. "She's nice."

Eloise thought everyone was nice. "I made coffee," I said. "Want a cup?"

"I'd love one," she said, and we made our way to the kitchen. The circles under her eyes were a shade lighter, and her face wasn't quite as puffy. She smiled a real smile for the first time since I arrived, and it was comforting to see a glimpse of the old Eloise.

She took some kind of salad from the fridge and ate it with her coffee. I ate another chicken leg and told her about Sheriff Bagwell's visit, saying he thought the killer, or killers, were probably meth-heads who came upon Grandfather when he stopped there to relieve himself and saw an opportunity to rob a helpless old man for drug money. Killing him was just a senseless side effect of an addled doper's brain. I kept the real reason he came—*to check on her*—to myself and didn't mention my trip to Morton's garage and the murder site, either. The former, because I'd kidded her enough about Arlen Bagwell's amorous intentions already, and the latter, to keep from having to think about that little patch of white sand.

"I guess we need to make funeral arrangements," she said. "Will you help with them?"

"Of course, I will," I said. "Or I can handle them myself."

"No, we can do it together," she quickly added.

I agreed with her and said so. "But we'll need the medical examiner to release him. According to Sheriff Bagwell, we can expect that to happen tomorrow afternoon. So, how about we try for Saturday or Sunday?"

"Saturday, if we can," she said. "I want the funeral to be as soon as possible. It may be weak of me, but I'd rather not linger with . . ."

She searched for the right words and seemed to fail. "This" was all she came up with. "What about a visitation at the funeral home?" she asked. "That would have to be Friday evening."

"Why do we have to do that at all?" I asked.

"But John David, people want to offer condolences and pay their respects, and we must let them."

"You know I'm not good at things like that, Eloise. If it were up to me, I'd shut all the doors, pull all the drapes, turn off all the lights, and wait for the funeral. I appreciate the fact that so many people admired Grandfather and mourn his loss, but I don't like it. That probably makes me an insensitive, unappreciative bastard, but he's gone. It's the family that hears the sentiments at those kinds of gatherings, and I believe that it only serves to stir grief anew, with the remaining family required to display brave faces and be gracious hosts for a cheerless party that none of us desire to attend. I think we'd be better off skipping it. If you want to do something, you can invite your closest friends over here after the funeral. At least we won't have to make small talk to a bunch of strangers across the room from an open casket. Let those people pay their respects at the funeral."

She smiled at me. "You can be so dark sometimes, little brother. "And way too philosophical. But okay. Let's have a closed casket at the funeral service. I'd rather not have that be my last memory of him."

I gave her a squeeze. "Then we'd better get busy," I said.

Eloise got on the phone with the funeral home and made the arrangements. The funeral would be at 1 PM on Saturday at Holly Springs Baptist Church, with burial in the church cemetery. I sat down and wrote an obituary, with Eloise's suggestion that instead of flowers, people donate money to a local charity that helps the environment. Eloise approved it, and I called the Greenville Newspaper and dictated it to them. They promised it would make tomorrow's newspaper.

"How long are you staying, John David?" Eloise asked when we'd finished with the arrangements and the obituary.

"As long as you need me," I said.

"Why don't you just stay for good?"

"There's nothing here for me, Eloise. You belong here, I don't."

"You could take over the paper. You know you could do it."

The subject was a tiresome road, overly traveled. "You know I'm not interested in that, Eloise."

"I know. I'm just being selfish. I guess I'm worried about what will happen to Mackenzie and me. The last job I held was at Finley's Drug Store in the tenth grade."

"Why are you worrying about a job?" I said. "I'm sure Grandfather left you well taken care of." I was surprised she would think otherwise.

"You may be wrong," she said. "Granddad never talked about it, but for some time, I think he was just getting by. At least, that's the impression I have."

"I don't believe that for a second," I said, trying to sound convincing. However, Eloise's comments disturbed me. I realized I knew nothing about Grandfather's financial condition.

"You've got Still Hollow," I said, "and I'm sure there's insurance. We can also sell the *Clarion*," I added as the idea came to me. "You don't want it any more than I do. We'll talk to Ellis Hagood if he's still the family lawyer. He must have the details of Grandfather's finances. You'll see; he will be able to arrange something, so you won't have to worry. We'll pay him a visit as soon as we can."

"Would you do that for me, John David? I know it's a lot to ask, but in the frame of mind I'm in right now, I don't think I could concentrate on it."

"I'll do what I can," I said, but if grandfather named you the executor of his will—which I'm sure he did—then legally, I wouldn't be able to do anything without your approval."

"Co-executor, maybe," she said. He wouldn't just leave you out."

"We'll see, won't we?" I said.

Eloise prepared a plate for Mackenzie and took it up to her. When she came back down, she said, "I think she's going to be okay. The poor baby just needs a little space to get everything worked out. She was worried about being so anti-social, but I told her you would understand."

"She's an incredible kid, and I do understand," I said. "You've raised her well."

We went back out and sat on the front porch again. The sounds of the receding afternoon were all around us. Cicadas were serenading in complete harmony in the woods, and somewhere in the hills beyond, a Whippoorwill called, its mate answering with the same lonely, lovesick sound. I was reminded of a much earlier time when Eloise and I first came to live here. A time when we'd both just learned that life could have a cruel streak.

"Tell me about Kelly Mayfield," I said. "I didn't think Grandfather would ever turn the position of editor over to *anyone*."

"She's very smart. She graduated from Smith College magna cum laude."

Smith. It figured.

"She joined the *Clarion* about a year ago from the *Charlotte Observer*. Granddad thinks— *thought* the world of her."

"*Charlotte Observer*? That's a major paper," I said, and I wondered if Kelly Mayfield was a victim of the downsizing occurring in newspapers all across the country, thanks to the Internet. Moving from the *Charlotte Observer* to the *Clarion* was quite a downward leap. "What on earth is she doing here?" I asked.

Eloise frowned at me. "Not everyone shares your low opinion of small-town newspapers, John David," she said, using her big sister voice. "Kelly doesn't. Granddad badly needed help, and since you wouldn't. . ."

I could feel her eyes on me. "What is it?" I asked.

"I think it's time you tell me what happened."

"What are you talking about?" As if I didn't know.

"That damned thing between you and Granddad."

I stared at the floor, thinking about why I'd never shared the sordid episode with her. The truth was, I was afraid to put a crack in the pedestal my sister kept me on.

"Something happened during your last year in college, and the two of you were never the same afterward," she said. "I know you got into some kind of trouble, but I don't know the details. Granddad wouldn't talk about it, and now he can't. That leaves you."

"Do we really need to get into this now, Eloise?" I asked.

"I think we do. Maybe for you as much as for me."

A gap of uncomfortable silence fell between us. She stared at me while I concentrated on a time I'd just as soon forget.

"I did the unspeakable," I finally said. "I disappointed him."

Eloise played her eyes over my face. "What could you do that would be so bad?"

Dear, faithful Eloise. I took a deep breath and studied a spot on the floor between my feet.

"I guess things kind of went to my head. The football. The attention. Big man on campus. I started doing some stuff I'm not too proud of."

"Drugs?" she asked.

"Among other things," I said as I saw the first look of disappointment on her face.

"You were young," she said, trying to hide it.

"I was old enough to know better," I said.

She sat waiting for me to continue.

"There was a party," I said, with a vision of me snorting coke off a bare breast in a hallway of a house off campus, a detail I would leave out of the story. "I met a girl from town," I began. "Not a student. She came with a guy, also a 'townie,' who always seemed to be hanging around. But she wasn't *with* him if you know what I mean. They weren't a couple. The guy was passing around blow like it was a sugar substitute, and we all got wrecked. After a while, this girl and I took the party to her place. Just the two of us."

Out of the corner of my eye, I saw Eloise suppress a smile.

"Probably not something you'd want to tell the preacher, little brother," she said, "but not the end of the world, either."

"I wish that was all there was to it," I said. "Later, I woke up in bed alone. I got up to go to the head and found her sitting naked on the toilet. At first, I thought she'd gone to sleep sitting on the john. Then I saw the rubber tube on her arm and the syringe still hanging out of a vein. She'd moved on to the industrial strength stuff sometime during the night. I put my hand on her shoulder, and she was cold, too cold to just be asleep."

Eloise brought her hands to her face. "She was dead?"

"Yes," I said.

"Surely the police didn't think you had anything to do with it?"

I sat and stared at her without speaking, watching slow realization spread across her face.

"You didn't call the police," she said.

"I called the guy from the party. Her friend . . . or whatever he was. He'd given me his number. He told me to just take off. Split. Said she was a junkie, and the police wouldn't look too hard into it. It's what I wanted to hear, I guess. I got the hell out of there."

Eloise looked away, but not quickly enough to hide what I saw in her eyes. She'd expected more out of me.

"A couple of days later,' I said, "when I was almost at a point where I could go five minutes without seeing her sitting on that toilet—the guy shows up."

"The guy from the party?"

I nodded. "He gets straight to it. He wants me to shave points off the upcoming game on Saturday, or he's going to the cops."

Eloise made a small, round circle with her mouth. "He was blackmailing you?"

"I think he was trying to set me up from the beginning. He had pictures of the girl and me doing lines at the party, but her death presented him with an even more propitious moment."

"But what could the police do to you? It wasn't your fault."

"The scandal alone would have destroyed me, Eloise. No more scholarship. No more football. No more 'big man on campus.' Hell, probably no more college. He made sure I understood that."

"Oh, John David."

"We were favored by two touchdowns, and he wanted it closer. He made it all sound so easy and insignificant. Fumble a snap . . . sail one over a receiver's head . . . turn the wrong way scrambling out of the pocket. He wasn't asking me to throw the game, he said. He just wanted me to keep it from being a runaway. I was so thrown by it I didn't know what to say, which, I guess, let him leave thinking I'd do it."

Eloise watched me with sad eyes.

"That was Wednesday," I continued, "and I didn't hear from him again until Friday. He called the frat house, and I told him to go fuck himself."

Eloise smiled at me as if no other course of action on my part was ever possible. "What did he say to that?" she asked.

"He added another incentive. He said he had friends who were counting on me. He said they had already placed bets, and they were the kind of guys who'd end my football career more abruptly than the cops or bad publicity would."

"Oh my God, John David."

"By game-time Saturday, I was a basket case. My timing was shot, and I felt like I was playing through a brain fog. Not only that, but the opposing team was better than anyone thought. We barely squeezed by, winning the game by a field goal, 20-17. On Monday, the guy strolls into my room at the frat house like he owns the place, hands me an envelope with three thousand dollars in it, and starts talking about the next game."

"So, he thought you shaved the points?"

"Yes, he did, and nothing I could say made any difference. I realized that everybody else would think I did it too if it ever came to my word against his. But I couldn't let it go any further. I stuffed the money in his shirt pocket and dumped him in the parking lot. Then I phoned Grandfather and told him everything. I didn't know who else to call."

"What did Grandfather do?"

"He listened quietly, asked a couple of questions, then expressed his absolute disappointment in me in as few words as possible, and hung up."

"You explained that you didn't shave the points?"

"Dammit, Eloise, don't you see? Even if he believed me, it didn't matter. I'd pitched my tent across the battle line. I had fallen in with the devil's brigade: gamblers, drug dealers, addicts, and whores. I was morally corrupt. He took it as a grave, personal insult. The question of benefit of the doubt or second chance was never an option with him."

"So, what happened?"

"As it turned out, I didn't need his help—or anyone else's. The guy never came back to me, and neither did these 'friends' of his. Maybe he got the message when I threw him out. Or maybe the cops were on to him for the drug dealing, or gambling, or whatever. I don't know. I heard later that he left town. I never saw him again."

"The irony of the whole thing is that on the third play from scrimmage that following Saturday, I took a helmet to the ribs that knocked me out of the rest of the season. I lost my job to a red-shirted freshman who went on to make first-team All-American and played a few years in the NFL. I was no longer in a position to shave points, willingly or not. I'm sure Grandfather would have said it was God's way of getting *His* licks in. But I wouldn't know. We never spoke of it again, or for that matter, about much of anything else. He never asked how it all turned out, and I never told him. I let him think what he wanted—which would always be the worst. The rest, you know. As soon as I graduated, I headed to Atlanta. Months turned into years . . . and here we are."

"What did he say to you when he came down?"

"What?" I said.

"He went down there and stayed a couple of days. What was that all about"

"You're mistaken about that, Eloise. He was only on that campus twice.

When he took me down my freshman year and when I graduated. You were with him for graduation."

"Eloise sat frowning. "I could swear that several days after you called him, he went to see you," she said.

"Well, he didn't," I said. "He basically turned his back on me."

Eloise slowly shook her head. "I can't believe that, John David. Maybe he just didn't know how to help and was heartbroken to see you suffer. Maybe he thought he failed *you.*"

"If so, he had a damned funny way of showing it."

She shook her head again. "The two of you were just alike. One of you should have found a way to talk about it, but you were both too pig-headed."

"Well, it's too late now, isn't it?" I said.

She slid her chair over to mine and draped an arm across my shoulders.

"I'm going to give you some advice, little brother, and I want you to listen. You can't undo what's been done, and you can't live the rest of your life being sorry about it. Worse, you can't hate him—or yourself—for it. It won't do any good. You've got to get over it. I know you're strong enough to do that. You've always been my hero, little brother."

I came home to comfort and support *her*, and here she was, trying to console *me.* Something was turned around here.

"I need to go to bed," she said. "Tomorrow's going to be a long day. I'm sure there will be a lot of people dropping by."

I sat for a while longer, listening to the creaks and groans of the old house and the sounds of the night before going to bed. But sleep was a long time coming. Fitful, troubled thoughts circled in my head, echoing with fragments of regrets of things left undone and words left unsaid—and a fleeting glimpse here and there of a little white patch of sand.

CHAPTER ELEVEN

Wednesday morning, Grandfather's death made the Greenville newspaper's front page (albeit below the fold), delivered with a thump on the doorstep by someone in a noisy car. The obituary made it, too, as promised. I brought the paper into the den and read it, and when Eloise came down, I gave it to her. Mackenzie came and sat next to her on the sofa, reading over her shoulder. There were a few tears as they read, but little comment. When they were finished reading, Eloise put the paper down, her eyes red. She quietly mouthed the word "breakfast" and got up and went into the kitchen. Mackenzie went to help her.

The story didn't add much to what I already knew. Law enforcement agencies were quoted as saying that grandfather was shot and killed during a robbery and that he died at the scene—but nothing was written about why he was at the location in the first place. There were no suspects yet, but a multiple-state manhunt was underway. A highly complementary synopsis of his journalism career followed, then a listing of Eloise, Mackenzie, and me as surviving family members. I was described as an investigative journalist residing in Atlanta. Calling me anything other than a sportswriter for a weekly tabloid would have made Grandfather happy.

After breakfast, Eloise gave me Grandfather's long-time lawyer Ellis Hagood's phone number. I called him to make an appointment. I needed to get this estate-settling thing started. When the soft-spoken southern woman who answered his phone learned who I was and what I wanted, she put me on hold for a minute; when she returned, she said Mr. Hagood could see me as soon as I could get there.

Eloise and Mackenzie went into town for the unpleasant task of purchasing appropriate funeral clothes. It seemed neither owned any somber colors. Eloise would also deliver Grandfather's burial suit to the mortuary and sign whatever papers needed signing. She refused my offer to do that for her, and while I felt a bit guilty about it, I didn't fight too hard.

After they left, I donned a navy blazer to add a little business to my casual for lawyer Hagood. A silver late-model sedan came up the drive as I locked the front door. An old friend was behind the wheel, and seeing him made me smile. Bucky Streeter was my best pal growing up, a neighboring farmer's kid who was the closest thing I ever had to a brother. Together, we'd sown our share of wild oats across our teen years, much to Grandfather's dismay. He didn't approve of Bucky, thinking him a bad influence—which only encouraged my friendship with him. And as to who was influencing whom, it was probably a tie.

When I went away to college, time, distance, and different interests began the natural erosion of boyhood friendship. I couldn't even remember the last time I saw him.

I walked out to meet him. He'd put on a few extra pounds, and someone called a "stylist," not a "barber," was cutting his hair these days. But other than that, he was the same old Bucky.

We shook hands and did a man hug.

"How the hell are you?" I asked.

"The question is, how are you?"

"I can think of a better reason for a homecoming," I said.

"Terrible news," he said. "I can't believe it. Do they have any ideas about who did it?"

"They seem to think it was somebody looking to score money for dope."

"Well, I hope they get the S.O.B."

"We'll see, won't we?" I said. "I heard you lost *your* old man a while back."

"Yeah. He died in his sleep. Heart attack. I guess there are worse ways to go."

"Sorry, I didn't hear about it in time to make the funeral."

"Wasn't much of a service. He was cremated, and we scattered his ashes below the falls on Whitewater, where he loved to fish."

Bucky looked uncomfortable talking about it. Sorrow was a subject the two of us had never shared. Bucky's dad always struck me as a man irrevocably worn out by life. He seemed to approach each day as if in a chronic state of exhaustion.

It was probably brought on by thirty years of trying to scratch a living out of a hundred acres of red clay and rocks. I could picture Mr. Streeter in sweat-stained overalls, coming in from the fields at dusk, a well-worn hoe slung over his shoulder, walking like he was about to buckle under the burden of it as if it bore the accumulated weight of all the years of cleaved rows of cotton and corn.

"I thought I'd come out and see if there's anything I can do," Bucky said.

"You can buy me a drink somewhere before I return to Atlanta," I said. "We can catch up on things."

"Consider that done," he said. "When are you going back?"

"I don't know. Grandfather was helping me with a story I'm working on, and I guess I'll stick around a little while and try to finish it."

"What kind of story?"

"Oh, it has to do with a famous pro golfer and a woman up here he allegedly assaulted. The man's an asshole, and I'd like to prove it. Grandfather was helping me find her."

"Did he? Find her?"

"I don't know. Unfortunately, he died before I could find out."

Well, I can't help you with that," he said, "But let me have your cell phone. I'll program in my number and address. There are probably a lot of other world problems we can solve over a couple of stiff catch-up drinks. When you're ready, give me a call."

I gave it to him, and he added his number to my phone contacts.

"You were obviously going somewhere," he said, "so I'll let you get to it." He turned to leave and said, "Call me anytime, John David. I'm always available for an adult beverage."

He smiled and wagged his eyebrows at me, which returned the feisty boyhood look I remembered so well. He got in his car and drove away.

I stood and watched. I forgot to ask him how he was making his living these days. A few years ago, he was working as a fishing guide on the lake, but he didn't look like a fishing guide anymore. He had a more prosperous look about him. If anybody deserved prosperity, it was Bucky. He'd come a long way from that hardscrabble farm he grew up on.

I thought back to a summer when we were about thirteen years old, and we got the idea to try to make muscadine wine. Muscadines grew wild in the woods on Bucky's Dad's farm, and we picked and squeezed enough juice to fill a gallon jug, threw in some sugar and yeast, and hid it in the barn so Bucky's old man wouldn't find it.

We left it there for a week; it was August, with the temperature in the nineties every day. When we finally got the nerve to sample it, it was awful, and it was a miracle that it didn't poison both of us.

Bucky told me to pour it out in the woods, but I poured it on a pile of fodder in the pasture instead because it was closer. Bucky's daddy's old mule got into it, and we later found the animal standing in the middle of the fodder, legs all spraddled out, her head almost on the ground, and piss drunk.

I thought it was one of the funniest things I'd ever seen and laughed until tears came. Then I noticed that Bucky wasn't sharing my humor. The next day he told me that after I left, his daddy took a fishing rod and beat him so hard it left bloody marks from the guides on his back and legs.

I knew Bucky's old man beat him often, but Bucky always took it and never complained or changed his ways. He remained a wild and rebellious kid, full of good-natured devilment, and constantly in one kind of trouble or another. He knew when he'd gone too far with his old man and took his beatings with nonchalant resignation. I always felt like that was just an act, but even so, Bucky was a tough kid.

Later, I spent time thinking about that mule and what I'd done. I realized that Bucky's dad's anger wasn't at the wine-making but was stoked by the fear of losing the mule. That plow-mule put food on their table and was the only thing that stood between them and an even bleaker life. And there we were, feeding it something that could have easily killed it. It never crossed my mind that the mule would eat the wine-soaked fodder, so the fault was all mine and a stupid, unthinking thing to do.

What struck me the hardest was something else I'd never given much thought to. How different our lives were. I lived in a big house with an abundance of food and amenities, and meals better than most restaurants, and here was Bucky, only a mule away from not having enough to eat.

He could have blamed the whole mule episode on me, but he didn't. He kept his mouth shut and took a beating for it. I grew up owing him for that, a debt that had never been paid. I'd never had a better friend than Bucky Streeter.

CHAPTER TWELVE

Time had stood still in the small town of Pickens. The courthouse dominated one side of Main Street, and a row of two-story shops and stores with different colored brick fronts returned the morning sunlight with the starkness of a Hopper painting.

Whenever I looked at the courthouse, I always felt a sense of what I think is called Weltschmerz—the loss of something never experienced. The present courthouse replaced an older, statelier building that was torn down before I was born, but I'd seen photographs of it. It was an imposing structure of a bygone era, a majestic construction surrounded by oaks that shaded old men on benches who sat and talked about crops, boll weevils, and politics. As a kid, I always thought that whatever happened inside a building like that had to be important. This courthouse, however, with its commonplace redbrick façade, skinny white pillars, and tiny cupola on top, seemed to diminish the importance of anything that went on inside.

The law office of Ellis P. Hagood was behind the courthouse, two blocks south, near the old Pickens jail—originally spelled g- a-o-l. The antiquated spelling seemed appropriate since the small castle-like structure, no longer a functioning jail, was now the county's history museum.

I found the place easily and parked in a small lot next door. Inside Hagood's office, a gray-haired receptionist sat behind a desk. I walked up and announced myself. She told me that Mr. Hagood was with someone but would be available shortly. I recognized her voice as the one I spoke to earlier.

I sat down and picked up a magazine. I could feel her eyes on me, but every time I glanced up, she busied herself with something on her desk. I had the feeling she was struggling with whether or not to comment on Grandfather's passing.

Ellis Hagood's relationship with my grandfather went back to when he purchased the *Clarion*; they also had more than just an attorney-client relationship. They were close friends. As a boy who watched too much TV, I always thought the dapper little lawyer, in his customary tweed jackets, suspenders, and bow ties, should speak with a British accent rather than the clipped twang of an Upstate South Carolinian.

The door to an inner office opened, and the elderly man in coat and tie came out, followed by a young man in a golf shirt. I stood to greet the older gentleman and extended my hand, but he walked right by me and out the door. I looked back at the younger man, now standing by the reception desk, looking at me.

"It happens quite often," he said.

"What happens?"

"People confuse my great uncle Walt with my grandfather."

"Who is your grandfather?" I asked.

"Ellis Hagood. Who did you think?

"I'm here to see him. I'm John David Bragg."

"Oh, he isn't here. He's in Florida."

"But I just called this morning and understood he would see me." I looked to the receptionist for help.

"My grandfather retired," the young man said, "I took over his practice." He offered his hand. "He was Ellis Hagood Sr. I'm Ellis Hagood III."

"John David Bragg, I said and took it reluctantly. The guy didn't look old enough to shave. I thought he might be pulling my leg.

"What happened to Ellis Hagood number two?" I asked.

"My father is in the insurance business. The law gene skipped him, I guess. You don't think I look old enough to be an attorney, do you?" he asked, smiling.

"Well . . ."

"It's the same reaction I got from your grandfather the first time we met. I might add that he and I eventually became good friends . . . once he got over the shock that I looked like one of Mackenzie's classmates. Follow me," he said and went into his office.

I tagged along. He stood waiting by several framed diplomas on the wall.

"Look, there's no need to . . ."

"Humor me," he said and pointed to the top diploma. "William and Mary." He moved to another one. "Columbia Law School. And below that, my acceptance to the bar of the Great State of South Carolina." He walked over and took a seat behind his desk. "At Columbia, I graduated number three in my class and turned down offers to join some of the country's most prestigious law firms."

"Why?"

"Because I wanted to." He gave me a look that dared me to say anything else.

I didn't.

"I assume you're here about your grandfather's will," he said. "If not, what else can I do for you beyond offer my heartfelt sympathies over the tragic death of a fine man?"

I sat down across the desk from him. "Yes, the will. That and anything else you can tell me about his business and financial affairs."

"Is Eloise joining us?"

"No, she isn't. It's just me."

"I think it might be better if both of you are present for the reading," he said.

"She wants me to handle everything for her."

Hagood reached for the phone caddy. Looked up a number and dialed it. He swiveled around in his chair and stared out the window, his back to me.

"Eloise, hello," he said after a moment. "This is Ellis Hagood. First, allow me to offer you my deepest sympathies. Yes, I know, it's a terrible tragedy. We will all miss him."

Hagood's voice was kind and respectful. I got the feeling he meant what he said.

"Eloise, your brother is here with me, and he tells me that you have no wish to be present for the reading of your grandfather's will. Is that correct? Yes. All right, but I'll send along a copy. And please don't hesitate to call if you have any questions . . . well, that's nice of you to say. Goodbye."

He swiveled back around and yelled to the woman outside: "Margaret, bring me the Bragg file." Then he sat quietly, looking at me unblinkingly through his tortoiseshell glasses as we waited.

"Did we get off on the wrong foot?" I asked.

"Don't take that call personally, Mr. Bragg. I'm required to do that. In fact, I probably should have it in writing just to be correct, but I think we can waive that procedure in this case."

"I didn't mean to get your back up over your age. Or lack of it, as the case may be. I was just surprised, that's all."

Hagood smiled. "You'd think I'd be used to it by now. I apologize for the bullshit about the class ranking and the offers."

"You mean it isn't true?" I asked.

"Of course, it's true. But it's still bullshit."

The receptionist delivered a file folder that contained a sheaf of papers. Hagood fumbled among them until he found a document, pulled his glasses closer to the end of his nose, and peered at it. "Do you want me to go through all the legalese gibberish or cut to the chase?" he asked.

"Cut to the chase," I replied.

He looked at me and frowned. "In anticipation of this meeting, I took the liberty of reviewing the file. The will, I have to admit, has me intrigued. My grandfather drew it up for your grandfather long before I began working here. I have not come across another one worded quite this way. But then again, words were your grandfather's business, weren't they?"

If he was looking for some kind of comment from me, I couldn't give him one. I had no idea what he was talking about or what lay in my grandfather's will.

"I'll read one part of it verbatim if that's okay."

I didn't think he was really asking for my permission, but I nodded anyway.

"To my beloved granddaughter Eloise and my precious great-granddaughter Mackenzie, I leave a love that is far more lasting than my time upon this earth, along with my trust that if there is anyone in this world who will understand my actions here, it will be them."

Hagood shifted in his seat and glanced at me over the top of his glasses before resuming. "To my grandson, John David, I leave all my worldly possessions in the belief that he will discover my love and trust through my deeds. By this act, I place Eloise and Mackenzie in his hands."

"What?" I almost shouted.

"Well, it's really quite simple," Hagood said, looking up. "He's left everything to you."

"I don't understand," I said flatly.

"There's nothing to understand. You get," Hagood said, turning his eyes back to the will, "two hundred acres of land, located approximately ten miles north of the township of Pickens in the community of Sunset, including the family residence, commonly known as Still Hollow, and all other constructions, dwellings, household goods and artifacts thereon; plus all monies, policies, investments, valuables, and collectibles personally held by Garnet Quincy Bragg—including the business and property, dwellings, equipment, and holdings in the 300 block of Pendleton Street, Pickens, South Carolina, otherwise known as the *Clarion*." He looked up from the will and added, "There are no stipulations as to what you do with any of it."

I was numb.

"It looks like he left it entirely up to you to decide if Eloise and Mackenzie share in the bequeathal," he added.

"It looks like he had gone senile," I said.

"I know that isn't true," Hagood offered.

"It's a test," I said. "Even in death, he's giving me a goddamned test."

"Forgive me for saying so, but if it's a test, you're already failing it. To me, it's more proof than a test. Proof that he had a lot of faith in you."

I didn't care what it was called: test, proof, or the act of a crazy old man who had to be right no matter how different it made him or who suffered because of it. It was another of his experiments in morality, a final lesson for his most difficult pupil. I stared out the window, trying to collect my thoughts while Hagood watched me quietly.

"What I have to do is quite easy, actually," I finally said. "I don't want anything but Still Hollow, and I really don't want that. I just want it to stay in the family."

I turned to Hagood. "I'd like your help in preparing something that will guarantee Eloise has Still Hollow as long as she lives, then Mackenzie after her. And I want you to help me sell the newspaper. It has to be worth a substantial sum, and the proceeds and everything else can go into a trust fund for Eloise and Mackenzie so they can maintain Still Hollow. Will you help me do that?"

Hagood took his time answering. "I'd be happy to, but are you sure this is what you want to do? Your grandfather had on several occasions indicated that one day you might return to take over the newspaper yourself."

"He actually told you that?" I asked, failing to keep the surprise from my voice.

"He told my grandfather. My grandfather told me. I understand that you're also a journalist?"

"I'm a sportswriter."

Hagood gave me a look that suggested he found the distinction negligible.

"I have no interest whatsoever in the *Clarion*," I said flatly. "I want it sold as soon as possible."

He studied me for a moment. "Well. That answers that I guess, but there are complications."

I waited for him to continue.

"The bank is holding a lien on the newspaper for outstanding loans, which must be taken care of before any sale.

"Loans?" I said. It was the first I'd heard of it. Was Eloise right about Grandfather having financial trouble?

"Is the newspaper making money?" I asked.

"The newspaper has always shown a modest profit," Hagood replied, "which would be greater if your Grandfather's editorials didn't occasionally anger people in the community, often resulting in the loss of advertising revenue."

He wasn't telling me anything I didn't already know about Grandfather's knack for pissing people off. "What were the loans for?" I asked.

"Mostly for capital improvements, which occurred in stages over the years: a new press, computer and other equipment costs, expansions, and so forth.

"Then we'll just build them into the sale price. That's another reason to sell it."

"It may not be that easy," Hagood said. "The bank may not be willing to wait for it. I'm afraid that Garnet being . . . well, who he was, the bank was quite lenient with him. Most years, when annual interest payments were due, they would allow him to fold it back into the notes, increasing the principal rather than paying it down. They may not be quite as understanding with anyone else."

Meaning me, I thought. "So, what are you telling me? Are we in trouble here?"

"Anticipating your arrival, I took a quick look at things earlier and saw that one of the notes is due soon. If you could pay the interest on it and maybe a bit of the principal, we might get them to roll it over for another year. It would give us more time to sell the newspaper. How much money can you raise now, Mr. Bragg?"

I didn't have to think too long." I have about eight-hundred bucks in the bank, an old jeep that the finance company and I own, and a baseball card collection worth about two grand," I said. "There may be an insurance policy on the old man, but if there is, it sounds like it may be all Eloise and Mackenzie will have to live on for a while."

Hagood unsuccessfully tried to hide his disappointment. "The *Clarion* has an operational account," he said, "but I don't know what the balance shows. You'll have to check on that."

"How much is the *Clarion* worth?" I asked.

"I don't know, but I think it's enough to cover these loans and then some. An audit would help us determine that. But how much it's really worth might not matter. The real question is how much a buyer is willing to pay—especially with this debt hanging over your head. They might think it smarter to wait until foreclosure and then pick the place up at a fire-sale price."

"Would you know if anyone has ever expressed an interest in buying the paper?"

Hagood briefly chewed on his lip, his eyes inwardly focused on something that wasn't too pleasant.

"There was someone about a year ago," he finally said, "but I don't think he's what we're looking for."

"Why, wasn't it a serious offer?"

"Oh, I'm sure he was serious. This person already owns a string of small papers across the country."

"Great. Let's call him up and see if he's still interested."

"Maybe we should see who else is out there first."

"What's the problem? I want to sell; he wants to buy. Sounds like a perfect match to me."

"Garnet wouldn't even return the man's calls. It seems the two didn't share the same political views. In fact, your grandfather was quite vocal in his distaste for the man. I think he referred to him as an imbecilic neo-Nazi. I took it to mean that this fellow uses his newspapers to espouse an extreme political view."

"And my grandfather didn't?" I said.

My sarcasm wasn't lost on Hagood.

"Your grandfather was nothing like this man. Garnet's editorials would often ruffle feathers, but I always found them to be fair and—"

"Look," I said, cutting him off. "I really don't need you to defend my grandfather to me right now. I need you to help me find a buyer for the *Clarion.* I don't care if it turns out to be Heinrich Himmler reincarnated."

Hagood's face colored slightly. He thumbed through the file on his desk with more energy than was required, found a letter, slid his glasses toward the end of his nose again, and peered at it. "The man's name is C. Wilson McCrary. He is headquartered in Des Plaines, Illinois. We can draft a letter of inquiry to him if you'd like."

"Do that," I said. I'll listen to any offer."

Hagood finally nodded, but it took an effort.

"Then we need to begin an audit," he said, "and an inventory to help determine what the paper is physically worth. It would help if you could deliver the *Clarion's* books to me as soon as possible. I have an accounting firm in mind that should be able to handle that part of it rather quickly—if they meet with your satisfaction. I'll give you their number, and you can talk to them if you'd like."

"I'm sure they're fine. I trust your recommendation. I'll get the records as soon as I can—today if possible."

"Good. And, of course, we'll need to find someone with knowledge of the equipment to estimate what that's worth, and we'll need a real estate appraisal. I can see to that, too, if you'll allow me."

"Of course, thank you." I offered him my hand.

CHAPTER THIRTEEN

Feeling like that old comic strip character that went everywhere with a small dark raincloud over his head, I headed to the *Clarion*. It was located several blocks south of Hagood's office in a sprawling one-story white clapboard and brick structure with so many helter-skelter add-ons that if viewed from an airplane, it would look like pieces on a scrabble board.

There were two things I wanted: the necessary financial records to set the sale of the paper into motion and whatever I could find to help me track Grandfather's movements from when I called him to the message he left me. During that time, he had located the woman I was looking for, and I hoped a clue would turn up here as to how he did that.

But the offices looked closed; the only car in the lot was a Volkswagen Jetta, the color of blue ink. I tried the front doors anyway and was surprised to find them unlocked. The reception area was just as I remembered it: it featured well-used antique furnishings in dark shades—a décor similar to the study at Still Hollow—complete with Grandfather's black and white landscape photography on the walls. There was no one about, but I could hear the clatter of computer keys coming from down a hall.

Doris Mozingo's nameplate still sat on the reception desk, but her responsibilities, I knew, went well beyond that of a receptionist. She had been with my grandfather since the beginning and was his personal assistant, office manager, confidant, and generally mother hen to the staff. Any duties of a more personal and undisclosed nature were unimaginable if you knew either of them.

Grandfather's office was to the left of the reception desk, the door closed, the room beyond the frosted glass panel dark. I walked over and reached for the doorknob.

"Excuse me." The voice came from behind.

I turned to find a young woman standing there, her arms folded under her breasts.

"May I help you?" she asked.

She looked at me with undisguised hostility.

"I'm John David Bragg," I said, feeling like I should have a hat to roll and squeeze in my hands.

"I know who you are," she said.

"And you must be Kelly Mayfield," I said.

My mental picture of her couldn't have been more wrong. This woman was no candidate for spinsterhood, far from it. The only thing I'd guessed right about were the glasses, which were thin-rimmed, small, and fashionable, and gave her both an intelligent *and* a sexy look. She wore her hair long and straight with the kind of black that shined with blue highlights. With her dark eyes and high cheekbones, I wondered if she had Native American in her family tree.

She pointed toward my grandfather's office with her chin. "I'd rather you didn't go in there. I've been trying to sort through some advertising contracts, and it's a difficult task as it is without someone moving things around. Garnet had a rather unusual filing system."

"He was an unusual man all around," I replied, opening the door. "I promise not to disturb anything."

The hostility flared in her eyes like a power surge.

"I said I'd rather you didn't."

I turned and faced her. "I seem to be getting off on the wrong foot with everyone today, but I'm not quite sure what I've done to you. Maybe you could clue me in."

She glanced out the window before casting the full force of her bottomless black eyes on me. "You've done nothing to *me*, Mr. Bragg."

"But you don't like me," I said.

She didn't answer one way or the other.

"Most people get to know me before they dislike me," I said.

Her expression didn't change. My self-deprecating charm had absolutely no effect on her.

"Your grandfather was a wonderful man," she said. "I think you caused him a lot of heartache."

I felt the anger warm the back of my neck like rising bathwater. "You don't know anything about me," I said.

"I knew Garnet," she said.

We glared at each other for a moment, and then she said, "If you want to go into his office, I guess I can't stop you. But please don't move anything. Now if there's nothing I can do for you,

I'd like to get back to work. The office is closed, but we will still have an edition to put out—eventually."

"There *is* something you can do for me," I said. "You can get me the paper's financial records for the last five years."

My request visibly startled her.

"Financial records? What on earth for?"

"I'll also need the assistance of the company bookkeeper, accountant, financial officer, or whatever you call that person here to help explain these records to an outside accounting firm."

"Just a minute—"

"They should also be prepared to meet with my attorney, Ellis Hagood, as soon as possible."

"I'll do no such thing," she said, her cheeks turning a lovely shade of pink. "I'm going to speak to Eloise about this," she said, moving toward the telephone.

"I would be upset if you bothered her right now," I said.

She picked up the phone and began dialing. "I can't be responsible for your emotions, Mr. Bragg. But I am responsible for this newspaper. I'm not going to let you walk out of here with the records of this company without Eloise Bragg's approval."

"She knows what I'm doing," I said, a small lie since she really didn't know—at least not in detail. "I don't think my request is out of line since my grandfather left this newspaper entirely to me—not to my sister."

She reacted as if I'd slapped her.

"I don't believe that," she said, staring wide-eyed at me.

"To be perfectly honest, neither do I," I said. "But that's beside the point. If you must call somebody, make it Ellis Hagood, our attorney. My sister has enough to cope with right now."

She put the receiver down slowly, the dawn of a suspicious idea showing on her face. "Why do you want the books?" she asked.

"So I can get some idea of what the place is worth."

"You plan to sell the *Clarion.*" It wasn't a question.

"I have no choice."

Those dark eyes blazed again. "Then you have my resignation, effective immediately."

"I won't accept it."

Her jaw dropped. "You won't . . . you don't have a choice!"

"I don't want your resignation. I want your help," I said. "Somebody has to run this place until I can sell it."

"Now there's an attractive offer. My resignation stands."

"How many people are employed here?" I asked.

She started to turn away, but the question stopped her.

"Fourteen. Why?"

"Don't we need to think of them too?"

"Just what do you mean by that?"

"If you leave, it won't help them," I added.

Her eyes became narrow slits. "You're using them to blackmail me? You're lower than I thought."

For a moment, I thought she might physically attack me.

"That isn't it at all," I said quickly. "I'm trying to say that the best thing for everybody is to keep this paper operating without a hitch. That way, all the employees—including you— will have more job security once new management takes over. Taking over a successful, well-run business will give the new owner less reason to screw with it. It's the best way I know to protect everyone's jobs."

"What you really mean is that a successful newspaper will fetch a better price, right?"

"So what? It doesn't change what I just said."

"Then don't try to con me. Don't stand there pretending you only want me to stay because of the welfare of the staff. At least have the courage to tell the truth. Admit that you don't give a damn about what happens to any of us. You just want to grab the cash as fast as you can and be on your way."

I felt the back of my neck getting even hotter.

"Some of these people have been here all their lives," she continued. "Otto Williams, our pressman, is a second-generation employee—taking over from his father when *he* retired. Doris Mozingo has been here for forty years. She's given her whole life to this paper. A half dozen others have been here twenty years or more. If these people lose their jobs, some will find it hard—if not impossible—to find another one. They would have nowhere else to go, with families to support and mortgages to pay." She looked at me sadly. "But you don't care about that, do you?"

I shoved my hands in my pockets and tried not to let her see how much she was getting to me.

"Look," I said. "I didn't ask for this newspaper, but I've got it. And when I said I have no choice but to sell, I meant it for Eloise's sake. I need to raise a lot of money for her, and I don't know any other way of doing it."

"I'm supposed to believe that?"

"I don't give a damn what you believe."

"Now he speaks the truth," she said, walking toward the door.

"Wait," I said, with enough force to stop her. "I'm sorry. We're all under a lot of strain here. You deserve a better answer than that. Do you know about the loans?"

"Loans? What loans?"

"The *Clarion* is mortgaged to the hilt," I said.

I could tell by her expression that she didn't know that. "Eloise doesn't know it either," I said. "The bank will probably want these debts settled right away. I don't have it. *We* don't have it. I've got to sell this newspaper, or we lose the *Clarion,* and Eloise and Mackenzie will have no income. I will not allow that to happen."

Her eyes locked with mine, then faltered slightly as if she was beginning to believe me.

"I'll try to do everything I can to safeguard the jobs of the people who work here," I added, "but the bottom line is, I *must* sell the paper."

She was still glowering at me, but she was listening.

"I don't intend to take a nickel of it,' I said. "But I need someone to help keep the place going. I would prefer it to be you, but if not, I'll just have to find somebody else. Either way, I have no choice."

"And I'm supposed just to take your word about this," she said, but the defiance in her voice was gone.

"If you don't believe me, just stick around and find out. At least it'll give you a chance to show your resume to the new owner. Look on the bright side: the faster we sell, the faster I'll be out of town. That prospect alone should be reason enough for you to help me."

"I'll think about it," she finally said.

CHAPTER FOURTEEN

Although Kelly Mayfield remained less than friendly, she was at least cooperating. She called the *Clarion's* accountant at home, and in fifteen minutes, a bespectacled and prematurely balding young man named Raymond Brown showed up. With an impressive display of raised eyebrows, he listened to me explain what I wanted and why and went to work without argument. He informed me that gathering everything I needed would take him at least a day—maybe more—but he could probably have some ballpark figures within an hour. I agreed, and Kelly Mayfield went with him to lend a hand, if for no other reason, I suspected, than to speed my departure from the premises.

I stood and listened to the sound of file cabinets opening and closing, the pecking of computer keys, and the drone of a copier coming from down the corridor. Satisfied that Mayfield and Brown were laboring diligently, if not willingly, to fulfill my request, I went to Mrs. Mozingo's desk and found her appointment calendar.

As expected, one of her duties was scheduling my grandfather's appointments. Monday showed a breakfast with the Downtown Business Alliance, a ribbon cutting for a new Pizza Parlor, and a meeting of the Rotary Club—nothing atypical or noteworthy. Tuesday, the day he died, there was one appointment in the afternoon, a school board meeting, but she had drawn a line through it. Perhaps it had been canceled after I called him and changed his afternoon agenda.

Next to the appointment calendar was a three-ring binder with a ballpoint pen connected to a small chain. It was a log to track staff members' comings and goings during office hours. There were sign-out sheets with spaces to record the time of their departure, their destination, and their return. Monday and Tuesday showed a number of entries bearing Grandfather's name, written in a small, neat hand that matched the appointment calendar—perhaps Mrs. Mozingo's attempt to keep track of him.

On Tuesday, she signed him out at eleven-thirty, which would have been right after I called, and he was back at twelve-forty-five. His destination was noted as the "Register of Deeds Office and lunch."

The part of my call that interested him the most was clear because as soon as he got off the phone with me, he made a beeline for the land office, most likely to find out who was buying and selling land in Eastatoe Valley.

Eloise said she called him that afternoon, and at six, according to the sign-out log, he left for the day. Thirty minutes later, he'd called me from Grady Morton's garage. So, somewhere in between, he got a line on my missing girl and came across something that "troubled" him. Impressive work for the short amount of time spent.

I put the sign-out register back where it belonged and went into his office, quietly closing the door behind me to avoid another run-in with the disagreeable but comely Ms. Mayfield. The office was as cluttered as I remembered it, with every surface and shelf filled and spilling over with books, files, magazines, and stacks of old newspapers yellowed enough to have been there for a while.

The walls held forty years of mementos in cheap metal frames. Grandfather posing with the famous and the infamous: lawmen, politicians, dignitaries, a lantern-jawed minor Hollywood actor, an evangelist as popular in the bible belt as the Pope is in Rome, and plaques, citations, and awards of all shapes and sizes, garnered throughout the years for one journalistic accomplishment or another.

The most significant award, of course, was the Pulitzer. It was displayed among the others as if it held no more importance than the plaque from the local United Way that hung next to it. I sat at his desk and opened a drawer, careful not to disturb the advertising contracts stacked on the desktop, presumably the work in progress of Ms. Mayfield. Inside the drawer were several pouches of pipe tobacco at various stages of depletion, the mellow aroma bringing an instant vision of Grandfather so clear I expected to turn and find him standing in the doorway.

Underneath the tobacco was a large loose-leaf book that I first thought was a photo album, but when I took it out, I saw it was a scrapbook. Evidently, the artifacts on the wall weren't the only mementos he collected. The first thing in it was an old newspaper clipping dated August 15th, 1943, long before his time with the *Clarion*. It was a story about some area families with sons serving in the military. The Braggs were featured, with four boys, all single and all in service at the same time—three in the army in Europe and one in the Navy in the Pacific. These were my great uncles, my grandfather's older brothers.

In later years, multiple family members would be prohibited from serving in combat simultaneously; it was a rule adopted too late for my great-uncles. None of them would return to Pickens County alive. Luckily, the war ended before Grandfather was old enough to enlist since his overly developed sense of honor and duty would have surely compelled him to join up at the first opportunity. Considering the bad luck that befell his brothers, he could have been killed too, preventing the eventual entry into this world of my father and, therefore, one John David Bragg.

I studied the yellowed photograph accompanying the article, picturing the Bragg sons, grandfather included, posing with my great-grandfather, the old bootlegger himself. They were standing in a group by the barn at Still Hollow, an American flag suspended from the eaves. My great-uncles were resplendent in their uniforms, and my great-grandfather was clad in overalls and wearing a snap-brim hat. A young Garnet Bragg kneeled at their feet. They all stared into the camera with matching bleak looks as if they had somehow caught a glimpse of their future.

I thumbed through the pages to an article from the late fifties announcing the sale of the *Clarion* to a local journalist named Garnet Bragg. The young publisher promised "sweeping changes" in reporting the area's news and events.

Several pages later, I came across an article about the Pulitzer. I didn't have to read it; I knew the story by heart. Grandfather won it for a series of editorials he wrote in the sixties about the last lynching in Upstate South Carolina—a shameful event that occurred back in 1947. What wouldn't be in the article was that in addition to all the accolades that Grandfather received for his editorials, he was also receiving a lot of hate mail from the local bigoted citizenry. I remembered my father telling me about the night, as a teenager, he awoke to find a fiery cross burning on the front lawn of Still Hollow.

His editorials recounted the story of a black man who was arrested for the murder of a white cab driver. On a cold, dark February night, a mob of about fifty white men stormed the Pickens County jail, hauled him off to a grove of Cottonwoods by a railroad track in Greenville County, and lynched him. Thirty-one men were arrested, charged with murder, and brought to trial. But even though many of them confessed to their part in the lynching, a white jury acquitted them all.

That verdict left a smoldering coal of outrage burning within Grandfather. He revisited this ugly episode in upstate history as the civil rights movement became a raging storm in America in the sixties. He chronicled an event that brought out the worst of the human condition with a series of articles. The editorials dredged up names and memories that some people in the upstate would rather have kept in obscurity and proved unpopular in certain circles—as the cross burning on the lawn of Still Hollow would prove.

I quickly flipped through the rest of the pages, stopping to glance at things that caught my attention. Many of the clippings were about the newspaper and the recognition and awards it had received over the years. I made a mental note to photocopy some of them, thinking they might impress a prospective buyer.

I skipped past anything about my parents' fatal car accident—another story I obviously knew all too well. I scanned a paragraph about a plaque I'd won in a creative writing contest in the sixth grade and a second-place ribbon a year or two later for a science project entered in the state science fair. There was nothing in the book about my prowess on the gridiron, but that was no surprise.

Near the album's end, my name jumped out again as the byline of a story I did a few years back during a brief stint with the *Atlanta Journal-Constitution*. It was about an insurance scam among thoroughbred horse breeders. Several unscrupulous owners were killing their horses for insurance money, and my investigative efforts were responsible for their arrest and conviction. I reread it, thinking it was some of my best work. There was a positive, honest energy there that lacked the cynicism that would eventually creep into my writing. I closed the book and placed it back into the drawer. Finding the horse-breeder story that I wrote was a surprise. I didn't know that grandfather had ever read anything I'd done, much less clipped it out and saved it.

Searching the other drawers turned up the usual assortment of pens, pencils, and miscellaneous office supplies, but nothing to reveal how grandfather spent his last hours. I was about to give up my plundering when I noticed the edge of a yellow legal pad peeking out from under a stack of advertising contracts on the desktop. I pulled it out and recognized the old man's wild scrawl, his handwriting like a doctor's, almost impossible to decipher. As kids, Eloise and I got the idea that his scribbles weren't the result of poor penmanship but a way to keep his notes from prying eyes. We spent an entire summer working like two Egyptologists interpreting hieroglyphics and learning to read his writing. I examined the page and saw I hadn't lost the knack.

At the top of the page, he'd written "red car," "Eastatoe Valley," and "Barry Beal." This was obviously done while talking with me on the phone. Next was a list of what I recognized as several area hotels and their phone numbers. The list was surrounded by a maze of geometrically shaped doodles and wildly drawn stars, the kind of thing you might do while on the phone. Toward the bottom of the page were the letters "WS" and below that, the name "Cecil Hood" and a phone number with an Atlanta area code. A line of doodled question marks followed both these last entries. I knew Cecil Hood. He was an old farmer who lived in Eastatoe Valley and a life-long friend of Grandfather's, but I didn't understand why he would have an Atlanta phone number. I knew Cecil Hood. He was an old farmer who lived in Eastatoe Valley and a life-long friend of Grandfather's, but I didn't understand why he would have an Atlanta phone number.

I looked at his name again and saw it was Carl Hood, not Cecil. Carl, I didn't know. I also didn't know what the "WS" meant or why Grandfather had written either on the pad.

The rest of the pages were blank. I looked back at the list of hotels. Their locations appeared to range from the college town of Clemson in the west to the city of Greenville in the east; one was in the north, just over the state line in North Carolina. All of them were within a thirty to forty-minute drive from where I was sitting. The only other thing they seemed to have in common was that they were all among the area's priciest, most upscale lodging. There wasn't a budget motel in the bunch. Was this list related to Grandfather's search for Beal's victim? If it was, I couldn't see the connection. I tore out the page, folded it, and put it in my pocket. If there were a clue here as to how Grandfather found my missing woman so fast, I didn't see it. Maybe it would come to me.

I went back out to the reception area. Mayfield and Brown were still at work as I quietly moved past them along the row of small offices where the rank-and-file employees labored— writers, advertising sales, accounting, circulation, and so on.

At the end of the hall, I descended the stairs that led to the archive room in the basement, known as "the morgue," to anyone in the newspaper business for more than fifteen minutes. It was where all past articles, clips, and back issues of the *Clarion* were stored. Management types at the big papers were continually trying to change the name "morgue" to fancier monikers like "resource retrieval center" or "data archives resource." Most old hands resisted this, knowing that it was just a thinly veiled attempt to justify to a board of directors the cost of the scanners, computers, and man-hours needed to bring a newspaper's archives into the age of technology.

The *Clarion* was yet to fully enter this area of the hi-tech world. The paper's repository of a hundred years of upstate history remained stored mostly on spools of microfilm in several battle-ship gray filing cabinets lining the wall. An old microfilm viewer sat near them, a tall metal stool the same color as the cabinets perched in front of it.

A couple of microfilm boxes sat on the side shelf of the viewer, the film from one of them still threaded through the sprockets of the machine. The label on the box read "June - August 2003." Mostly out of curiosity, I switched on the projection light and leaned toward the screen. What I saw was an article dated July 15th, 2003, that bore the headline, "Local man sentenced in Atlanta." I sat down and read it.

> Carl Edward Hood, the Pickens County native convicted of second degree murder in the beating death of Leon E. Waldrop outside an Atlanta nightclub last year, was sentenced yesterday by 5th District Georgia Superior Court Judge William Horton III. Hood was sentenced to twenty years in the Georgia State Prison at Reidsville, with the possibility of parole in ten years. Hood, 35, with a lengthy record of prior arrests and convictions previously served time in the Pickens County Correction Farm for aggravated assault. Carl Hood is the son of Cecil Hood, a respected farmer and lifelong resident of the Eastatoe Valley Community. (please see Hood, A3).

Now I knew who Carl Hood was. He was the son of Grandfather's friend, Cecil Hood. I never knew the man had a son. Since this Carl appeared to be quite the recidivist, he probably wasn't around much when I was a boy. Maybe Grandfather knew him, but he never mentioned him to me.

I heard footsteps on the stairs behind me. I turned to find Kelly Mayfield descending the stairs, showing signs of renewed irritation.

"So, here you are," she said. She dropped a file folder in my lap. "Most of what you asked for is in there. Anything else will take more time."

She leaned over my shoulder and peered at the article on the viewer. I could smell her perfume and feel the warmth of her breath behind my ear. I turned and looked at her, which placed our faces so close together that I could see tiny flecks of amber in her otherwise dark eyes. Aware of the sudden closeness, she took a step backward.

"Please return the microfilm to its proper place when you're finished doing . . . whatever it is you're doing," she said and turned to go.

"This was already on the viewer when I got here," I said.

She returned and looked at the screen again, her pretty brow wrinkling.

"Garnet must have—"

Whatever she was going to say, she didn't finish.

"Garnet must have what?" I said.

She continued with a puzzled frown.

"I was going to say that Garnet must have left that out when he was writing the story about the accidental death of his friend Cecil Hood. But that was several weeks ago."

"Old man Hood is dead?" I said. "He and Grandfather were close."

"Yes, I know. Garnet was quite upset about it."

"You said accident. What kind of accident?"

"He fell out of his barn loft," she said, still looking at the microfilm.

"Well, he had to be about ninety years old," I said. "He probably shouldn't have been up in a barn loft in the first place. I guess Grandfather forgot to put the microfilm up."

She gave me a look that said that wasn't even remotely possible.

"I was down here Tuesday morning, and this wasn't here. If he looked at this, it would have had to be that afternoon."

The afternoon Grandfather died. I turned back to the screen with a newfound interest. What was it about Cecil Hood's son, Carl, that would make Grandfather, on the last day of his life, write his name and number on a pad, then come down here to look up the man's checkered past?

I noticed Ms. Mayfield was staring at the screen as if she were wondering the same thing. She straightened up, gave me a stern look again, and motioned to the file folder she'd given me.

"This should answer most of your questions, Mr. Bragg, so unless you need something else, I'd like to get back to my work."

Before she left, I asked, "You wouldn't happen to know a girl about your size and shape sporting a black eye and a busted lip, would you?"

She looked at me as if I might be dangerously wacko and made a hasty retreat.

"I guess not," I said and watched her go.

I spooled down to page A-3 and read the rest of the Carl Hood story. A photograph from the trial showed Hood leaving the courtroom with a man I assumed to be his attorney. Hood was caught glaring into the lens with a fierce look. He was lean, dark, and broad-shouldered, with a bad-boy look that some women find terribly appealing.

I rewound the microfilm, put it back in the box, and returned it to its rightful place in the file cabinet—a gesture to the comely Ms. Mayfield's sense of order.

As I left, computer keys were clattering again from down the corridor. I didn't bother to say goodbye, quite sure no one there expected me to.

#

Ellis Hagood III was waiting for me when I returned with the *Clarion's* financial records. He was now wearing white shorts and a blue jersey with "Legal Eagles" written on the front. He looked about sixteen years old and mumbled something about softball practice. I fought to keep my remarks to myself.

Ronnie Burns of the accounting firm, Burns and Galloway, was also present. He had already been briefed about his task. Burns took the file and departed, promising to get back to us as soon as possible. After he left, Hagood motioned me to a leather sofa across from his desk.

"I've managed to contact C. Wilson McCrary, the prospective buyer we discussed," he said. "He informs me that he's still interested."

I was about to say "terrific" when I noticed Hagood studying his Nike cross trainers and wearing a hangdog look.

"You don't seem too happy about it," I said.

He was slow to look up.

"If it were my newspaper, I don't think I'd sell it to this man. The more I learn about him, the more I feel that your grandfather's reservations about him have merit. In addition to his extreme political views, his business model is to strip the papers he acquires to a bare minimum, especially staff-wise, with quality and substance taking a backseat to low budget and his canned editorials. If a guy like that gets his hands on the *Clarion*, he'll turn it into something I don't believe will benefit the community. I live here; you don't."

He dropped his eyes from me again when I didn't comment and sighed. "As soon as we get a better idea of what the paper is worth," he said, "we'll open a dialog with him."

I was getting tired of people judging my character.

"Just for the sake of argument," I said, "how much would it cost to run ads in the Atlanta, Greenville, and Charlotte papers— and maybe the *Wall Street Journal*? Can we tap into some kind of industry trade publication or publishing grapevine?"

Hagood finally smiled. "Whatever the cost, I think a good accountant like Ronnie Burns could find a way to write it off."

"And maybe there's a broker somewhere who specializes in these sorts of things."

"An excellent idea." Hagood was practically beaming now.

"Then do it," I said. "And make any other inquiries you think necessary. But please hurry." I left him to pursue alternate avenues for potential buyers, which he obviously preferred to C. Wilson McCrary. I thought that Kelly Mayfield would hate me even more if I sold the paper to someone like him, and I was surprised to find that what she felt about me mattered.

CHAPTER FIFTEEN

I stopped by a greasy spoon on Main Street, ordered a chili cheeseburger, and asked the teenage waitress for directions to the County Registrar of Deeds Office. She hadn't a clue and went to consult the elderly fry cook in the kitchen. He came out and personally gave me directions, taking the time to draw a map on a napkin, illustrating Southern hospitality. The office was located, he said, in the County Government Complex, several miles south of town. I paid the check, tipped generously, and headed out.

At the edge of town, I went too far into a yellow light to stop before it changed to red, so I sailed through it. My mind had wandered off into some other zip code. I quickly searched the rearview mirror for signs of a cop car among the cars lining up at the light. It appeared I'd lucked out. There wasn't a cop in sight. Suddenly, a white pickup truck, three cars back in the line, pulled out, sped around the other vehicles, and ran the red light too. Once through the light, the truck settled down to a reasonable speed and fell in behind me. I couldn't see the driver clearly, but it was someone in a billed cap. I guess he thought if I could do it, he could too.

"Rednecks," I said to myself. There was no explaining them.

A couple of miles later, I walked into the Registrar of Deeds Office and found a pleasant-looking older woman replacing a book the size of a coffee table on a shelf with dozens of others just like it. Plat books, I presumed. I walked around a long table and a bank of cabinets with dozens of small drawers to stand next to her. She turned and smiled. A nameplate on her blouse front read "Betty Roper." I asked her if she was working last Tuesday afternoon. The question obviously surprised her; it was a moment before she answered.

"Why yes, I was," she said. "Why do you ask?"

"I'm trying to find out if my grandfather was in here that afternoon."

She stopped and looked at me. "Who is your grandfather?"

"Garnet Bragg," I said.

She quickly brought her hands to her face. "Oh, my word," she said. "Yes, he was here. We were all so sorry about what happened. Oh, my word," she said again.

"Do you happen to know what he was looking for?" I asked.

She was shaking her head, "He knew his way around in here," she said, "and he didn't seem to need my help. He just said hello and went right back to the records."

"Did you notice what record or deed he may have looked at?"

"No, but I got the feeling whatever book he wanted, Darryl Watson already had it out."

"Darryl Watson?"

"Yes. Mr. Watson is here all the time," she said, with a tone that left no doubt that Watson was not one of her favorite people.

"Mr. Watson was sitting at the table looking through one of the deed books when your grandfather came in," she continued. "Your grandfather sat down with him, and they looked at the book together. They didn't sit there long. Mr. Bragg seemed to become disturbed about something and left rather hurriedly. It was probably something that Darryl Watson said to him. He has a way of irritating people."

I felt sure that one of the people Darryl Watson irritated most was Betty Roper.

"I don't think I know Mr. Watson," I said.

"He's a local realtor. His office is on West Main in Pickens, next to Blue Ridge Power. Watson Realty."

I thanked Betty Roper for her help and left to pay Watson Realty a visit. But as I approached the intersection with the road that would take me back to town, I spotted a sign pointing to the Pickens County Sheriff's Department straight ahead. I decided to go there first since I was so near. I soon came upon a two-story brown brick building with a sign out front announcing that it housed the County Detention Center, County Traffic Court, the Office of Magistrate, and the Sheriff's Office. Next to the building, a chain-length fence enclosed several automobiles. One of them was Grandfather's old Cadillac.

I parked and went inside, where a woman behind a cluttered desk listened politely as I explained who I was and what I wanted. I told her I needed the odometer reading of the Caddy so I could put the car up for sale. That was basically true. I did want to sell the old car, but I left out the part where I needed the odometer reading and Grady Morton's oil change sticker to find out how many miles Grandfather drove after leaving the garage.

She said she'd have to go get someone to answer that. She then, as everyone else seemed to be doing, proceeded to tell me what a great man my grandfather was, how sorry she was at his tragic death, and how much everyone would miss him. All these platitudes were starting to wear a little thin. Or maybe I was just anti-platitude because they were directed at Grandfather.

The woman went down a hall and returned a few minutes later with a plain-clothes detective in tow. He was introduced as Lieutenant Jud Chapin of the Criminal Investigations Department. He said he was one of the detectives working Grandfather's case.

I told him the same story I'd given to the woman about wanting to sell the car. "Bad memories," I added. The detective seemed to understand that.

"I've got the odometer reading in the paperwork," he said and asked me to wait while he went to get it.

"Lieutenant Chapin," I called out, stopping him. "I'd also like to look at the tires and general condition of the car. Would it be too much trouble to let me see it? I noticed it in the lot outside. I can copy down the odometer reading from there."

I got the feeling that I was pushing the limit of his professional courtesy a bit, but he was trying hard not to show it.

"I guess that'll be all right," he finally said and went to find the keys.

As we walked to the impound lot, I asked, "How did you get the car here? Did you tow it, or did someone drive it in?"

He gave me a sharp look as if insulted by the question.

"Driving it in would be against procedure. We towed it."

"What did you use, a regular wrecker or a flatbed?"

"Flatbed," he said.

"We would never use a tail-dragger to haul in a crime scene vehicle. That could impact the evidence."

He stopped walking and looked me in the eye. "Mr. Bragg, if there happens to be some physical damage to the vehicle—which seems to be what you're getting at—it was done prior to our taking custody. Only the crime scene unit and forensics have touched the car, and it hasn't moved from the spot where it presently sits."

His words were said with a clipped tone that suggested I'd now strained his professional courtesy efforts to the limit.

"You've misunderstood me, Lieutenant Chapin," I said. "I'm sorry if I came across that way. I was just curious about how things are done." I'm sure he didn't believe me, but that was okay. He'd answered my real question: *did the Caddy's odometer accumulate mileage on the way in from the turnout*? It didn't.

We went inside the fence, and he unlocked the car for me, standing back while I gave it the once over, inside, and out. Except for the dark smudges around the windows and doors, which I guessed was fingerprint dust, the old Caddy proved to be as dent-free and perfect as always—right down to the almost new tires. I went through the charade of taking a few notes—for the ad copy, of course—while getting what I really came for: the odometer reading from the speedometer and the one from Grady Morton's oil-change sticker. I thanked Lieutenant Chapin for his help and could tell he was happy to see me go.

Back in the Jeep, I looked at the Caddy's odometer readings I'd taken and did some quick math. Ignoring the 3000 miles Grady Morton added to the oil change decal as a reminder of when the next service was due, Grandfather drove a total of 30.4 miles after he left the garage. Okay, so I knew how far he drove after he left Morton's. The trick now was to use it to find out *where* he drove. I headed for Watson Realty to see if I could learn anything there.

As I left, I noticed another white pickup truck behind me. From the distinctive crossbar grill, I recognized it as a Dodge Ram, the same make and model as the one that ran the red light earlier. It followed me all the way into Pickens. Maybe it was the same guy, and he was going back to run some more stoplights.

CHAPTER SIXTEEN

Watson Realty was precisely where Betty Roper said it was. I found a short man with a large stomach and a jowly red face standing on the sidewalk, locking up the small storefront office. He had a wrinkled brown paper bag and a thermos tucked under an arm.

"Mr. Watson?" I called out, taking a chance that I had the right man.

"Yes," he said, turning to look at me. A brief look of irritation was quickly replaced by the wide, plastered smile of the perpetual salesman.

"I hope I didn't catch you at a bad time," I said.

He looked at the keys in his hands, then back at me. "No, not at all. How can I help you?"

"I'd like some information if you can spare a moment."

"What kind of information?" he asked and turned to wave enthusiastically to a passing motorist who looked right at him but didn't return the greeting.

"I'm John David Bragg. I think you knew my grandfather, Garnet Bragg?"

He assumed a perfect tragic face. "Of course, I knew him. A fine man and a great loss to the community."

He offered his sympathies, and I thanked him.

"You know, I saw him on the very day it happened," he said, shaking his head sadly. "We were looking at deed books at the land office together."

He stood staring at the pavement as if contemplating his own mortality and then shifted his tragic expression into one of concern. Watson seemed to be a man of many faces but a lousy actor.

"Now, what can I do for you, Mr. Bragg?"

"I'm trying to settle my grandfather's estate, and I need some idea of his property's worth."

"I see. Are you talking about Still Hollow?"

"Yes, I am."

Watson beamed with delight—yet another expression displayed.

"Beautiful place, and I know it well. Been in your family for generations, hasn't it?"

"Since the late seventeen hundreds."

"My goodness. Where is *your* home, Mr. Bragg?"

"Atlanta."

"Atlanta. That's a far piece, as my grandma used to say. I don't get down there much. Too much traffic. Scares me to death just to drive through on the interstate."

He was buying time with small talk, but I could see him thinking the situation through, his face failing to conceal the eagerness in his voice. Wheels were turning in his head, probably figuring out how much the six percent commission on a property like Still Hollow would be.

"You're considering selling it?" he asked.

He wanted to hear that, so I said, "Thinking about it. If I can turn it over quickly."

"Mr. Bragg, you have come to the right place. And exactly at the right time."

"Oh? Why is that?"

He gave me a conspiratorial look.

"A man named Roy Habersham recently sold over 500 acres not all that far from your granddaddy's place. And Cecil Hood's place was sold, and it had been in the Hood family about as long as Still Hollow's been in yours. Son, where you find a couple of quail, there's likely to be a covey. There's some serious movement going on up there."

The Hood name seemed to be coming up a lot today.

"Did you say anything to my grandfather about the sale of these properties when you saw him?" I asked.

Watson stared at me as if I'd missed the point entirely.

"I may have mentioned it," he finally said.

"What did he have to say about it?"

"Nothing, really. I think he was late for a meeting or something. He sort of left in a hurry."

I'd bet he did. That news would have lit my grandfather's tail on fire.

"When they damned up the Keowee River and built the lakes, it changed everything, son," Watson said. "It ain't been all that many years ago you could buy land for six hundred dollars an acre up there. Now they're getting six-hundred thousand—if it's on the water."

"But Still Hollow isn't near the water," I said.

"Hell, that don't matter. It's close enough. That whole area is taking off, and the sale of the Habersham property proves it." He stood beaming at me as if he'd just explained everything in crystal clear terms.

I gave him my blankest look. "I don't follow you, Mr. Watson," I said.

"That whole parcel is on the side of a *mountain*, don't you see?" He held up a hand and ticked off his points, finger by finger. "You can't farm it. You can't build factories on it. Hell, it's so steep you can barely climb it. The only thing it's good for is to be *on* it, looking *off*, so you can enjoy the view. It's a pretty picture from up there. It overlooks Eastatoe Valley. So, it's got to be for some fancy housing development, and a sizable one, based on the acreage."

Watson took out his keys and began unlocking the door of his office.

"Why don't we go inside and get the paperwork started," he said. "You don't want to miss out on this one. Timing is everything in the real estate business."

"I thought it was *location*," I said.

If he detected any sarcasm, he didn't show it. He continued to work at the lock and talk over his shoulder.

"Some of them fellers up on Wall Street or wherever keep saying real estate is still in the tank, but that just ain't true. Especially with what's going on around here right now. If you snooze you lose, Mr. Bragg. You've heard that, haven't you?"

"Once or twice, Mr. Watson," I said, "but before I sign any papers, I need to discuss this with my sister."

That stopped him. "Your sister?" he said, unable to hide his disappointment, probably the first genuine expression he'd shown during our conversation. "Is the property in her name?" he asked, his voice going up an octave.

"No, it's in mine, but I don't want to do this behind her back. I'll talk to her about it tonight."

That news seemed to mollify him a bit, and he appeared to resign himself to the fact that I was determined to do it my way. "Then I'll hear from you?" he asked, thrusting out one pudgy hand to seal the bargain while offering a business card with the other.

"You have my word," I said, taking his hand and his card.

"By the way, who's been buying this land?" I asked.

Watson removed his hand from my grip and gave me a sly look.

"Don't take this the wrong way, Mr. Bragg, but if I tell you that, you may decide you don't need me."

"I think you can trust me not to do that, Mr. Watson."

He looked uncomfortable and tried to smile. "It's not a matter of trust, Mr. Bragg; it's just how things are done. I assure you I mean no disrespect."

"Then I'll find out myself," I said. "And because I'll have to go to that trouble, I'll probably want to work through someone else."

He was shaking his head even before I finished.

"Now, Mr. Bragg, you don't want to do that. Besides, if you're talking about just walking into the land office and looking up the records, that won't work. Nothing's been posted yet, and if things go as usual, it could be a while before that happens. Also, the property was never listed, so there's no record there either. The buyers evidently approached them directly and made an offer."

"I don't need the records," I said.

Watson cocked his head and gave me a puzzled look. "Then how do you plan to find out?"

"I know Roy Habersham," I lied. "I'll go ask him."

Watson stared at me for a moment, then laughed.

"I guess you've got me there. Me and my big mouth. It always has cost me money. But I can guarantee you that you won't get the price I can, even with my commission. Plus, I do all the work, arrange everything, handle the closing, and so on." He looked at me with pleading eyes.

"I have no desire to sell the property on my own," I assured him. That was the truth since I had no desire to sell it at all . . . ever. But he didn't have to know that.

"Then what's the problem?" he asked.

"There is none if you give me the name of the buyer."

Watson sighed. "I can't."

"Then we do have a problem."

He gave me an embarrassed look. "I don't mean I won't. I mean, I can't. My grapevine says it's a company called Red Hills Developments, and they've bought most of Eastatoe Valley, but so far, I can't find anything about them. No published transaction history, no website, and nothing comes up when you Google them. But I'm just getting started. I'll find them, don't you worry. If we advertise a little, and they're interested, they'll come to us."

"Habersham wouldn't tell you who bought his land?"

Watson looked even more hangdog. "Roy Habersham and me don't talk," he finally said. "Has to do with an automobile I sold him a few years ago when I was in that business."

"So, where are you getting your information?"

Watson tried another unsuccessful smile. "That's confidential, Mr. Bragg."

"I thought we'd already been through that."

He wouldn't look at me when he spoke.

"A certain lady friend of mine who works in a beauty parlor told me about the Habersham sale. Habersham's wife gets her hair done there. She said they'd sold their land and were moving to Florida. I heard about Hood's property from a guy who bought Hood's livestock after he died. But he didn't know who bought the farm, only that it was sold."

"Who sold him the livestock?"

"Mr. Hood's son. I guess everything went to him. But I haven't been too successful there either. He ain't exactly a talkative man. He won't return my calls."

"You told all this to my grandfather?"

Watson gave me a forlorn look. "Yes, I guess I did," he said.

Watson reminded me of an old fox prowling around an impenetrable henhouse. He could smell the chickens inside but couldn't find a way in. Something told me it was a life-long predicament.

But Watson's news would have kicked Grandfather into an emotional high gear, and I knew he wouldn't have taken it quietly. The prospect of someone coming into Eastatoe Valley and paving over even more of God's original creation would send him charging into the field with a newfound ecological zeal.

But how did this help him locate my missing woman? And why did it pique his interest in Carl Hood?

I called Eloise from the car as I sat outside Watson's real estate office. "Do you know a man named Roy Habersham?" I asked when I got her on the line.

"Ronald and Randy Habersham," Eloise said.

"No, Eloise, I said *Roy* Habersham."

"Roy is Ronald and Randy's daddy, John David. You went to grade school with them."

The Habersham twins. Of course. Real hill people. I remembered them bringing a rifle to school in sixth grade to shoot squirrels at recess. This was way before Columbine, but they still scared the shit out of the teacher and class alike.

"They're both married with gangs of children now," Eloise said. "I always see Ronald at the Pickens Flea Market when I go looking for things for my crafts. He's out there almost every day. He sells old junk and calls it antiques. What's the big interest in Roy Habersham?"

"Someone mentioned his name, and I thought he sounded familiar."

#

The Pickens Flea Market was still where I remembered it, out the Walhalla highway just past the bridge over the Twelve Mile River, a narrow stream that some called Twelve Mile *Creek* instead. Evidently, they believed it wasn't large enough to claim a river. But I guess those who made the maps were obviously of a different opinion.

Rows of long, low buildings open on all sides like picnic shelters sprawled across the entire length of the river bottom, but only one seemed to house any vendors today. A large sign by the roadside explained why. The main trading day was Wednesday, which was yesterday; this probably meant that the odds of finding Ronald Habersham today were slim.

As I slowed to pull in, I noticed a white pickup truck approaching from behind. It was a Dodge Ram, just like the one I'd already seen twice today. I stopped inside the gate and waited until it went by. The driver was a man in a billed cap, just as before, but he turned his head away as he drove past. I sat and watched the truck until it disappeared around a bend in the road. The Cherokees who once lived in this area believed that all things are interconnected and were skeptical of coincidence. I'm no Cherokee, but I tend to share some of their beliefs, especially about coincidence. The guy was tailing me. But I had no idea who he was or how we were connected.

I joined the fifteen or twenty vehicles huddled in a corner of the unpaved lot, which was large enough to hold a thousand, and parked between a battered old pickup and a gleaming new Mercedes. Another Mercedes and a couple of BMWs were in the lot, looking haughtily out of place among aging SUVs and pickups with their obligatory gun racks. It was easy to distinguish the buyers from the sellers. The pickups and old SUVs came with loads of inexpensive junk, hoping the Mercedes and BMWs would take it home as expensive junk. However, everyone would probably go home happy with the price paid; I guess that was the point of a flea market.

A couple dozen people milled about, the building divided into stalls to give each vendor a space for their wares; while it might not have been the main sale day, there was still enough merchandise on display to warm the cockles of any bargain-hunters heart. Goods were hanging from racks on hooks from the ceiling, stacked high atop and under tables, and in some places, spilling out onto the ground in front of the stalls. There was furniture, tools, antiques, old clothes, paintings, glassware, doodads, knick-knacks, and almost any other object made by man, old or new. The place looked like a small village reduced to ruin by an earthquake.

A bearded fellow wearing a wide-brimmed hat made of rattlesnake skins manned the first stall I visited. Behind him, a row of old musket loaders and cap and ball pistols were stacked in a display rack against a backdrop of Confederate flags and old army uniforms. He looked like the perfect man to know Ronald Habersham.

"You wouldn't know if old Ronald Habersham is around today, would you?" I asked in the best down-home phonation I could muster.

The man looked me over carefully and answered with a thick New York accent—Bronx or Brooklyn. "He's in the stall with the what's-it on top. The weathervane."

I looked in the direction he pointed. Attached to one of the stalls was a weathervane shaped like a rooster. "Thanks a lot," I said.

"Don't mention it," he said, smiling from under the rattlesnake hat. "Youse come back now, ya heah?" he added.

Who was conning whom around this place? I wondered.

At the stall under the weathervane, I found a man bent over a cardboard box. He was taping the lid shut. A gleaming new Chevy pickup sat in the back; the bed filled with more boxes. He appeared to be emptying out the place.

"Excuse me," I said.

He turned, and I saw the red hair, impish face, and buckteeth of Ronald Habersham, twenty-something years later. He still looked like a kid who would bring a rifle to school.

"You're Ronald Habersham," I said.

"I know that," he said.

"I'm John David Bragg."

He gazed at me with a blank expression.

"We went to grade school together," I offered.

His expression still didn't change. "I'm out of business here," he said louder than he needed to. "Closed up for good." He spoke with that mournful native accent of the Blue Ridge, tuned to a chord of high mountain places and long-forgotten dialects.

"I'm sorry to hear that," I said.

"What the hell *you* sorry for?"

I didn't know how to reply to that.

"You see that there truck?" Habersham nodded at the Chevy over his shoulder.

I looked. It still bore dealers' paper plates.

"Bought and paid for in cash. So, I don't have to work this damn jockey lot no more."

"I guess I'm happy for you," I said. "Business has been good, then?"

"Hell no, business ain't been good," he said, reeking of whiskey that I could smell even from where I was standing. "My Daddy finally sold that goddamned mountain we wuz all born and raised on." He turned and spat on the ground. "He done give us our shares, and now this damn place can kiss my ass."

"Who did he sell it to?"

Habersham stopped taping a box and looked at me. "Who'd you say you wuz?"

"John David Bragg."

"Any kin to Garnet Bragg?"

"He was my grandfather."

"He got hisself killed, didn't he?"

"Yes, he did."

His expression softened a bit. "You got my sympathy."

"Thank you," I replied.

"Why would you be wanting to know who bought my daddy's land?" he asked.

I told him the lie I'd told Watson. "I'm considering putting our place up for sale and thought that whoever bought yours might be interested in ours."

He studied me for a moment, squinting his eyes at some inner thought. "You know, land's a funny thang," he said. "Most of it ain't worth shit until somebody wants to buy it. We been land rich and dirt poor all our lives, then some damn fool comes along and offers us more money for it than a show dog can jump over. And that's for a goddamned steep-as-shit mountain."

"What was this fool's name?" I asked.

"Company called Red Hills Developments. Guess they think they can build houses up there."

"Who handled the purchase for them?"

"A lawyer named Pitt and a young woman named Melissa something."

Arthur Pitt's presence officially connected Barry Beal to the development, and Melissa was most likely my missing woman. "You don't remember this Melissa's last name?"

He thought for a minute. "Nope. I don't recollect. But she was a purty thing. Built like a brick shithouse with Venetian blinds. But Daddy handled all the dealings with them. I wuz just there at the closing."

"Do you think your daddy would talk to me about this?" I asked him.

"He probably would, but him and Mama are down in Florida looking for a place to buy. I don't even know exactly where he is. Can't get him to buy a cell phone. He's still living in the past somewhere."

I gave him my cell phone number and asked him to give it to his daddy when he heard from him. I noticed he was suddenly eyeing me with new interest.

"Say, you like carnival glass?" he asked, pulling a piece of colorful orange glassware out of a box. "I'll sell it to you by the pound. Got some real nice pieces the womenfolk love to set out just to look at."

"I don't think so," I said and turned to go. "I like your truck, though," I added. Habersham didn't reply. He was busy admiring it himself.

Leaving the flea market—or jockey lot as Ronald Habersham called it for reasons unknown to me—I called Eloise and told her I would grab a bite in town, so she shouldn't expect me for dinner. I wanted a stiff drink and a little time to figure out my next steps. At this time on Tuesday, Grandfather already had a line on my missing woman. All I had was a first name, and I couldn't even be positive about that. What was I missing?

CHAPTER SEVENTEEN

Darkness was falling quickly, and to the west, a line of black clouds gathered, pushing gusts of wind that ruffled the tops of the trees along the roadside. Rain was coming. I went in search along the streets of Pickens for a place of shelter that might serve a cocktail and something to eat.

The white Dodge Ram pickup wasn't behind me anymore, or at least I couldn't see it. Maybe whoever it was gave up once he thought I was on to him. But since I didn't know why he was following me in the first place, how could I know why he would quit?

On the outer edge of town, I spotted Kelly Mayfield entering a small roadside diner. I whipped in, parked, and watched her take a booth by the window. I felt like a voyeur and was about to leave when she saw me. She lifted her head, and our eyes met. Even from where I sat, I could see her cheeks redden. Something told me I'd been the subject of some of her thoughts, none of them pleasant. I got out of the Jeep and went inside. Maybe this place would serve a fellow a drink. She watched my approach, her expression solemn.

"Expecting someone?" I asked, gesturing to the empty side of the booth.

"No," she answered. "Least of all, you."

I looked down at her and raised an eyebrow.

She shrugged and tilted her head at the vacant seat as if too tired to resist my company.

A waitress came over, a short middle-aged woman with a curly hair-do. She handed us a couple of menus.

"Just coffee," Kelly said to her. "Black."

"And for you?" the woman said, looking at me.

"Unless you have a scotch on the rocks, I'll have a coffee, too," I said.

"If we sold booze, I'd have one myself," she said. "But we do have some fresh-made apple pie that would go great with that coffee."

We both declined.

"You lovebirds don't know what you're missing," she said and went to get the coffee.

I smiled at the *lovebirds*, but Kelly didn't.

"Hope this won't start any ugly rumors," I said.

The woman behind the counter was still smiling at us.

"What do you want, Mr. Bragg?" Kelly asked.

"For you to call me John David," I said.

"What do you want, John David?"

"I want you to stay on at the *Clarion*."

She took a sip of coffee and studied the cup. I waited.

"I'll stay," she said quietly. "It's the only way I can help the others. And Eloise. If it helps you too, so be it." Her black eyes bore into my face. "But I have one condition. *You* stay out of the way. I run the paper; you don't. I don't want to show up one morning and find you with your feet up on Garnet's desk. If that happens, I'm out the door."

"No problem," I said. "I assure you I have no intention of spending any more time at that paper than I have to. You'll only see me with the lawyers or the accountants if need be—and maybe with any potential buyer who wants a tour. I will probably need your help with that. As far as the operation of the paper goes, you're the boss."

"Then it's settled," she said.

She turned to stare out the window as if there were nothing more to say. I let my eyes follow hers, and we sat quietly for a moment. It was raining now; the only sounds were the low rumble of faraway thunder and the occasional whine of tires on the wet pavement. I finally broke the silence and said, "I guess the sidewalks are officially rolled up and put away."

"Not what you're used to, is it?" she said, looking at me. "Down in Atlanta, they're probably just getting started about this time."

"Not me. I'm usually in bed by 9 o'clock."

"And always home before daybreak," she added.

I shook my head. "Give me a break, will you?"

She shrugged.

"What can I do to change your opinion of me?" I asked.

"Why should you care what I think of you?"

"I have this need to be liked."

"You must get disappointed a lot."

"Yeah, but the fun is in the trying."

"Well, stop trying with me. I find it insulting."

"Are you suggesting that I'm hitting on you?"

"I think that would be your style, yes. What's it been, one whole day since Garnet's death?" She looked sorry the second she said it. "I'm sorry, that was cruel. Even you don't deserve that."

"I forgive you," I said.

She stared out the window again, the moisture in her eyes reflecting points of light from the street. Then she stood up, tossed some bills on the table, and walked out.

I sensed the waitress standing over my shoulder.

"Lover's quarrel?" she asked.

"No such luck," I replied, adding a couple more dollars to the table. "Say, where can a man get a drink around here?"

"I'd say my place, honey, but my husband would probably frown on that," she said and chuckled. "Try the Silver Dollar east of town. It's down the hill from the old high school. A billboard at the edge of town will point the way. But watch yourself, darlin'. That place can get a little rough sometimes."

CHAPTER EIGHTEEN

The rain slackened, but the world was still streaming water when I found the Silver Dollar. A large neon sign lit up the cars in the parking lot—which was full—something I didn't expect on a weeknight. Not all the sidewalks were rolled up, it seemed.

Inside, country music played loudly behind a door fronted by what looked like a movie box-office window. A young lady with bleached-blonde hair and exposed cleavage sat behind a window. She seemed pleased to catch me looking at her exposure.

"Business seems to be booming," I said. "What's the attraction?"

"Loud music, cheap drinks, and good barbeque. Hell of a combination," she said. "But you've got to be a member to get in. It's a private club."

"How does one become a member?" I asked.

"Pay me five bucks and sign this," she said, pushing a cheaply printed wallet-sized card at me.

"No price is too high for exclusivity, I always say."

"It's what we have to do to get around these dumb-ass South Carolina liquor laws. There's also a five-dollar cover charge for the band," she added as I was signing the card. I handed my money over and went inside.

I ordered a Macallan on the rocks at the bar and got an "are-you-kidding" look from the bartender. If there was a place in Pickens that stocked Macallan, obviously, this wasn't it.

Macallan was my one extravagance, and while I couldn't afford it, once tried, forever hooked. I settled for a popular blended Scotch, put my back against the bar, and looked the place over.

The band was playing a rowdy Hank Williams Jr. tune and doing a fair job of it. The dance floor was packed with gyrating bodies, stomping feet, and flying arms. A blackboard behind the bar listed tonight's special of baby-back ribs and all the fixings. While tempted, I decided that a couple of drinks was all I wanted. The fridge at Still Hollow was still full of food and free.

A gorgeous redhead who looked barely over the legal drinking age shouldered up next to me at the bar and waved a twenty at the bartender. She turned and looked at me with the bluest eyes I'd ever seen. She smiled, and I smiled back. She was dressed like a cowgirl. She wore a western shirt with mother-of-pearl buttons, a hat, boots, and tight-fitting jeans. The lyrics to an old song came to mind, something about "Sweet Doreen from Abilene" and one's ability to read the dates on the nickels in her jeans.

"You by yourself, slick?" she asked, cracking her gum loudly.

"Alone, but not lonely," I said.

She wrinkled her freckled little nose and studied me. "You're not a regular here, are you?" she asked.

On the dance floor, an overweight woman lost her footing and sat down hard on her derriere. A shoving match broke out between her dance partner and another man.

"Is anything regular here?" I asked.

She took off her cowboy hat and carefully placed it on the bar, crown down. "Not exactly your cup of tea, huh?" she said.

"Not tonight. My pistol's in the shop getting the trigger filed."

Her blue eyes seemed to turn a slightly darker shade.

"Why are you being such a smart-ass when I'm just trying to be friendly?"

She had a point. "I apologize," I said. "I'm sorry if I was rude."

"Apology accepted. I'm Darla."

"I'm J.D."

"Why don't you come over to the table and meet my friends? We don't allow strangers to drink by themselves in here."

Why not? I thought. There was no reason to be unfriendly, and it was too loud to do any serious thinking about what, if anything, I'd learned today. Moments later, I was sitting at a table with a Nick, a Tommy, a Jill, and a Lisa, all of them closer to twenty than thirty. The table was covered with lime wedges, empty shot glasses, and the sweet-sour smell of Tequila. Darla scooted her chair over and said, "You dance, J.D.?"

Before I could say, "Not if I can help it," a guy built like a tree trunk came over, pulled a chair from a nearby table, and squeezed in on the other side of her. He bumped fists across the table with Nick and Tommy, threw an arm around Darla's neck, and looked at me.

"Who's this?" he asked her.

"J.D., meet Bobby Paige," Darla said and made a show of removing his beefy arm from her shoulders.

Bobby, several years older than the others, had no neck, a permanent crease between his eyebrows, and a white-blonde buzz cut. He didn't offer to fist-bump *me*.

"What are you doing with my gal?" he asked and smiled, but it didn't reach his eyes.

I picked up my glass and looked at it. "I'm having a drink. What else?"

"I don't know what else. That's why I fucking asked."

"You've got to overlook Bobby, J.D.," Darla said, turning her back on him, "he can't help being born an asshole."

"What's the matter, Darla?" Paige said, keeping eye contact with me. "Hometown dick ain't good enough for you anymore?"

She spun around and slapped his face. He was quick; he slapped her back and was about to do it again when I grabbed his wrist. To my dismay, he broke free with no apparent effort and stood up, knocking his chair over and tumbling down a pyramid of shot glasses stacked on the table. I ducked a wild swing and moved inside and behind him, getting my arms under his armpits and locking my hands behind his thick neck. I rode him down like a falling horse, upending the table with a clatter of breaking glass and flying objects.

He slipped my grip with confidence-destroying ease, flipped me over like a hotcake, got on top, pressed a meaty elbow into my throat, and bore down. Pinpoints of white light flashed like cartoon stars behind my eyes as he seriously attempted to crush my larynx.

Suddenly, his elbow was off my throat. I sat up, trying to catch my breath between coughing fits, and saw two big guys with Hulk Hogan arms struggling to keep a red-faced Bobby Paige at bay. Finally, Paige calmed down.

"This over?" one of the big guys asked him.

Paige stared at me for a moment and then shrugged his shoulders.

"Then get on out of here, Bobby. I want you completely off the property for the rest of the night."

Paige brushed himself off, scowled at me, and left.

"You okay?" one of the big guys asked me.

"You the bouncers?"

"We try to be."

"You eighty-sixing me, too?" I asked, my voice raspy in my ears.

"You didn't start it."

"How do you know that?"

"With Bobby Paige? You don't strike me as that suicidal."

I thanked them for saving me from speaking through a battery-powered voice box for the rest of my life and walked Darla to the bar.

"Thanks for sticking up for me," she said when the drinks we ordered came.

"What was that all about?"

"Bobby's crazy. That's why I broke up with him. But that was long ago. This was weird, even for him. He's seen me with other guys since then and has never acted like that. I don't know how Nick and Tommy can stand working with him."

"What do they do?"

"Bobby's a civil engineer, I think. He's in charge of construction or something like that for a big company here. He's Nick and Tommy's boss. But he's got *bigger* ideas," she said mockingly. "Something about starting his own construction company with backing from somebody with a lot of money. He never told me who, so I figured it was just more of his bullshit."

I noticed Darla looking at me, a slight curl at the corners of her mouth.

"What?" I said.

"How about me buying you lunch tomorrow to say thanks. I'll show you what I look like in the daylight."

"A rain check, maybe? I've got things to do tomorrow."

She stuck out her lip. "Promise to call me?" she said.

I didn't promise, but I did take her number. Maybe I'd see her again just to stir Bobby Paige's pot.

The curl was at the corner of her mouth again.

"I was going to make the invite for breakfast," she said. "At my place. But I chickened out." She got up and left without looking back, waving goodbye over her shoulder with a waggle of fingers.

I sat and watched her walk away. Maybe I couldn't read the dates on the nickels in her jeans like the song said, but it sure would be entertaining to try. Maybe Kelly Mayfield was right about me having the thoughts I was having only a day after a death in the family.

In the parking lot, I heard a step behind me and something cold and hard pressed against the back of my neck, followed by the distinctive metallic click of the cock of a hammer.

"Where are you going, motherfucker?" Bobby Paige said.

"Home to bed?" I said.

"I don't think so. Turn around, asshole."

I did and found Tommy and Nick standing behind him.

Sweat beaded on Tommy's upper lip, although it was a cool night. Neither he nor Nick would meet my eyes. Paige pointed the gun at my navel and held it there.

"Okay, Paige, you've had your fun," I said. "You've scared me. So, what do you say we call it a night?"

"This ain't over until I say it's over."

"You're not related to Yogi Berra, are you?" I said.

"What?"

"Never mind."

"You think I won't blow your ass off the planet?"

"Come on, Bobby," Nick said behind him. "Let's just fuck him up some, then boogie."

"Shut the fuck up, Nick," Paige said.

"Okay, Bobby," I said. "You're not going to shoot anybody for having a drink with an ex-girlfriend. You're not that crazy," I added, sincerely hoping I was right. "So, let's stop this before that thing accidentally goes off."

There was a flicker of something in his eyes that I didn't recognize, and I gave him a second look. There seemed to be more to this than just the girl.

"Go back to Atlanta, hotshot," he said. "I don't want to see you around here again. And believe me, you don't want to see me either."

Paige turned to walk away, then took a step back and hit me in that soft place just below the sternum, hard enough to knock the air out of my lungs and send me to my hands and knees to make sounds like a drinking straw that just hit the bottom of the cup. While gasping for air, I tried to remember if I'd mentioned to anyone in the Silver Dollar that I was from Atlanta. I was pretty sure I hadn't.

CHAPTER NINETEEN

"What's wrong with your voice?" Eloise asked. She was sitting in the den reading when I returned to Still Hollow. I suspected she was waiting up for me.

"Hay fever," I said, hoping she wouldn't notice the red marks on my throat that went with the hoarseness. I didn't feel like explaining my fight with Bobby Paige right now. In fact, I didn't know if I really could. The whole thing was wrong somehow.

I gave her the copy of the will Hagood gave me. She sat and read it while I sat beside her and ate a bowl of beef stew I warmed up from the fridge. The fact that Grandfather left everything to me didn't seem to surprise her. She actually seemed to understand it, which was more than I could claim. Her confidence in me to do the right thing was a weight almost too heavy to bear.

I filled her in on the money we owed, and she took everything calmly, listening quietly as if nothing fazed her and with absolute faith that I'd work it all out. I asked her about any insurance policies that Grandfather may have. She went into the den and came back with a policy for $100,000, which could prove to be a lifesaver. With that, we might be able to pay the interest on the loans and roll them over, giving us time to sell the *Clarion*. The rest we could use for living expenses for Eloise and Mackenzie until the sale.

I told her about stopping by the *Clarion* and finding a scratchpad on Grandfather's desk where he'd written down a list of hotels in the area. I showed it to her and asked if she had any idea why he would have done that.

She chuckled. "So, you can still read Granddad's handwriting? I'm amazed. Remember all that time we spent as kids decoding it like a couple of spies?"

"Yeah, I thought about that when I was trying to decipher it," I said.

"But hotels?" she said. "I don't know unless he was writing a story about them or recommending one to somebody."

"What about the letters 'WS?' Does that mean anything to you?"

I waited as she gave it some thought. "I'm drawing a blank there, too," she said. "What's this all about?" You sound like you think it's important somehow."

"I'm just trying to find out how he got such a quick lead on this woman Barry Beal assaulted. I still need to find her."

She looked at me for a moment but didn't comment on that. Instead, she asked, "What were you doing at the paper in the first place?"

"I was gathering the documents we'll need for the lawyers and accountants in order to sell it," I said. "I met Kelly Mayfield. She wasn't too happy with me or the reason I was there. You're probably going to hear from her."

"Oh my God," Eloise said. "I was so wrapped up in Granddad's death when you brought up selling the paper that I wasn't thinking about what it would do to *her*. I want her involved in whatever we do, John David. Will you promise me that?"

"Of course, Eloise. Nothing will happen without her knowledge," I said and wondered if that was a promise I could keep. "By the way, I learned that Cecil Hood died."

Eloise cast me a sharp look.

"Granddad ran the story on the front page. You didn't see it?"

"I guess I missed it," I said. "I didn't tell her that I let my subscription to the *Clarion* expire long ago. Eloise would look upon that as a treasonable act. Grandfather would have too, but if he had known, he obviously didn't tell her.

"Mr. Hood fell out of his barn loft and landed on a tiller, or a set of harrows, or something like that," Eloise said. "Whatever it was had sharp blades, and he hit them headfirst, cleaving his head open. His body lay on the thing for at least a day before anyone found him."

"That's terrible," I said.

"It really hit Granddad hard. He loved Mr. Hood. They could sit and talk about the old days for hours—about the times before the old mountain people died out or moved away. Before anybody even thought of damming up the rivers into lakes and building million-dollar homes on the shores." Eloise sighed. "Just two old men grumbling about what once was and what nobody else but them gave a tinker's damn about." She blew her nose on a crumpled tissue from her pocket. "Now they're both gone."

"Did you know Mr. Hood had a son?" I asked.

"I knew it, but I never met him. I think he'd already left home when we came to live with Granddad. Mr. Hood's wife died years ago," she said, "and I think they lost a daughter way back, too. I have the impression that the son was sort of the black sheep of the family. Granddad said Mr. Hood rarely talked about him."

I told her about the microfilm newspaper article I read about him—his conviction for murder and criminal history—and said I could see why Mr. Hood didn't speak of him. I sat pulling up old memories of Cecil Hood. One, especially, came to mind. My old friend Bucky Streeter and I spent a lot of time one summer fishing the stretch of Eastatoe River that bordered Mr. Hood's property. When Hood's watermelons came in, we would sneak into his patch and nip a ripe melon or two, submerge them in the icy waters of the stream until they were cool, then eat the hearts out of them along the creek bank, the illicit nature of the act making them taste all the sweeter.

We prided ourselves on our stealth and cunning and repeated the larcenous act several times, thinking that Mr. Hood was never the wiser. So, it came as a surprise to learn that he knew about our thievery all along and had told Grandfather about it. But Mr. Hood made him promise not to punish me, saying that one of the reasons he grew watermelons was so boys could steal them. I had liked Cecil Hood and was sorry to hear that the old man had gone in such a dreadful way.

My thoughts turned to his farm. If I remember correctly, it was at least two hundred acres and practically the center-cut of Eastatoe Valley. This meant it would be a necessary ingredient for anyone planning to build a golf course there.

"So, Mr. Hood was still living on his farm when he died?" I asked. "I thought with Barry Beal's plans for the valley, Mr. Hood would have sold the place some time ago."

"I think he almost did," Eloise said. "I know Mr. Hood was offered a lot of money for it and went as far as signing an option contract. But then he changed his mind for some reason."

"How do you know all that?" I asked.

"Because I heard Mr. Hood tell Granddad right out there on the front porch. It was the last time he came to visit. He said with the money they were offering, he could afford to buy a place anywhere he wanted, put a rocking chair on the porch, and put his feet up for the rest of his life. But after thinking about it for several months, he realized that he was already living exactly where he wanted to spend the rest of his life. He returned their honest money along with the news that he wasn't selling, and they threatened to sue him. He told us he was planning to get a lawyer and fight them. He said he was born on that old patch of land, and that's where he would die. He said anybody wanting to get their hands on his farm would have to wait until after he was gone."

She stared vacantly out at the lawn for a minute and then added, "Two weeks later, Mr. Hood was dead."

I had a sudden, disturbing thought. "Maybe he didn't fall out of that barn," I said. "Maybe he was pushed."

The look of disbelief on my sister's face told me exactly what she thought of that idea.

"What on earth are you talking about, John David?" she said. "It was an accident."

"Who says? Was there an eyewitness?"

"No, but Sheriff Arlen Bagwell and the coroner . . ."

"You don't think they can be wrong?"

"Why would someone kill poor old Mr. Hood?" she said. "

"For his land, Eloise," I said. "Somebody just killed Grandfather for a camera and pocket change. If a big development goes into Eastatoe Valley, then Cecil Hood's farm would be worth a million times more than that." The lengths the human species would go to for monetary gain were not part of my good sister's psyche. On the other hand, I was capable of darker, more suspicious thoughts.

My sister was shaking her head, still showing disbelief. "Who'd do something so terrible, John David?"

"I'd start with who has the most to gain. A company called Red Hills Development . . . or even Mr. Hood's son Carl. Did Mr. Hood say who he was dealing with in all this?" I asked.

"I didn't hear anything about that," she said, "but he may have told

Granddad. It was cold out on the porch, and I came inside and left them talking."

"There's a coincidental chain of events here, Eloise, that can't be ignored." I spelled it out for her: "Developers wanted Mr. Hood's farm; Hood wouldn't sell. Hood dies. Developers get the land. Hood's son Carl—with a resume for murder—gets rich."

Another thought hit me like an oncoming train. "Without climbing too far out on a conjectural limb," I said, "I could take this chain of events to an even more sinister conclusion. I could see Grandfather thinking the same thing I was thinking and saying it to the wrong person. A person who would kill him before he could tell anyone else."

Eloise sat staring at me with wide eyes. Finally, she said, "Are you saying Sheriff Bagwell is wrong, and Granddad's murder wasn't because of a robbery?

There wasn't a single shred of evidence to prove what I was thinking. But that didn't stop me from thinking it. My gut instinct didn't always listen to the facts. "I'm just saying it's possible. That's all."

"Shouldn't we tell Sheriff Bagwell about this?" she said.

"It's probably too early to cry wolf, Eloise. Everything I said is just conjecture—pure speculation. Anyway, I don't think Sheriff Bagwell would listen. He seems to have his mind made up about things."

"Then what do we do, John David?"

"*We* don't do anything. *I* do. I'm going to backtrack Grandfather's steps on the day he died and find out how he found my missing woman so quickly. Then I will get her to confirm Barry Beal's assault on her and tell the world. I can't let that guy get away with it. If I come across anything that proves Grandfather's murder was connected in any way to Cecil Hood's death—*then* I'll talk to Sheriff Bagwell."

Eloise was staring at me again. "But, John David," she said, "if you go walking in Granddad's steps, how do you know that what happened to him won't happen to you? This scares me, little brother."

I thought of Bobby Paige's threats and the white Dodge Ram pickup following me. Did my sister have a point?

After Eloise went to bed, I sat at Grandfather's desk computer and searched the Pickens County "Online Tax Search and Pay" site. I entered the name

"Paige" and clicked "search all properties." I came up with a Robert L. Paige, 215 Ridgeland Circle, Pickens. As only one Robert was listed, the odds were good that this was my Bobby boy.

The record showed he pays taxes on his home and one vehicle—a 2012 Ford F-150—not a Dodge Ram pickup. A Dodge Ram looks nothing like a Ford F-150, so Bobby Paige wasn't the one tailing me unless he had another truck he wasn't paying taxes on. But this didn't explain why he tried running me out of town. Maybe I should find out what Carl Hood drove— and if he and Paige knew each other.

CHAPTER TWENTY

Thursday morning, I awoke at the crack of dawn with a fist-size bruise on my upper abdomen and a voice like Gollum from *The Lord of the Rings*. After cursing Bobby Paige for a moment or two, I went down to the kitchen, made a pot of coffee, and lathered a couple of pieces of buttered toast with some of Eloise's homemade fig preserves, hoping it could relieve some of the raspiness. It actually worked a little.

I heard the morning Greenville newspaper hit the porch and went out to get it to read with my breakfast. The sports page showed the Masters' tee times for today's second round, and Barry Beal was listed for the afternoon at one o'clock. I guess he wasn't as upset over my allegations as lawyer Pitt had indicated and had decided to play after all.

Neither Eloise nor Mackenzie was up yet, so I left Eloise a note on the kitchen table saying I had things to do and would call her later. I took an old road map from Grandfather's desk, a ballpoint pen, and a couple of sheets of stationery and went for a drive north on Highway 178.

As I sailed by Morton's Garage, I clicked the mileage counter on the Jeep's odometer to zero. When I reached the turnout where Grandfather died, I pulled in and killed the engine. According to the counter, the distance between Morton's and the murder site was 1.2 miles. I then subtracted that from the 30.4 miles that the Cadillac's odometer showed it had traveled after leaving Morton's Garage. That left 29.2 miles that Grandfather drove before returning to the spot where I sat. Halve that, and the potential distance traveled from the turnout would be 14.6 miles out and 14.6 miles back.

Considering that Sheriff Bagwell said the Caddy was facing south when they found it, I assumed that wherever Grandfather went, it was north of this spot. I got out and spread the map on the Jeep's hood. With a sheet of the stationery, I created a handmade ruler with a series of hash marks. The marks represented 14.6 miles, according to the map's legend. Using the turnout as the center and the paper ruler as a radius, I traced a 14.6-mile semicircle around the north side.

There were two noticeable possibilities along the circumference where Grandfather could have gone: into Eastatoe Valley via the Cleo Chapman Highway—the entrance a half mile ahead—or to the small town of Rosman, up 178 and just over the North Carolina line. Rosman was 14.6 miles on the button. Eastatoe Valley was closer than that, but if Grandfather drove around the valley a bit, maybe looking things over, going there was also possible.

I set the Jeep's odometer to zero, drove to Cleo Chapman Highway, and turned left, descending into the eastern entrance to Eastatoe Valley. After a few hilly twists and turns, the valley opened up like a small, lovely crease in the green hills. The road crossed the clear, cold waters of the narrow Eastatoe River and then turned sharply to parallel it for the valley's length. The odometer at that point was less than the 14.6 miles maximum, so Grandfather would have had to zigzag back and forth across the valley to rack up the necessary miles. Possible, I thought, but not definite.

Beal had chosen a great spot to launch his golf and real estate development career. The little valley was perfect for a golf course community, beautiful and idyllic, surrounded by steep-sided mountains, but not so much as to prohibit building houses along their flanks. The valley was also an excellent geographic choice—halfway between the population centers of Atlanta and Charlotte and not all that far from the interstate and the Greenville-Spartanburg Airport.

With the lakes and all the development going on to the west, progress had marched into the northwestern tip of South Carolina wearing heavy construction boots. The development of a scenic little valley like Eastatoe was inevitable. If Barry Beal didn't seize the opportunity, someone else would, eventually. It rubbed my fur the wrong way to think of that son-of- a-bitch Beal as the one to profit from it.

The only nullifying possibility was the economy. Although it seemed to be gradually improving of late, there was always the chance of another downturn. I caught myself almost hoping for it if it meant Barry Beal losing his ass on the deal.

But if changes were coming to this little valley, they still lurked behind the scenes. I saw no flagged stakes to indicate surveyors applying their trade, no fresh scars in the landscape, and no advertisement of a developer's future plans. The only signal that anyone had designs on the place was that no one seemed to live there anymore. New weeds grew in the yards of the several seemingly vacant farmhouses and summer cottages, the driveways without cars, the porches lacking the usual rocking chairs and hanging flowerpots, and the barns and outbuildings void of farm machinery and implements. No new crops grew in the fields, and no livestock roamed the pastures. From the look of it, the Hood place wasn't the only property sold and vacated.

A rusty mailbox on the side of the road signaled the Hood farm with faded red letters. Behind it, a sandy drive led up to the old two-story farmhouse, partially hidden behind a towering grove of ancient oaks. Beyond the house, I could see the edge of the barn where Eloise said Cecil Hood fell to his death.

The bulk of Mr. Hood's farmland lay across from the mailbox on the other side of the road, toward the river. Looped over one of the posts on either side of the driveway was a length of chain with an open padlock threaded through the links. Both the lock and chain looked new. I drove through the open gate and up to the house.

A large yellow rental truck was backed up to the front porch, and two men were crab-walking a sofa into it. One was a beefy kid barely out of his teens, wearing a faded Metallica t-shirt; the other was twenty-five or thirty years older. The older guy was tall and lean, with broad shoulders. His arms were corded with muscle and covered with blue jailhouse tattoos. His long black hair was slightly gray-streaked and tied into a ponytail. A diamond stud sparkled in his left ear. Older, a little grayer, and more tattooed, it was the man who stared defiantly at the camera from the courtroom shot I'd seen on the microfilm reel. *Carl* Hood—Cecil Hood's black sheep son.

I got out of the Jeep and walked to the edge of the porch. Both of them saw me, but neither spoke. They continued to struggle with the sofa until they had it wedged into the back of the truck against more of Cecil Hood's furniture. Behind Hood, the younger guy spread a furniture blanket over the sofa. Hood jumped down off the porch, dusting one hand with the other.

"Yeah?" he said to me.

"I heard this place has been sold," I said, which was a spur-of-the-moment attempt to start a conversation.

"You heard right," Carl Hood said.

"I was out this way and thought I'd stop. It's been years since I was here."

The young boy came out of the back of the truck, plopped down on the tailgate, and pulled a pack of cigarettes from his jeans. I smiled a broad hello at him and got a vacant look in return.

"I ain't paying you to sit on your butt Jimmy," Hood said without even looking over his shoulder at him.

Jimmy got up and went quietly into the house. I didn't blame him. There was something about this guy that discouraged backtalk. I might have been taller, heavier, and younger, but I knew I wouldn't want to tangle with him.

"I'm John David Bragg," I offered and stretched out my hand. "I knew your father. He and my grandfather were good friends. Hood's only response was a hint of something—recognition perhaps—that moved behind his eyes.

"What's wrong with your voice?" Hood asked. "You gotta' cold or something?"

"Something got stuck in my throat," I said. "Better now." For some reason, I got the feeling he already knew who I was. I withdrew my hand and shoved it in my pocket. "Mind if I look around a little?" I asked. For old time's sake?"

He studied me for a moment longer, his face occupied with thoughts he didn't turn into words. "Knock yourself out," he said and went back inside.

I went around the house and walked toward the barn. A stand-alone garage sat off to the side, the door closed and locked with another shiny new padlock and chain. Just beyond was a corncrib, empty of grain, the nail heads in the walls leaving rusty tails down the side of the weathered wood. A hog lot, long absent of livestock, sat beyond that. The ground underneath the troughs—once mire and muck—now looked as dry and hard as set cement. The barn was just ahead, the pasture beyond sprouting clumps of wild onions and dandelions to a line of trees in the far back.

The old barn, gray, weathered, and with a rusted tin roof, was typical for the southern highlands, built with hand-carved tree-size timbers meant to stand the test of time. However, a different kind of time was overtaking it, a time defined by the harsh test of usefulness. Long before age could tumble the heavy walls, the structure would be knocked down for a fairway or a two-story brick colonial with a three-car garage. But for now, the smell of old hay and horse manure lingered in the air around it like a final tribute to the old man who toiled and died here.

I walked through the hallway. The walls inside were as smooth as soap in some places from the body oil of years of horses and mules rubbing their flanks against them. Overhead, clusters of dirt daubers' nests stuck to the ceiling like miniature Pueblo towns. I turned at the back of the barn and looked up at the open hayloft door. According to Eloise, Cecil Hood had fallen through it and died, probably about where I was standing. But the packed earth beneath my feet bore no sign of it. Eloise said he was found with his head cleaved by some kind of farm machinery, but that was gone too. I turned to find Carl Hood watching me from the corner of the barn. He gave the loft door a quick glance.

"They don't build them like this anymore, do they?" I said.

He neither agreed nor disagreed.

"But I guess they won't need a barn on a golf course, huh," I said.

He looked at me for a long moment, saying nothing.

We're about to leave," he said. "I'll be putting the chain back up.

He followed behind silently as I made my way back to the Jeep.

CHAPTER TWENTY-ONE

On the way out of the valley, an idea popped to the surface of my mind like an air bubble from the depths of a pond. Something that held no meaning a minute before now made perfect sense. I dug the note page from Grandfather's office out of my pocket and looked at the hotel list again. They took on a whole new meaning if I added Barry Beal to the equation. All of them were within comfortable driving distance of Eastatoe Valley, and all were places Beal would choose if he were staying in the area on business—upscale places likely to pamper a narcissistic asshole like him. That had to be why Grandfather was looking into them. I marveled at his ability to uncover a lead—but then I'd never found him lacking in his professional capacity. It was his personal skills I always had a problem with.

Halfway down the list was the Transylvania Inn, the catalyst for my sudden "moment of clarity." I'd never been there, but I was aware of it. Obviously, the eerie-sounding place wasn't in Romania. It was in the town of Rosman, in Transylvania County, North Carolina. And I would bet my whole collection of baseball cards (which included the entire starting lineup of the 1969 "Miracle Mets" that the hotel lay precisely 14.6 miles from the turnout.

I returned to the turnout again, reset the mileage counter on the Jeep to zero, and headed north. This time I drove past the intersection with the Cleo Chapman highway and continued to climb the mountainous road toward the North Carolina line. After a couple of miles, I crested a summit before traversing the small summer community of Rocky Bottom, the few scattered cottages along the highway tucked among the tangles of mountain laurel and rhododendron. The doors of the roadside cottages were closed, and the windows were dark as if the owners were yet to return for the summer.

The old Rocky Bottom camp lay off to my right, out of sight behind the trees, a meeting place for church groups and schools in earlier years. According to a sign along the highway, it was now a summer camp for the blind. Just past the entrance to the camp, another sign by a narrow gravel road pointed the way to the forestry lookout tower up on Sassafras Mountain, the highest point in South Carolina.

Leaving Rocky Bottom, I followed the highway up another steep ascent, then down and across the bridge over upper Eastatoe Creek. From there on, it was all heavy forest, sheer drop-offs, and mountain vistas to the North Carolina state line.

The heavily forested road continued to ascend and switch back on itself until the mountains gave way to a wide valley and the small town of Rosman. Off to my right, a single-engine airplane made a landing approach to a country airstrip. If Beal were looking at property in the area, I would think he'd want to see it from the air as well, and a handy airstrip nearby would be another reason to choose his lodgings here.

A small ornate sign on the right announced, "The Transylvania Inn," and I turned into the narrow road beside it. It led to a sprawling old Victorian Inn, the entrance bordered by rows of azaleas in red, white, and fuchsia, looking like strips of ribbon candy.

The three-story building was a postcard from another era when Rosman was a prosperous lumber and logging town. It bore the look of a recent renovation, painted a bright white with a porch wrapped around three sides, the posts trimmed with ornate woodwork. A croquet game was underway on the lawn, with the participants dressed in all white. I half expected someone on a unicycle to come peddling down the drive to greet me. The Jeep's odometer showed I'd driven exactly 14.6 miles from the turnout.

I had a hard time picturing Barry Beal at a place like this, but given the choice of a budget motel or here, and with an airstrip for a plane or helicopter nearby, I guess it made sense. However, a guy like Beal would have been one bored puppy here. Bored enough to chase some local skirt—like the young woman I was looking for.

I parked in a spot in front labeled "visitors." Out on the lawn behind me, the clack of a mallet against a ball brought a small round of applause as someone evidently made a good shot—if *shot* was the right thing to call it in croquet parlance. I'd never covered a croquet game. I could almost hear the grizzled long-hunters and mountain men who traversed these hills 250 years ago chuckling in their graves.

Inside the tall glass-paneled front door was a room that looked more like a parlor than a hotel lobby. The front desk was a low table with a computer in an alcove. A young man not much past college age sat behind the table, watching me approach.

"May I help you?" he asked as I walked over.

"I'm supposed to meet Barry Beal here," I said.

"Mr. Beal?" he said with a genuine look of surprise. "I don't believe he's presently a guest."

He said it as if Beal was well known to him. Again, I was impressed with my Grandfather's investigative abilities. He'd made short work of placing Barry Beal in the vicinity.

The desk clerk began punching keys on the computer keyboard. "I wasn't aware that he was expected," he mumbled, gazing at the screen. "No, he isn't with us,' he added, "and I don't even see a reservation for him."

He looked up and smiled, obviously pleased to know he was still in the loop on the guest list.

"What about his associate? She was supposed to be here too. Maybe the room's in her name. Melissa something? I can't remember her last name. Young . . . pretty. Long dark hair?"

"Melissa *Raines*?" he asked.

"That could be it," I said, trying not to look too smug at how easily I had ferreted the name out of him.

He went back to his computer. Miss Raines often handles arrangements for Mr. Beale, but it's still usually in his name, but I'll check."

After a minute of punching keys and watching the screen, he said, "Nope, there's nothing here from her, either. "Are you sure about your dates?"

"I thought so," I said. "Do you happen to have Miss Raines' phone number there? Maybe I can give her a call."

"Oh, I'm not allowed to give out personal guest information, sir."

And I was doing so well, I thought. But at least I had Melissa's last name now. *Raines.* I wasn't ready to give up here just yet, so I casually placed a ten-dollar bill on the desk in front of him and said, "If you don't tell, I won't either."

"Are you, by any chance, a reporter?" he asked with a sly look.

"Why would you think that?" I said.

"Because you aren't the first person to come in here this week asking about Mr. Beal and Melissa Raines."

"Was this person a distinguished-looking elderly gentleman from a newspaper over in South Carolina?"

"Yes, he was, and I'm telling you what I told him. It's against our policy to share that kind of information about our guests."

I took a twenty out of my pocket and placed it on top of the ten. He studied it for a moment before making it disappear into a pocket. He tore a sheet off a pad on the counter, pulled out a pen, and began writing, glancing back and forth from the computer screen to the paper. Then he pushed the note at me. He'd written down a phone number and an address—the address in Pickens, not far from the *Clarion* offices. I took it, tipped my chin at him, and left.

In the car, I called the number, and it was answered on the second ring.

"Miss Raines?" I said.

There was a tentative "Yes?"

I gave her my name and told her I was with *SportsWord* Magazine.

"What do you want?"

"I want to know about Barry Beal."

Another pause. "What about him?"

She didn't deny knowing him, so I didn't see any point in beating around the bush. "I know he physically attacked you, Ms. Raines, and I wondered if you would talk to me about it."

"I don't have anything to say," she said.

"Did he rape you?" I asked.

"Nobody raped me. I don't know what you're talking about."

"Beal is a bad guy, Miss Raines. I don't think you want to be protecting him. Even if he didn't rape you, what he did was at least assault and battery with intent to rape, and that's just as serious. He deserves to pay for that."

I could hear her breathing, but she didn't say anything.

"Perhaps he's already paying," I said. "Has he offered you money to keep quiet?"

"Absolutely not. Just leave me alone, will you?"

"I'm afraid I can't do that, Miss Raines. I'm not giving up until you talk to me."

"I'm hanging up now," she said and did.

I called her back, but she didn't answer. Another call produced the same results, but this time I left a message, telling her again what a lousy guy Beal was and why talking to me was the right thing to do. I needed to find a way to speak to her face-to-face. She sounded emotionally stressed to the breaking point, but perhaps she'd open up if we talked in person.

I drove the twenty-five miles from the Transylvania Inn down to Pickens and found Melissa Raines' house on the east side of town on a street lined with other small houses, all strikingly similar: faded white clapboard siding, the same shape and size, and small porches in front. They were all built precisely the same distance from the street, and a view from the side was like sighting down one long wall. They had to be old company houses remodeled, built originally for workers from the textile mill that used to be nearby. Her place looked deserted—the blinds were drawn, no car was in the driveway, and no one came to the door when I knocked.

I walked to the house next door, thinking a neighbor might know where she was, but no one answered my knock there either. And the house on the opposite side had a for-rent sign in the yard. So, I left.

The road quickly became winding and narrow as I left Melissa Raines' house, and I suddenly realized this wasn't the way I came in. Lost in thought, I'd turned the wrong way out of her drive.

I found a place to turn around, and as I was reversing, I came

face to face with a white Dodge Ram pickup as it barreled around the curve. With a yelp of tires and a violent swerve, it barely missed hitting me. A man in a billed cap was behind the wheel as the truck flew by without so much as a wave or horn honk. His hat was pulled down low, so I couldn't see his face. But I could tell he was a big guy by the width of his shoulders.

CHAPTER TWENTY-TWO

As I started back to Still Hollow, I had a wild idea and pulled over to the side of the road. I'd seen the Friday tee times for the Masters tournament in the Greenville newspaper that morning and remembered Barry Beal's one o'clock tee time. Starting late meant he would be finishing up late. Pickens to Augusta was a little less than a three-hour drive, and if I left right now, I could be there about the time Beal finished his round. If I could catch him in the locker room or somewhere afterward, it might be interesting to get his reaction to the convenient death of Cecil Hood and the quick sale of that property.

Also, I wanted to tell him that I knew who his assault victim was and had talked to her. I wanted him to know that even if he'd probably paid for her silence and thought he'd gotten away with it, I wouldn't stop until she opened up. If that did nothing more than cause him to worry, I would consider it a small victory.

When I got to the Augusta National Golf Club, the site of the most famous golf tournament in the world, The Masters, I found that Beal had just finished his round with a miserable score and had failed to make the cut for Saturday. My press pass got me into the locker room, and I spotted him sitting on a bench changing his shoes. I cut a direct path toward him. He saw me coming and abruptly stood up. Even from across the room, I could see his face take on the color of a fresh-boiled lobster.

Beal was shaking his head from side to side as I neared.

"I'm not talking to you," he said. No interviews."

"You need to answer some questions, Barry. And I won't leave you alone until you do."

"Will someone call security?" he said, raising his voice as he looked toward the room behind me.

"What about Melissa Raines, the woman you assaulted?" I asked. "Can you comment on her? She was your employee, wasn't she? Or was she more than that?"

That stopped him for a moment.

"That's right, I know who she is. I've talked to her. Even if you've paid her to keep her mouth shut, I'll eventually get her to open up."

He began stuffing clothing and things from his locker into a travel bag.

"Here's another question for you," I said. "It's about an old farmer named Cecil Hood. He owned property vital to your development. Property that he pledged to you but then changed his mind and refused to sell. Then he suffered a fatal accident, and the property dropped right into your lap. Most people would have been a little suspicious about the convenience. One was my grandfather, and I think it got him killed. You seem to be the only one around who doesn't find these deaths suspicious. My question is, why not?"

Inside a vein in his forehead Beal's pulse was leaping like a cricket. He glared at me for a moment, tossed a last item in his travel bag and closed it as if he were trying to rip the zipper off.

There was activity behind me, and I turned to see two serious-looking guys in matching blazers and club ties coming my way. Security had been called. Beal saw them, too, and leaned in so close to me that I could smell his aftershave.

"Listen to me, you fucking worm," he said, his voice little more than a guttural whisper. "I don't give a goddamn about some old farmer—or your grandfather. And I don't give a goddamn about you. You'll never work again, anyway. I'll make sure of that."

We stood for a moment staring into each other's eyes. His were shockingly void of compassion or regret and as cold and detached from anything human as a reptile. I knew then that any expectations of ever getting to him were futile. This man may not be a murderer, but he was inherently evil. And if justice ever found him, it wouldn't be because of anything I could do.

I turned and walked away, one step ahead of the security guys.

CHAPTER TWENTY-THREE

The funeral began at two on Saturday, and by the size of the crowd at Holly Springs Baptist Church, half the county must have turned out. The church was standing room only, with many more people waiting outside to attend the following graveside service.

The eulogy was delivered by the pastor of Holly Springs and was praising to the point of fiction—at least in my mind. I felt he was speaking about a total stranger as he talked of my grandfather's boundless warmth and caring nature. Mackenzie and Eloise obviously disagreed with me, emitting snuffles at various salient points.

SportsWord sent a wreath with a card signed by Joe Dennis, Burt Lowe, and others, but none came to the funeral. I didn't expect them to. Several friends and drinking buddies sent cards or called. I talked them out of coming, telling them to go to some dive bar and have a drink or two in my name. My ex-girlfriend, Rosita, neither called nor sent a card. I wondered if she even knew about the funeral—or cared.

From the church, the procession moved to the gravesite across the road, the crowd forming a semi-circle around the tent erected for the family. Since only the three of us could claim that title, friends of my grandfather and Eloise joined us under the tent. We sat in folding metal chairs and stared somberly at the flower-laden casket before us, a row of slender gray monuments just beyond, all bearing the Bragg name. My mother, father, great-grandparents, and great-uncles were all there under the bright blue Carolina sky. Time and tragedy denied me the chance to know most of those whose blood flowed through my veins. Now another Bragg was taking his place beside them, and I wondered if I knew him any better.

In the sea of faces that circled the gravesite, Kelly Mayfield stood staring at the casket, clutching a lacy white handkerchief she used to occasionally dab at her eyes. She caught me watching her. She held my gaze momentarily and then returned to the service. I lost sight of her in the crowd when it was all over. I collected Eloise and Mackenzie, and we began to make our exit, moving slowly through the lingerers who continued to issue their sentiments and regrets for our loss.

Bucky Streeter was waiting by the side of the gray limousine the funeral home provided for us. The sight of him made me smile for the first time that day. I thought with some irony that this was the first time we'd ever seen each other in coats and ties.

"I didn't realize you were here," I said, shaking his outstretched hand.

"I couldn't get into the church. Some turn out."

My eyes followed his to the sea of automobiles all trying to leave at once, the cars parked along either side of the road jockeying for a slot in the traffic streaming from the church lot.

From inside the car, Eloise tapped lightly on the window, waved at Bucky, and motioned for me to get going.

"Why don't you come to the house? A small group of Eloise's friends are coming over."

"Now?" he asked.

"Yeah. We're holding the wake like they do in Australia—*after* the funeral. Eloise doesn't know it, but I picked up a bottle of Scotch in town the other day. I need somebody to help me drink it."

"Why didn't you say that first?" he said and held the limo door for me while I got in. "I'll be right behind you."

Inside the car, Eloise sat huddled in the corner, staring out the window. Mackenzie's head was on her shoulder, her eyes closed.

"How are you doing?" I asked my sister.

She turned to face me, her eyes red and puffy.

"I guess I've cried myself out," she said softly. "I sit here feeling like I'm still crying, but the tears won't come. It's like I've run out of water. Is that silly or what?"

I took her hand and squeezed it.

Mackenzie stirred, and I looked across the seat at her.

Eloise followed my gaze. "My baby," she said, gently touching the sleeping girl's hair.

"She's a remarkable young lady," I said.

"She's going to miss him. They loved each other so much. Maybe he was mellowing in his old age; he was different the past few years: kinder and gentler. He seemed to take more interest in us." Eloise smiled. "He thought I was too lenient with Mackenzie, of course, and we argued constantly about my spoiling her. But there was a lot of love there."

"Sorry I missed that," I said before I could help it.

"John David, will you stop it," Eloise said, loud enough to wake Mackenzie. "You're my brother, and I love you, but I won't listen to this anymore. I never knew you to feel sorry for yourself, but right now, you are wallowing in self-pity. You can't change what happened. And whether you want to believe it or not, he loved you in his way. He *was* what he was."

"Eloise . . ." I wasn't sure what I wanted to say, but it didn't matter; she wasn't listening.

"And whether you want to admit it or not," she went on, "you loved and respected him too. Now grow up and see things for what they are. I swear you're just as stubborn as he was."

I locked eyes with her and then noticed Mackenzie watching us.

"Does your mother ever talk to you like that?" I asked her.

"Hardly ever," Mackenzie said. "Only when I act dumb."

I studied my niece and smiled. "Okay, you've both made your point, so stop picking on me." We rode the rest of the short way home in silence, each thinking our own thoughts and recalling our own memories of the life and death of Garnet Quincy Bragg.

CHAPTER TWENTY-FOUR

Several of Eloise and Mackenzie's friends were waiting for us on the front porch. Bucky came in right behind us and followed me into the kitchen, with Eloise and Mackenzie congregating with their friends in the den.

I pulled the bottle of Scotch from the cupboard where I'd hidden it. It was a twelve-year-old Macallan I was surprised to find in a liquor store in Pickens.

"Macallan," Bucky said. "You must be doing pretty well, old buddy."

"Not really, but this is worth going into debt for."

"I can't believe Eloise let you bring a bottle into the house," he said.

"We're not drinking in the house," I said, grabbing two glasses from the kitchen cabinet. "We're going outside."

We went out back to a weathered old picnic table under a spreading oak and sat on the tabletop with our feet on the bench. I poured us both three fingers of Scotch, neat.

"So, have you been staying out of trouble down there in Hotlanta?" Bucky asked.

"The only place I ever get into trouble is up here," I said. "I wasn't here a day and a half before I got into a fistfight."

"You're kidding. "Who with?"

"A guy named Bobby Paige. A perfect stranger."

"Bobby Paige? Jesus J.D., you got a death wish? How the hell did you manage to tangle with him? Paige considers himself the biggest badass in the county, and he ain't all that wrong."

"He picked a fight with me at a place called the Silver Dollar."

Bucky grinned. "The Silver Dollar? That was your first mistake. What the hell were you doing in that redneck joint?"

"Failing to use good judgment," I said. "Sounds like you know this Paige guy."

"I do," Bucky said. "He works for my father-in-law."

"Who's your father-in-law?" I asked. "I heard you got married, but not until after you'd already tied the knot."

"Sorry about that. Her family did the invitations, and I didn't get much say in it."

"Somebody I know?" I said.

"I don't think so," Bucky said. "We never ran in Casey's circle back in the day. At least I didn't. She's the daughter of Bailey McDaniel."

I couldn't hide my surprise. "*The* Bailey McDaniel?"

"One and the same."

The McDaniel family, I knew, was Pickens County's American royalty, our downhome version of the Rockefellers or Vanderbilts. Everyone knew the McDaniel family history. They practically taught it in school. It began with Ezra McDaniel, a carpetbagger who traveled south after the Civil War to build a factory on the west bank of the Saluda River to manufacture buggies and firearms. After Ezra's death, at around the turn of the century, his son converted the factory into a textile mill and, upon its success, began building them one by one across the county, luring farm boys out of the cotton rows for ten cents an hour and the promise of company housing with indoor plumbing.

This company housing, clustered around the mills, formed villages local folks called "Mill Hills." As McDaniel and others built new mills near one another, the mill hills merged like joining cells, spawning entire towns. Textiles would become the lifeblood of the Piedmont region for three-quarters of a century and the financial mainstay for a majority of the people who lived on the southern fringe of the Appalachians—from Alabama to Virginia.

At one time in Pickens County, most people made their living either farming or in a cotton mill—everyone else worked at a business that served them. But that way of life was gone. The Japanese entered the game in the fifties, followed by the Chinese. Now the textile industry in the South was all but extinct. Most of the original multi-storied plants were gone—either torn down, in ruins, or turned into condominium lofts. And many of the old Mill Hills were now the ghettos of the new south.

Bucky's father-in-law Bailey McDaniel was the great-grandson of old Ezra. And he still ran the company, which was only a shadow of the original textile empire. However, Bailey McDaniel was still looked upon with great deference by anyone in the county over the age of fifty. Also, he still had hordes of family money in various investments—from real estate to Wall Street.

"How did a hillbilly like you ever meet Bailey McDaniel's daughter?" I asked.

Bucky laughed. "She and a couple of her friends were slumming one night at a club in Greenville, and I asked her to dance. The rest, as they say, is history."

"You got kids?"

"We're waiting a while on that," he said, leaving it at that.

"What's her old man like?"

Bucky looked somewhere out over the lawn and seemed to struggle for an answer. After a moment, he said, "Let's just say I'm not the son-in-law he wished he had."

That seemed to take something out of him, I noticed. "You still have the marina?" I asked as much to change the subject as anything else. The last time I saw Bucky, he was trying to make a success of a small marina on Lake Keowee, barely making ends meet and living in a little house on the property.

"That all ended when I married Casey," he said. "It wasn't anything but an excuse to go fishing anyway."

Bucky stopped talking long enough to pour us three more fingers of Macallan, then said, "Although I did love that fucking marina. I always thought I could have made something out of the place. Expand. Get into high-end boat sales. Maybe build a restaurant and some condos."

He sighed and waved the vision away. "But I met the fair Casey McDaniel and had to get into something more *dignified*."

"So, what is the *dignified* thing you're doing now?"

He studied his drink for a moment. "I'm Vice President of Operations at McDaniel Mills," he finally said.

I saw him looking for my reaction. "That's great, Bucky," I said.

He smiled. "It's a crock of shit. I know it, and you know it. Hell, the whole goddamned world knows it. If I weren't the son-in-law of Bailey McDaniel, I'd be lucky if they let me sweep up the place. It's Bailey's way to keep me from embarrassing him too much."

I didn't know how to respond, and he didn't seem to expect a reply. So, what's with this Bobby Paige?" I asked, deliberately changing the subject.

"He's been working with my father-in-law since before I even met Casey. Paige heads the construction crew for building and maintenance at the mills. I guess I'm his boss, but I don't think he knows it. Or acts like it. He still considers himself to be working directly for my father-in-law. In addition to his responsibilities at the plant, he's the old man's personal 'go-to' guy. He does personal work around Bailey's house—built some stables out there last summer—that sort of thing. Sometimes I think Paige is more a part of the family than I am." Bucky chuckled. "And maybe he is. But he's a hard worker; I'll give him that."

"I'm sure he's a regular employee of the month when he's not trying to bash somebody's skull in," I said.

"I think he does do a bit of that. We leave each other pretty much alone."

Bucky went silent for a moment and then said, "Terrible thing about your granddad. You said they think it was probably some doper stealing to feed a habit."

"Sheriff Bagwell does," I said.

I felt him studying the side of my face.

"You sound like you don't," he said.

"Let's just say I'm not as convinced as he is that the motive was a robbery."

"Why is that?"

"Just a theory based on some things I can't prove yet."

He let his eyes linger on me for a moment.

"If it wasn't a robbery, then what was it? Old Mr. Bragg was a pain in the ass, but what other reason would anybody have to shoot him?"

"My gut tells me he stumbled across something he shouldn't have."

"Your gut," Bucky repeated and gave me a skeptical look. "What does your gut tell you this *something* is?"

"You know a guy named Carl Hood?"

"Now there's a name out of the past. Old man Cecil Hood's son."

"So, you know him?"

"I know *of* him. Don't really know him. He's a few years before our time but a local legend. They say that at the old Bloody Bucket across the tracks in Easley, guys who thought they were badass would scatter like cockroaches under a light when he came in. They would leave their beers on the bar and just walk out." He gave me a questioning look. "Are you saying he's got something to do with this?"

"He sold his daddy's farm in Eastatoe Valley almost before they could sod over the old man's grave," I said.

"So?"

"Mr. Hood had refused to sell it. He told my grandfather that."

"I repeat, so? Cecil Hood's dead. What's wrong if his son sells the farm if he legally inherited it?" Bucky paused a moment at a thought he seemed to have. "He *did* inherit it, didn't he?" he asked.

"As far as I know," I said. "But it's not that."

"Then what is it? I guess I don't understand."

"The whole thing is just too damned convenient. It's not public knowledge yet, but a large real estate development is coming to Eastatoe Valley. The developers are paying big money for land. The whole valley has pretty much been sold. Hood had told them he would sell but then changed his mind. He told Grandfather they would have to wait until he was gone to get their hands on it. And that's exactly what happened. He conveniently dies, and his son Carl sells the land almost immediately."

"Whoa. You're saying what? That Carl Hood killed his old man for the land? And then he killed your grandpa because he found out about it? Jesus, J.D., that's a fucking serious thing to lay off on somebody. What've you got to back that up?"

"It wouldn't be the first time Carl Hood has killed someone. He did time for murder in Georgia and hasn't been out all that long."

"That just makes him capable, John David. It don't make him guilty. Besides, last time I heard, old man Hood's death was an accident."

"Just like Grandfather's death was a robbery," I offered and met his gaze.

"You tell any of this to the cops?" Bucky asked.

"Yes, but Sheriff Bagwell doesn't think much of it."

"Well, now, there's a big surprise," he said. "Look, J.D., the fact that this area has great development potential isn't exactly a secret. My father-in-law has been trying to get aboard that train since they dammed up the Keowee River and people started building million-dollar lake-shore homes on it. So, it's really no surprise that something's finally happening in Eastatoe Valley. And as far as Carl Hood selling his daddy's land so quickly, real estate agents would have been all over him before his old man's funeral was over."

Bucky looked like he wanted to say something else but thought better of it.

"What?" I asked.

"Naaah, I'll just keep my mouth shut.

"Say it."

It took him a moment, but he finally said, "My advice as your old friend is to leave this thing to Sheriff Bagwell. He's no Sherlock Holmes, but he ain't Barney Fife, either. If he thought this was anything other than what it seems, he'd be all over it like grease on a chilidog."

"Maybe you're right, Bucky," I said. "Anyway, there's one thing I still need to do, and if I'm right, it may shed new light on things. Do you know a Melissa Raines?"

Melissa Raines? "I don't think so. Who is she?"

"She's a pretty young thing I need to talk to for a story I'm working on. This famous pro golfer assaulted her, and I'm trying to prove it. Grandfather was helping me locate her. It wouldn't surprise me if she knows something about what's happening in Eastatoe Valley that Sheriff Bagwell doesn't know."

At that moment, Kelly Mayfield came to the kitchen door and looked out at us. Bucky held up the bottle of Macallan, smiled, and gave her a questioning look. She smiled back, shook her head, and turned and walked away.

"Speaking of pretty young things," Bucky said.

"True," I said. "But unfortunately, she despises me."

"You mean there's a woman around that you can't charm? You losing your touch, old buddy?"

"I haven't given up on her yet."

He drained the last of his Scotch and said, "I've got to go. Let's do this again before you leave." He smiled and added, "Have a drink, I mean. Not a wake."

I stifled a laugh, given the present funerary circumstances, and agreed. "I'll call you," I said.

After he left, I went into the house and put the Macallan back in its hidey-hole.

CHAPTER TWENTY-FIVE

Eloise and Mackenzie were lost in conversation with friends and neighbors, most of whom I didn't know. I would have liked to talk with Kelly Mayfield, but I didn't think that would work. It usually takes two to converse.

I tried to call Melissa Raines again, but she still wasn't answering. I decided to give her house another try. I sneaked out the back, got into the Jeep, and drove to her house. Her place was still dark, but her neighbor was home. I could hear a child crying through an open window on the toy-strewn porch. I walked over and rapped on the door. It was opened by a tiny woman with a toddler balanced on her hip. The kid's chin was covered with something that looked like mashed carrots, and he was wailing like a fire engine. The woman looked up at me and blew a wisp of hair out of her face.

I had to shout over the screaming kid to be heard. "I'm looking for Melissa from next door," I said.

"She's not at home," the woman shouted back. "She's gone away for a while."

I understood what she said by reading her lips than by hearing her.

"Can you tell me where she's gone?" I yelled.

I must have startled the baby because the crying stopped immediately, and the kid looked at me with eyes the size of half-dollars.

The woman swung the kid to the other hip and gave me a long, hard look of appraisal. "She didn't tell me that," she said.

She was a terrible liar. I knew it, and she knew I knew it. "Did you see her after she got back from Atlanta?" I asked. She gave me another long look.

"Yes," she said.

"She didn't look too good, did she?" I asked.

"No, she didn't," she said, looking at me like I might be the one who did it.

I took out my press ID and showed it to her. Underneath bold red letters that spelled the word PRESS was my photo and name, and below that, in smaller letters, the name of *SportsWord* magazine.

"I need her to help me nail the guy that did that to her," I said. "But I can't do that unless she talks to me. I'm on *her* side."

She looked from my card up to me. The baby was starting to whimper again. I could see the woman wanted to believe me.

"Melissa told me she slipped and fell on an escalator in a shopping mall," she said. "I take it that isn't true."

"No, it isn't," I said.

The baby began an ear-splitting lament again, and the woman held up a forefinger and disappeared inside. When she returned, she handed me a slip of paper with "Litchfield Beach Retreat" written on it.

"She's gone to the beach," she said over the baby's squall. "Don't tell her I gave you this, but I think she needs help."

I mimicked a zipping up of my lips and thanked her. Litchfield Beach was a little south of Myrtle Beach in Georgetown County on the South Carolina Coast. I'd been there before. It was less lively than Myrtle Beach and a good place for someone to visit if they wanted to be alone and go unnoticed.

The woman said something I didn't catch, and I pointed to my ear and frowned.

"She motioned to the screaming kid and smiled apologetically. "It's time for his nap," she shouted.

"Good luck," I offered and returned to the Jeep, thinking maybe I'd postpone fatherhood a while longer.

When I returned to Still Hollow, all the guests had left except Kelly Mayfield. I found her sitting alone in the den.

"Where's Eloise?" I asked her.

"She and Mackenzie are upstairs changing clothes."

I took a chair opposite her. We sat without speaking long enough for the moment to become awkward.

"Why the change?" I finally asked.

"What do you mean?"

"You're no longer treating me like I'm something to avoid stepping in."

"You mean, why have I stopped acting like a bitch?"

"That would be another way of putting it, yes."

"Eloise tells me I've got the wrong opinion about you. She says you're not really as bad as I think. So . . . I decided to try to be more open-minded about you."

"My sister is a wise and perceptive woman."

"You must understand; your grandfather was one of the finest men I've ever known. I not only respected him, but I grew to love him like a second father. So, when I saw this thing between you two causing him so much heartache, I couldn't stand it. He never once spoke ill of you, and I naturally assumed that whatever was wrong was your fault."

"The few times he talked about you, there was such a sadness in his voice that it got to me. It made me angry and . . . maybe even jealous. Obviously, he would've preferred to have you at the paper instead of me. I guess I didn't like you for that either."

"I never once promised him that," I said.

She brushed my words away with the wave of a hand. "So, when I met you," she went on, "I wanted to think the worst of you. I even tried to take my anger over Garnet's senseless death out on you. I'm at least smart enough to know that every story has two sides—and according to Eloise, you have yours. I'll accept that, even though I don't know what it is. I'll also admit the possibility that Garnet wasn't the saint I made him out to be, and, conversely, you may not be the prick I thought you were.

She looked at me, her pupils like perfectly round drops of India-ink.

"I know that you cared about him, no matter what happened between the two of you. I think his death has hit you harder than you let on."

"What makes you believe that?" I asked.

"I saw it in your face when you were going through his desk at the *Clarion*."

"You saw me in there doing that and didn't chew me out?"

"You were busy looking at his scrapbook, so you didn't see me stick my head in. I decided to leave you alone."

She seemed to understand something about me that I barely understood myself. She was a lot like Eloise in that respect.

She stuck out a hand. Truce?" she asked.

"Truce," I answered, and we shook on it. Her hand in mine was warm and silky smooth, and for a microsecond, I had the insane urge not to let go of it. But I did. She was thinking a little better of me now, and something as dumb as that was bound to reverse it.

"Eloise has invited me to dinner tonight," she said. "Do you have any objections?"

"Of course not."

"Good. I'd like you to bring me up to date on the sale of the paper. It would be nice to know how much longer I can count on a regular paycheck."

The look on her face when she said that was nowhere near as warm as her hand. Obviously, I still had a way to go to change her opinion of me.

CHAPTER TWENTY-SIX

Thankfully, Eloise suggested we forego the food from the fridge and grill steaks on the back porch for dinner, so she, Mackenzie, and Kelly went to buy some T-bones and fresh salad makings, leaving me to ramble about the house alone.

As the sun's last rays faded behind the hills, I went around, turning on a few lights. I sat down in the den and turned the TV on to ESPN to see what I was missing in the world of sports.

Suddenly, the large antique mirror on the wall across the room shattered. I dove to the floor, an automatic defensive reflex, as I heard the immediate echo of a gunshot from the woods behind the house. A small dark hole, about the size of a dime, appeared in the center of the mirror, a spider web of cracks spreading outward in a large circle. An identical hole had also punctured a windowpane on the other side of the room.

Rising slowly, I turned off the lamp, went down on my hands and knees, and crawled to the window to peek over the sill. Twilight had turned the backyard a deep purple and the heavy woods behind even darker. The shadows among the trees revealed nothing.

I looked from the hole in the window to the mirror. If someone tried to hit me, they were a piss-poor shot because the bullet missed me by at least ten feet. However, if they were just trying to scare me, they were a bit more successful.

Staying away from the windows, I crept over to the gun cabinet in the corner and took out a twelve-gauge shotgun and some shells. Breaching and loading as I went, I grabbed a flashlight out of a kitchen drawer and went through the back door, crossing the lawn with a bit of broken field running, like I was flushed out of the pocket by an oncoming defensive end and heading for the chains. I plunged into the woods and went to a knee behind a large tree. Over the sound of my heart trying to beat its way out of my chest, I heard the growl of an automobile engine start up and then fade away along the old logging road that bordered our property beyond the woods. The sound was throaty and large, and I wondered if it came from a white pickup truck. Whoever it was knew the area because the road back there wasn't on any map that I knew of.

Working my way inside the tree line to a place opposite the den window, I switched on the flashlight, examined the ground for several yards in either direction, then cast the beam back into the woods. I wasn't sure what I was looking for—a revealing clue like in the movies perhaps—like a carelessly dropped matchbook cover with the name of a bar on it or initials carved into a tree while the shooter waited for me to show my face at the window. But there was nothing like that. Not a broken twig, not a spent shell, and thanks to the carpet of old pine straw and dead leaves, not even a footprint.

The shot probably didn't come from too far back in the trees. The dense growth of thick pines and large, leafy hardwoods would have created an impenetrable wall between the shooter and the house, making the shot difficult, if not impossible, from that distance. The house must have been in plain sight when the shot was fired. Which also meant that the shooter was close. But, wherever the shooter was then, he was gone now.

Later, I was pouring water into the coffeemaker in the kitchen when Eloise, Kelly, and Mackenzie returned. I turned to find them staring at the shotgun lying on the kitchen table.

"What's that doing there?" Eloise asked.

"Somebody shot through the window in the den while you were gone," I said.

"Shot through the window? Who?"

"You got me. I got the shotgun and went looking, but whoever it was, they were already gone."

Kelly Mayfield wore a horrified look. "Do you think they were shooting at you?"

"They seemed to have it in for that big mirror on the wall," I replied. "I hope you weren't too fond of it, Eloise. It's shattered all to hell."

We all trailed my sister into the den, where she stopped and gazed at the broken mirror as if she expected to see an instant replay reflected in it.

"You were in here when it happened?" she asked, alarm all over her face.

"Over there," I said, pointing to the chair.

"Thank God you were on the other side of the room," Kelly said and glanced at the matching hole in the window. "Who would be out there shooting a gun at night?"

Eloise's eyes met mine, and we looked at each other for a moment, her face full of apprehension. I guess my theories and suspicions of murder made her quick to assume the worst. I wished now I'd never said a word. I discovered Kelly watching us, her face occupied with thoughts.

"Maybe it was the Medlin boys again," Mackenzie offered. They're not supposed to hunt back there, but they do. They shot one of Mama's goats last winter, thinking it was a deer."

Eloise seemed to brighten at the explanation as if she was anxious to accept Mackenzie's suggestion over any darker alternatives.

"I wouldn't put it past the little devils to fire toward the house," she said as she warmed to the idea. "Especially if some poor helpless creature got between them and us. I put out feed for the deer and turkeys back there, attracting all kinds of animals. It's probably just too much temptation for those boys."

"Jimmy's in my class, and Noel's two grades back," Mackenzie added. "When they shot the goat, Mama went and talked to their daddy, and he whipped their butts."

"You're going to call the police and report this, aren't you?" Kelly asked, still looking at me.

"Kids or not, they could have killed you."

I looked away quickly, not trusting my ability to conceal my doubts about it being a couple of kids who couldn't shoot straight. "I'm calling Mr. Medlin," Eloise said. "He's a good man. He'll do more to them than the law will."

"I heard a vehicle back there," I said to Eloise. "Can the Medlin boys drive?"

"Jimmy can," Mackenzie said. "He's been bragging about having his permit to everybody in class."

We all quietly watched as Eloise strode to the phone, got Medlin's number from 411, and made the call. She talked briefly, her back to us, then placed the phone back in the cradle as if it were made of eggshells. She turned and looked at me, her lips drawn in a thin line.

“Mr. Medlin says the boys haven’t been out since midafternoon. He says they were in their room playing video games.”

Her eyes probed mine, the unease back on her face. This was no longer just my problem, I realized. Whatever was going on, if I’d brought it into her home and endangered her and Mackenzie, I had to do something about it. I caught Kelly staring at us, her expression full of questions she seemed bursting to ask. “I’ll call Sheriff Bagwell,” I said.

CHAPTER TWENTY-SEVEN

Sheriff Bagwell arrived with a deputy he didn't bother introducing, sending him back to search the woods while he came inside to examine the den and listen to the rest of my story. After I went through the incident with him, he stood holding a baggy with the slug he'd just pried out of the wall behind the mirror.

"Thirty-ought-six or thereabouts," he said, showing it to us. "Deer rifle," he added. "You were sitting way over there?" he asked me.

I affirmed that I was and knew where he was going with it.

"It doesn't look like they were shooting at you," he said. "Unless you have some reason to believe differently, it looks more like a stray shot."

My thoughts went to Bobby Paige pointing a gun at me and then to Carl Hood, but I kept my mouth shut. I already knew what Bagwell thought of my alternative suspicions.

He shifted his focus to Eloise. "What you were saying about these Medlin kids, or somebody like them, sounds about right," he said, giving her a reassuring look.

"Kids today will shoot at anything and call it hunting. I know you talked to their daddy, but I'll double-check his story, anyway. See what kind of rifles he's got and if any of them have been fired recently."

The deputy came into the room, switching off the beam of a large flashlight before sticking it into his belt. He shook his head at the sheriff; Bagwell nodded and turned to us. "I'll send somebody out in the morning when it's light to get a better look," he said. "See if we can spot something on that old road you say is back there." The way he said it, it was apparent he thought nothing would come of it.

Bagwell lingered a while talking to Eloise, reconfirming his belief that this was likely just a wild shot from someone with no business possessing a firearm. The deputy put the shattered mirror back on the wall, and they turned to leave. As he passed me, Bagwell nodded ever so slightly toward the door, and I trailed him out to his car.

"Mr. Bragg," he turned and said, "Do you have any reason to believe there's more to this than what it looks like?"

"I guess I don't, Sheriff," I said, giving him the response that I knew he wanted.

He kept his eyes on me for a moment. "I heard about some trouble you had with Bobby Paige," he said. "You aren't thinking this has something to do with that, are you?"

"I don't know, sheriff. You seem to know him; what do you think?"

"I think of all the girls to hit on in Pickens County; I wouldn't have picked his," he said and grinned. "Bobby Paige is somebody to shy wide of."

I started to tell him that I wasn't "hitting" on anyone but decided it would be wasted words. I was tired of talking to him.

"If it makes you feel better, I'll see if Paige can account for himself at the time."

He tipped his hat to me, got into the car with the deputy, and drove away.

I grilled the steaks as Eloise tossed the salads and made garlic toast with help from Mackenzie and Kelly. The dinner conversation was subdued. Grandfather's funeral and the shot through the window worked like a dismal, ground-hugging fog that dampened most attempts at lighter topics. However, a rare steak was a welcome change from the covered-dish diet I'd been on. The only thing missing was a good bottle of red wine. But when in Rome . . . or Still Hollow . . .

After dinner, Mackenzie helped stack the dishes in the sink and then went to her room, leaving Eloise, Kelly, and me to sit over our coffees and make small talk. Kelly caught me staring at her more than once but didn't seem to mind. I wondered if she knew just how beautiful I thought she was. Or, more importantly, if she cared. Kelly went home, and Eloise and I stood on the front porch watching her leave. We went back inside, and I caught Eloise looking at me.

"In happier times, I'd be pleased about this," she said.

"Pleased about what?"

"You and Kelly. You two seem to fit."

"I don't see why you think that," I said. "I'm not even sure I like her. And I know she doesn't like me."

"I'm calling bull-hockey on that. You're a funny guy, brother of mine," she said, getting up from her chair. "And I'm going to bed. It's been a long and sad day with a scary ending."

After she left, I went outside and walked across the lawn to the edge of the woods again. I found a spot opposite the den that offered a clear angle of fire through the window at the old stuffed chair. I noticed that I couldn't see the mirror from there. But when I moved to a spot that revealed the mirror, I then couldn't see the chair. I thought about that for a moment. It would be impossible to aim at one and hit the other, which gave credence to Sheriff Bagwell's theory of an accident, a careless hunter with a stray shot, or a kid out with his daddy's rifle. Or was it a warning? Maybe Bobby Paige was trying to drive home a point.

Something made me look at the mirror again, not at the shattered glass, but at the reflection in it. The chair I was sitting in was perfectly framed there—the bullet hole squarely on a spot where my head would have been. Someone had nailed my reflection right between the eyes. A cold, invisible finger lightly touched a spot in the center of my forehead, and I went back inside. I didn't buy a coincidence, and I couldn't see Bobby Paige being that subtle if the shot was just meant to be a warning. Was it Carl Hood? I didn't really know him. My thoughts shifted to the worst-case scenario. Whoever it was thought they were shooting at me.

CHAPTER TWENTY-EIGHT

Early the next morning, I set out for the South Carolina coast to try to talk to Melissa Raines in person. First, I called the hotel and asked for her room. They put me through, proving, I guess, that she was still a guest there. I let it ring a half dozen times, but there was no answer.

Litchfield Beach is located northeast of the old city of Georgetown and just south of Myrtle Beach. I'd been there once, long ago. It was about a five-hour drive from Still Hollow, and I remembered it as a little less glitzy and crowded than Myrtle Beach but still part of the South Carolina coast known as the Grand Strand. There were a few more high-rises since my last visit, but the place remained basically unchanged. Hotels rose in multi-color pastels along the beach, interspersed with private beach houses, condos, and a barrier line of sea oats and sand dunes.

I rolled up in front of the Litchfield Beach Retreat around noon. It turned out to be posher than I expected. It looked beyond the means of a young working woman like Melissa Raines, another indication that she may have found a recent source of supplemental income.

I went inside the lobby and called her room from a house phone and, again, got no answer. I called her cell, but she didn't answer. I searched but couldn't find her in the lobby shops or restaurant, so I followed the signs to the pool. A couple of septuagenarians were swimming laps in it. The poolside chairs sat empty, a cloudy sky and an earlier downpour having removed the sun-worshippers from their race toward skin cancer.

I circled the pool and headed through the board-lined gap in the dunes toward the gray-green waters of the Atlantic. Wooden stairs led down to the beach, and I stopped at the top to look for anyone who might be Melissa Raines. Far to the north, a lone woman walked the water's edge, stooping to examine a shell or aquatic refuse that had washed up on shore. Even from a distance, I could see from her wide, squat shape that she wasn't Raines. Down the beach, a couple tossed a Frisbee, leaping and bounding after it like antelopes at play. Other than them, the weather had left the beach as deserted as the poolside.

Below me, a row of beach chairs with bright blue canopies sat facing the sun's position from an earlier, less cloudy day. The tops on all but one were folded back, and I could see they were unoccupied. I needed to get closer to find out if anyone was sitting in the chair with the canopy up.

I descended the steps and plunged into the soft sand, my shoes sinking above the heels with each step, causing me to walk like a man with leg braces. I walked around the covered chair to surprise a swimsuit-clad couple as young as my niece, Mackenzie, locked in a tangle of arms and legs. After a flurry of exclamations of "hey man" and "rude, dude," I left them to their previous activities and headed back to the stairs.

Up by the dunes, the couple still tossed their Frisbee back and forth. The woman, a petite bleached blond, was not Melissa. I watched as she awkwardly sailed the Frisbee over the man's head and past a large red and white sign that said: "STAY OUT." It landed in the environmentally protected hillocks of dunes and sea oats beyond.

The man stood looking into the dunes for a minute, then, sign be damned, went after the Frisbee. Suddenly he cried out and came stumbling back. He yelled several unintelligible words at the woman, then bent from the waist and threw up in the sand between his feet. She looked as baffled at his reaction as I was.

I made my way over and looked past them into the dunes. The first thing I saw was a mound of crabs. Small brown ones, larger orange and blue ones, and some spidery things that maybe weren't even crabs. I stepped closer for a better look. As I did, the crabs scattered, and the mound became the exposed head of a young woman, half buried in the sand. Stringy wisps of long dark hair matted her brow, her eyes dark hollow sockets. The skin on her face, what was left of it, was cracked and crusty with grit. However, I could still see a fading yellow bruise underneath one sightless eye and an old cut marring her lip. I was pretty sure I'd found Melissa Raines.

I called 911 and reported it. The couple and I stood around staring at each other without much talking until the cops showed up, followed closely by the media. I stood back, letting the couple do most of the talking, especially to the media. The Frisbee couple was credited for finding the body and became the center of their attraction.

I slipped into the background, avoiding the press, and never revealing to anyone other than the cops why I was there. I preferred to stay on the journalist's side of this story, rather than be a part of it. Finally, the police took me away with silent stealth, which I didn't mind, given the number of news vans that continued to arrive.

For hours, members of the Georgetown County Sheriff's Department, detectives from the South Carolina Law Enforcement Division (SLED), and an officer from the Litchfield Beach Security Police, hung on my every word. Even Sheriff Arlen Bagwell back in Pickens County got in on the act by conference call.

Another way of saying this was that I was held in a small windowless room at the Georgetown County Sheriff's Office for hours, with nothing to eat or drink since breakfast but bad coffee and crackers from a vending machine, while cops from one end of the state to the other fired questions at me.

The medical examiner had an early estimation of the time of death as between one and three in the morning. They'd found a maid at the hotel who saw someone who fit Melissa Raines' description walking to the beach a little after midnight, wearing a light jacket, jeans, and tennis shoes, like she was going for a nighttime walk on the beach.

At first, an annoying cynical detective from SLED gave me a rough time over my alibi; however, his attitude improved as Sheriff Bagwell placed me at Still Hollow last night, and I provided a gas and toll receipt showing I had driven down today.

Only then did they let me take a break and use the phone, but they kept me on a short leash, limiting me to a single call. I called Eloise, giving her a quick account of what happened, how I was doing, and when I hoped to be home.

They made me tell my story several times. Why I came looking for Melissa

Raines, who I thought was responsible for the old bruises on her face, and how and why I thought she was hiding out here. As to who may have killed her, I admitted that all I had were guesses but told them that a list of my "people of interest" would include Barry Beal, Bobby Paige, and Carl Hood. They listened, stared, pondered, made notes, and made calls but said little in return. I got the feeling from snippets of conversation that they were leaning toward none of my suggestions, but a stranger with evil urges, a good-looking woman, the middle of the night, and a deserted beach. They were waiting on a report to see if she'd been raped. The "random murder" conclusion was familiar, and I wondered if they were getting pointers from Sheriff Bagwell.

They finally turned me loose. Over a period of about four hours, I'd gone from being a "suspect" to a "witness with prior knowledge" and was expected to make myself available for further contact. I left tired and hungry, but after a black coffee and a roast beef sandwich from a Georgetown deli, I got a second wind and headed for the upstate.

Eloise was sitting up waiting for me when I returned. It was four AM. I went over everything that had happened sequentially and in detail, except for the crabs feeding on Melissa Raines' face. I didn't feel like describing that. I probably never would.

CHAPTER TWENTY-NINE

I managed to sleep past eleven AM, and with a cup of coffee and a donut, sat at the kitchen table reading today's Greenville newspaper's coverage of Melissa Raines' murder. Eloise and Mackenzie were out back feeding whatever gathering of domesticated beasts or fowl that depended on them for their daily sustenance.

The story was front-page news, albeit without much detail, and nothing about me being questioned about it. My guess was they'd picked the story off the wire services, filed early by those reporters who were first at the scene. Something they would have had to do to make this morning's edition.

The headline read, "Pickens County Woman Murdered at Beach." Eloise and I sat at the kitchen table, drinking coffee, and sharing the paper. Mackenzie was still sleeping.

The paper said that a Dan and Gail Ferguson from Columbia, South Carolina, were credited with finding the body. We'd never introduced ourselves, so it was my first time hearing their names. My name wasn't mentioned, for which I was thankful. A statement from the authorities said that the investigation was going as planned, and they were following several significant leads. It was similar to what Sheriff Bagwell told me when I talked to him about Grandfather's murder. Same bullshit, different murder.

I pondered the end of Melissa Raines. At the risk of insensitivity to the greater tragedy of a lost human life, her death had all but eliminated any chance I had to prove that Barry Beal assaulted her, thus—the end of my story. But whether the cops believed me or not, Raines had to be part of a bigger story. I was convinced of it. I'd not only lost the chance to prove Beal's assault but also the opportunity to discover any other iniquitous thing she knew about him.

The phone rang. I answered it and was surprised to hear the voice of Joe Dennis, my editor at *SportsWord.*

"How you doin', buddy?" he asked.

"Peachy, Joe, thanks for asking."

He asked me if we had received the flowers they had sent.

"Yes, we did," I said. "My sister and I both thank you."

"Well, it wasn't just from me. The whole staff pitched in. Including Burt Lowe."

"That was thoughtful."

"Look, J.D., I hate to ask this, but can you get back here?

"I thought I gave you enough material to get you through a couple of weeks," I said.

"It isn't that. Lowe wants to talk to you."

"About what?"

"All I know is he asked me to find out when you're coming back."

"C'mon, Joe, give me a clue. What does he want?"

I could hear him breathing, obviously laboring over how to best answer.

"It's Barry Beal. He says you came and hassled him at the Masters, and now the cops want to talk to him about a girl they found dead over on the South Carolina coast. They said you gave them his name as someone to talk to. He went apeshit. His lawyer came to see Burt, and now Burt wants to see you."

"Tell Burt I'll be down there this afternoon," I said.

"I didn't mean you had to come right this minute, John David," he said. "Later in the week will do just fine."

"I'm actually doing a down and back today, anyway," I lied. "Got a little time late this afternoon." I just wanted to get this over with, picturing myself standing in an unemployment line. "I can't get back for at least a week." Another lie. "I've got family business to take care of."

"Well . . . Burt *is* in the office this afternoon," Joe said.

"I'm getting fired, aren't I?" I said.

"John David, I . . ." Joe started to say.

"It's not your fault, Joe" I said. "I appreciate everything you've tried to do for me. I'll see you in a few hours."

I hung up and went upstairs to shower and change into my best *getting-fired* clothes. While in the shower, I heard the phone ring again. Eloise or Mackenzie obviously picked it up because it only rang twice. For about a second, I thought it might be Joe Dennis calling back to tell me I didn't need to come, as Lowe had second thoughts and said that people like Barry Beal didn't run *Sports Word*. Yeah, right.

I was sitting on my bed, pulling on my shoes, when there was a tap at my door.

"Are you decent, John David?" Eloise asked and poked her head into the room.

"No," I said, "but I *am* fully dressed."

My attempt at the old quip was lost on her. She seemed to have something more serious on her mind.

"I want to talk to you about something, and I'm not sure how you'll react," she said as she sat down in a chair by the window.

"Nothing you could say would provoke a bad reaction from me, Eloise. You know you're my favorite sister."

"I'm your *only* sister," she said, adding to another old quip we'd shared since kids. She took a deep breath, as if what she was going to say required more than the normal amount of air.

"I know you want to sell the *Clarion*," she said, "and I know you're doing it for me. But would you consider selling just a part of it?"

I wasn't expecting that. "I don't understand, Eloise. What do you mean?"

"Kelly wants to buy in. She thinks we could make the paper a more profitable business."

"*We*, Eloise?" I said.

"I also know you want nothing to do with the *Clarion*; you've made that perfectly clear. But I'm talking about Kelly and me as managing partners—with your approval, of course. I don't want just to sit out here and live off the income from a sale. Mackenzie will be off to college in a couple of years, and then what would I do? I want to live a productive life, John David, and I want to be able to earn it."

"Wow," I said. "This comes as a huge surprise. "Does Kelly have the money?"

"Family money," Eloise said. "Quite a bit, I think. We could use some of it to pay down the debt and some to make a few changes," she said, her enthusiasm building.

"Sounds to me like this isn't just some spur-of-the-moment idea," I said.

"We've been discussing it for several days," she said. "Kelly has such great ideas. You know how Grandfather felt about advertising revenue. It was just a necessary evil to him, and he never prioritized it. Kelly thinks she can double it. She also wants to add new sections and features to build circulation and create a digital version of the paper. And I think I'd like to try my hand at writing some articles. You weren't the only one to major in journalism, you know."

I couldn't remember the last time I saw my sister this excited. I stifled a grin, fearing that she would mistake my sudden flood of emotion for her as a rebuke of the idea.

"Granddad left the *Clarion* to you, John David, and if you think it's a bad idea . . ."

I didn't know what to think. But I couldn't dash cold water on her enthusiasm, so I said, "I think the thing to do is for the three of us to sit down and discuss it. It just might work."

She seemed pleased with that, kissed me on the cheek, and said, "Good. Kelly's on her way out here."

Thirty minutes later, Eloise, Kelly Mayfield and I were sitting in the den with fresh-made cups of coffee. Eloise and Kelly's focus locked on me.

"So, what do you think of our idea," Kelly asked me.

"Well, on the face of it, it's an intriguing idea," I said. "I really didn't expect something like this."

Kelly gave me a steely gaze. "So, does that mean your initial reaction isn't positive?"

"I didn't say that. I just need a little time to wrap my mind around it."

"I understand completely," she said. "We sprung it on you when you just returned from what sounds like a horrible experience. Let me put the plan down on paper, with some quick numbers and details, and we'll get back together if that's okay."

"Sure," I said. "I just want what's best for Eloise and Mackenzie's future."

"And I think you'll see this is it," she said with a wide smile.

A smile from Kelly Mayfield wasn't something I wasn't accustomed to. I found myself liking it . . . maybe a little too much. Looking back on things later, I would realize that she had me at that smile.

She took a pad and a pen out of her purse and said, “One more thing. I wouldn’t be much of a reporter if I didn’t ask you about this Raines woman and why you went to the coast looking for her? I understand you were there when the body was found. Is that right?”

Eloise must have told her. It looked like I would be answering a reporter’s questions after all. But this time, it was different than at the beach. It would be for a story in a newspaper whose success I had a vested interest in, and which, if present suggested plans came to fruition, would even be increasing for me.

“Yes,” I finally said, glancing at Eloise. My sister must have seen my discomfort for being on this side of a news story. She gave me an “I’m sorry” look and shrugged.

“What do you already know about it?” I asked Kelly, getting a question of my own into the mix.

“I know you wanted to talk to her about a story you’re working on. I know it involves an assault by the golfer, Barry Beal.”

“Alleged assault,” I said. “Now that the Raines girl is gone, there’s probably no way to prove it. So, I’d be careful about using Barry Beal’s name in anything you print. He likes to sue people.” *And he’d jump at that chance if he knew it was my newspaper he was suing*, I thought.

“Was Garnet involved in this in any way?” she asked.

I took a moment to answer, unsure of how much I wanted to tell her.

“Grandfather was helping me locate her,” is all I said. “And I’m going to have to leave it at that, for the time being. I’ve been summoned back to Atlanta today for a meeting late this afternoon, so I need to get going.”

I turned to Eloise. “I’m sorry to spring this on you, sis, but I just got the call. That’s why I showered and changed clothes. It’s a turnaround trip, I’ll be back tonight.”

“Sounds like you could use someone to keep you company,” Kelly said. “Mind if I tag along?”

The question surprised me until I realized that what she really wanted was to keep questioning me, and several hours stuck in a car together would give her that opportunity. I thought about it for a moment. There were worse travel companions.

“Why not,” I said. “If you promise not to use the time trying to sell me on you buying into the Clarion. I told you I need time to think about it."

"I'll try," she said. "But it's such a good idea that I'm not sure that's a promise I can keep."

"Well, at least you're honest about it."

"Honesty is one thing I can promise," she said.

I believed that about her. And found myself smiling at the thought.

CHAPTER THIRTY

Kelly climbed into the Jeep, buckled up, and looked around the interior. "A friend had one of these," she said, "but it had a soft top. The wind always whistled through it."

"The hard top is optional," I said. "I bought the Jeep used, and it came with it. And it doesn't whistle."

"Hmm," she said.

I didn't think the hard top made any difference in what she thought of it. You could dress them up, but they still rode like Jeeps. I could see her imagining a six-hour round trip in it.

"Still time to change your mind," I said, smiling.

She smiled back. "It'll be fun."

"Then wagons ho," I said, and we drove away.

Several miles west on Highway 11, I told her I wanted to make a quick side trip into Eastatoe Valley. I explained that I needed to look at something there and promised we'd be back on the road to Atlanta in fifteen minutes, tops.

"Fine by me," she said, looking puzzled.

I slowed down and turned right on Eastatoe Creek Road, the western entrance into the valley. When we came to Cecil Hood's farm, I pulled over and stopped by the gate. The chain and padlock were gone.

"I'll just be a couple of minutes," I said before walking up the drive.

The place looked even more deserted than before. A peek through a window showed the rooms were bare. The garage stood wide open and empty. If a white Dodge Ram pickup was ever parked inside, it was gone now.

I examined the tire tracks coming in and out of the garage. The treads looked all the same to me. I supposed it could have been a pickup truck, but what did I know? A modern-day Kit Carson, I wasn't. The only thing I could detect from the scene was that Carl Hood was gone, and he probably wasn't coming back.

"Nobody home," I said when I returned to the Jeep.

"When are you going to stop treating me like an idiot?" Kelly said as we drove off.

"I didn't know I was."

"This is Cecil Hood's farm. His name is on the mailbox. What are you looking for at a dead man's house?"

"A white pickup truck," I said.

"And this pickup truck is important to you how?" she asked. I sat and watched the landscape flow by the window for a moment. In for a penny, in for a pound, I decided. After bringing up the white pickup, I didn't see any way I could avoid offering an explanation, especially with someone like Kelly Mayfield.

"Someone driving a late model white Dodge Ram pickup has been following me."

"Well, we know it wasn't Cecil Hood," she said. "So, I'm assuming you think it was his son Carl, the ex-con. That's who I caught you looking at on the microfilm in the *Clarion* morgue, isn't it? But why would he be following you?"

"I don't know for certain that he is," I said. "I'm going through a process of elimination. Whoever drives a white Dodge Ram pickup gets tagged. I'll tackle the *why* when I've solved the *who*."

I could almost see the questions sprouting behind her pretty but now wrinkled brow.

"Why would *anyone* follow you?" she asked. "And why would you think it might be Carl Hood? You mentioned a 'process of elimination.' Who else is on the list? What else aren't you telling me, John David?" The questions came out in rapid succession.

"I keep forgetting you're a reporter," I said, looking across the seat at her.

"Was I grilling you?"

"Like a grouper filet."

"Well, I *am* a reporter. I can't help it. So, answer my question. Why is someone following you?"

"Because someone wants to know what I'm up to. And I don't believe Grandfather was killed during a simple robbery. I think he knew, or at least he suspected, that Cecil Hood's accidental death was really a murder. And knowing—or at least questioning it—got him killed. The robbery was just a cover-up. Now the killer is trying to see if I'm following in my grandfather's footsteps."

She stared across the seat at me for a long time before she spoke. "Assuming you aren't in the throes of a paranoid episode," she finally said, "what proof do you have for any of this?

"To quote a line from *Catch-22*," I said, "Just because you're paranoid doesn't mean someone isn't after you."

"Do you have proof or not?" she repeated.

"There are different kinds of proof, as you well know," I said. "The kind you need in a court of law, what you need for validation to go to press on a news story, and what you need to simply believe in something. All I have is the latter." I filled her in on everything. Barry Beal's alleged assault on Melissa Raines and my getting Grandfather involved. I laid out the steps of Cecil Hood's convenient death and Carl Hood's background and windfall. I told her about my fight with Bobby Paige and how he tried to run me out of town. And now, the fact that Raines had been murdered. We were well beyond the Lake Hartwell Bridge on I-85 and deep into Georgia before I was done.

"I can't help but believe everything that's happened leads back to Barry Beal's development in Eastatoe Valley," I said. "The only part I haven't been able to connect to the development is Bobby Paige, but I'm convinced he's involved somehow."

"The shot through the window last night," she said, "you don't think it was an accident, do you? I saw it on your and Eloise's faces."

"I think the only accidental thing about it was that they shot my reflection in the mirror instead of me," I said, then told her what I'd discovered on my second trip behind the house.

"Have you told Sheriff Bagwell any of this?" she asked.

"You sound like Eloise," I said. "Bagwell has meth-heads on the brain and isn't looking anywhere else. He thinks I'm a family-size box of fruit loops. The next time I talk to him, it will be with something concrete he can't ignore."

"What can I do to help?" she asked.

I was flattered she thought enough of my baseless theories to join in. Her respect obviously meant more to me than I realized.

"Nothing," I told her. "You shouldn't get involved."

"You can't believe I'd stay out of this now," she said.

The determination on her face defeated any argument I could come up with. I had a partner whether I wanted one or not. But hadn't I known this would eventuate when I decided to tell her everything? I'd ponder my reasons for that decision later.

"We start with Carl Hood," I said. "I want to know if he's driving that white Dodge Ram pickup. To do that, we need to find out where he lives in Atlanta and go look."

She fished a cell phone from her purse, and I listened as she called Mrs. Mozingo at the *Clarion* and asked her to pull up the file on Cecil Hood's obituary. While she waited, she said, "If Carl Hood submitted the obit info, we probably have his address on record."

She returned to the call, listened briefly, then hung up and grinned at me.

"Peachtree Villa Apartments, Peachtree Street NW, apartment 3-C," she said.

When she put her phone up, I reached into my pocket and retrieved the note page I'd found on Grandfather's desk at the *Clarion*.

"I found this in Grandfather's office," I said, holding up the page for her to see. "These notes from his search for Melissa Raines. He has a list of area hotels that helped me find her, along with Carl Hood's name and number. That's what put me on to him. But there's one thing I haven't been able to decipher, these letters, or initials, *WS*. Do you have any idea what that stands for?"

"I don't know. Website? Although I doubt that, as Garnet was somewhat technophobic when it came to computers. There's W.S. Merwin, a contemporary American poet I studied at Smith, but I don't think Garnet would have liked him. Do you think it's important?"

"It was right in the middle of all this other stuff, which he wrote down on the afternoon that he died."

"Maybe there's something in his address book," Kelly said. "I'll check when I get back. Perhaps we can swing by Carl Hood's place after your meeting."

As the mile markers on I-85 flew by, we fell into a pattern of small talk spaced with comfortable silences. She learned that I had a hard time hanging onto jobs and girlfriends, and I learned that she was born in a small town in the North Carolina tobacco country and joined the *Clarion* after seven years at the *Charlotte Observer*. I wondered why she left a major newspaper for a small weekly in Podunk; she didn't say, and I got the feeling she didn't want to talk about it. So, I didn't pry.

She was brainy but bore her intelligence with a self-deprecatory style that came off as anything but pretentious. I found myself liking her as a person. God knows I already liked how she looked. In fact, every time I could steal a glance at her, I noticed something new to admire. A tiny scar at the corner of her mouth that dimpled when she smiled, the lone amber freckle on the tip of her nose, the visible rhythm of heartbeat in her slender throat.

I was sitting there having extraordinarily embarrassing thoughts, all involving reaching across the seat and grabbing her, when the skyline of Atlanta appeared on the horizon, and the traffic around us began to slow and stack up. We both gazed at the road ahead for a while, lost in our own thoughts.

CHAPTER THIRTY-ONE

When we reached the offices of *SportsWord*, I pointed Kelly toward the lobby and hung around long enough to watch her select a magazine from a table, test the softness of a sofa, and settle in to wait for me. Out of everything I had told her, I omitted how badly I expected the meeting with Burt Lowe to go, probably because I was embarrassed to have her see me in such a predicament. When did I start worrying about what she thought of me?

Upstairs, Burt Lowe's secretary, Lydia Wells, barely glanced at me before motioning me into her boss's office. Lowe, the magazine's legal counsel, Stan Gilmore, and Joe Dennis were waiting for me, their faces grave.

"Hey, hey, the gang's all here," I said, taking a seat across the desk from Lowe.

I got nothing back but somber looks and silence. Whatever I was about to be charged with, I could already see that I'd been tried, convicted, and sentenced with no chance of reprieve.

"I'd like a cheeseburger, large fries, and an Eskimo pie if you're taking last requests," I said. "And make sure to honor my organ donor card after I'm gone."

"I see no humor in the situation, John David," Lowe said.

"No shit," I offered.

Burt Lowe shifted to a tragic face. "John David," he said, "allow me to extend, on behalf of the magazine and all of us, our heartfelt sympathies for your recent loss." Gilmore and Dennis nodded in solemn accord.

"I appreciate that, Burt, I really do, but I'm assuming you didn't ask me to come all this way just to tell me that."

Lowe's face colored, and the tragic look disappeared.

"Okay. We'll get straight to the business at hand if that's what you want."

"I don't think this meeting has much to do with what I want, does it?"

"Oh, but it does. We're here because you always do exactly what you want, with no regard for the wishes of others. And for that, we are terminating your employment, effective immediately."

Lowe looked at Joe Dennis for support, but Joe sat with his gaze glued to the floor.

"You wouldn't listen, would you?" Stan Gilmore said, slowly shaking his head. "You had to go to Augusta and rile up Barry Beal, and now you've mentioned his name as a suspect for this Raines woman's murder—for which he has an iron-clad alibi. You have placed this entire corporation in jeopardy."

I waited for a wellspring of anger to boil over, with clever, biting words sailing off my tongue like poisoned arrows to impale the hearts of all three of them, but I suddenly lacked the energy. I knew this could happen if I kept at the story, but I'd pushed that into a corner and pulled a rug over it. Now that the moment was here, I found I simply didn't care. In fact, a part of me was relieved to be free of them.

"We have a very generous severance package for you," Lowe said. "More than policy requires. But before we get into the details, there are a few papers to sign."

He pushed several contract-size documents toward my side of the desk.

"This is to protect the magazine if you continue to pursue this Beal foolishness," Stan Gilmore piped in. "Since our earlier warnings went completely unheeded, you should understand our reasons for wanting this." I looked at Joe Dennis, who hadn't uttered a word yet.

"It's a good severance, John David," he said, his voice resigned. "But if you don't sign, you don't get it."

In a rehearsed tone, Gilmore assured me that the magazine's problem with me was never the quality of my work but my unwillingness to embrace company dictates and policy, which resulted in irrevocable philosophical differences, etcetera, etcetera. I knew this was meant to cover their legal butts with an officially stated reason for my termination. I'd been there before.

I signed the papers. I needed all the severance I could get.

Joe Dennis acted genuinely sorry, and I guess I didn't blame him too much for his impotence to affect the outcome. He had a wife, a mortgage, and three school-age kids to look out for while trying to survive in an industry where cable TV, talk radio, and the Internet outdistanced the printed word by volumes every day.

When I returned to the lobby, Kelly surveyed the box of personal things I'd gathered from my office, examined my face for a moment, and said, "Bad day at the office, dear?"

I was beginning to really like this woman.

There are seventy-one streets in Atlanta with a variant of "Peachtree" in their name, which drives out-of-towners nuts and manages to confuse locals regularly. This turned out to be one of those times for the locals, namely me and was made worse by a thundering downpour that came out of nowhere, the sky suddenly darkening and unleashing torrents that beat down on the roof of the Jeep in a loud drum roll. After crossing back and forth between Peachtree Street, Peachtree Street NE, and Peachtree Street NW a few times, we finally found the apartment complex.

The Peachtree Villa was a sprawling compound of two-story spiritless brown brick buildings that began at the street and ran back about a hundred yards through a maze of drives and parking lots to border a small muddy creek in the rear. Each building carried a letter of the alphabet, and each apartment was numbered. Accordingly, 3-C was the third apartment in the third building. Parking spaces weren't designated, so residents were left to park anywhere they found a vacant spot. I checked the lot for a white Dodge Ram pickup but didn't see one. I pulled into a space by Hood's apartment and shut off the engine.

The rain stopped as suddenly as it started, leaving water dripping from the trees, streaming off the roofs, and running across the lot in a hundred miniature rivers. The windows inside the Jeep fogged up immediately. Kelly took a tissue from her purse, wiped a spot clear, and we sat looking through it at apartment 3-C. A middle-aged man wearing a wife beater and a pair of plaid Bermuda shorts came out of the apartment next door to Hood's, stood on the stoop, and gazed at the sky. I could see the food stains on his sleeveless shirt, even from where I sat. After a moment, he went back in and closed the door behind him.

"What now?" Kelly asked.

"We'll wait a while. If he doesn't show up soon, we'll come back later."

She wrinkled her nose at the suggestion.

"You have a better idea?"

"Yeah," she said, opening the door.

She headed toward the apartment where the man with the dirty shirt lived, and I started to follow, but she waved me back. I sat and watched as she banged on his door until he appeared in the doorway. They chatted for a minute. I was too far away to hear their words, but they seemed to be getting along well. She laughed out loud at something he said, and his face reflected how pleased he was with himself for it. She could be a charmer when she wanted to be, I realized. When she returned to the car, he stood in the doorway smiling and watching her leave.

I leaned over and held the door open. "Looks like you made a new friend."

"I thought he'd be more willing to talk to me without you along," she said as she got in.

She was probably right. "Well?" I said.

"He said he isn't sure what kind of car Carl Hood drives now. He did have an old clunker that, to quote him, 'had more rust on it than paint."

"Damn," I said.

"You aren't listening. He said *did have* an old clunker. After recently coming into an inheritance, it seems our Mr. Hood has not only quit his job as a welder at a machine shop, but he's also been shopping for a new automobile. But his neighbor hasn't been kept in the loop regarding any purchase."

"Does he know where we can find him?"

"He said to try a bar over on—you'll never guess—*Peachtree* Industrial Boulevard. Hood has a girlfriend who dances there. The place is called the Bareback Rider, and I think the name suggests what kind of dancing she actually does. My new friend in 4-C was kind enough to offer to escort me there, but I respectfully declined."

The Bareback Rider was just south of the I-285 loop, in the middle of a row of automobile dealerships. We couldn't have missed it if we'd tried. The windowless one-story building was painted hot pink and sat under a tall neon sign that pictured a nude woman astride a rearing horse. A dozen cars sat in the parking lot, several pickups, but none of them a white Dodge Ram.

I parked the car, and we sat for a moment, watching the place. A truck laden with lawnmowers and leaf-blowers pulled in, and several shaggy-haired workers in sweat-stained clothes hopped out and went inside.

"Sit tight, and I'll be back in a few minutes," I said, opening the door. "This one looks like man's work."

"Women don't go in these kind of places?" Kelly said.

"Sure, they do. But most of them are there to take off their clothes. If we go in together, we'll draw attention. It's best if we do this as inconspicuously as possible."

She didn't like it, but she agreed. As I exited the car, a carload of guys who looked like auto mechanics pulled in, already whistling and jeering. Behind me, I heard Kelly hit the door's auto-lock button.

The Bareback Rider was dark and loud, with the smell of stale beer and cigarette smoke lingering in the air. A bar ran the length of one wall, a single bartender behind it. On a runway that dissected the room, two girls were bumping and grinding to the music, wearing nothing but garter belts. Strips of bikini-waxed pubic hair rode atop their swaying pudendas like furry caterpillars. In the back, several pool tables attracted almost as many people as the dancers. I didn't see Carl Hood anywhere.

I walked over to the bar and spun a stool around to watch the girls. Both were striking blondes, prettier than I expected for a joint like this, which was a couple of steps down from some of the more infamous places around town. Atlanta's nude bars drew more convention business to the city than the Chamber of Commerce's PR department was willing to admit, and a hot dancer could make more money than a bank vice president. If the wad of bills stuffed beneath these girls' garter belts was any indication, they did well here, too, even though the clientele were mainly landscape workers from Chihuahua instead of computer salesmen from Toledo.

The bartender slapped a coaster on the bar behind me, and I turned and ordered a beer. When he brought it, I proffered a generous tip and asked him if Carl Hood was around.

"Don't know him," he said flatly and walked away.

"I don't think Carl will be too happy when he learns I was in town and missed him because of an unaccommodating dickhead bartender."

He turned, stared at me for a moment, and came back.

"You a friend of his?"

"We go way back."

"Ain't seen him for a few days," he said, his eyes flicking over my shoulder at the two dancers. "You might ask his girlfriend. Up there behind you. The blonde."

I looked. "They're both blondes," I said.

"The real blonde," he offered, without expression.

I saw what he meant. According to the caterpillars, one of them was actually a brunette.

"Think she knows where I can find him?"

"Probably," he said.

"Any problem with me asking her?"

"As long as you got five bucks for a table dance, you can ask her anything you want. She ain't on her own time right now." The music ended, and the girls stooped to pick up their clothes, re-hooking sequined bras and stepping ungracefully into panties that were barely more than strings. They made their way down a narrow set of stairs, passing two other girls on the way up, the music already blasting another driving bass line that rattled the glasses behind the bar.

I waved a five-dollar bill at the natural blonde and felt the bartender staring at me.

"The best place to get a table dance, Hoss, is actually to be at a table," he said over my shoulder.

I picked a table on the far side of the room. The bartender watched as I walked toward it as if I was severely retarded. I caught the girl's eye and waved her over.

"Table dance, Hon?" she asked.

"You bet," I said, offering her a hand as she stepped on a chair and climbed atop the small round table.

"You look like a man who likes to get straight to the point," she said, and re-shed her sequined top and stringed bottoms, dropping them on the chair and leaving me staring straight up into the caterpillar's very nest.

She began to move to the music, a vacant look on her face, the situation obviously more awkward for me than for her.

I inserted a five spot under her garter belt, and she knelt down and kissed the top of my head, bringing a pink nipple within inches of my nose.

"The bartender says you know Carl Hood," I said.

"Yeah, so what?"

"I need to get in touch with him."

"What for?"

"I'm trying to trade him out of that old rust bucket he drives."

"You a car salesman?"

"The best there is."

"Well, you're second best now, honey, cause he already traded it."

"He took his business to somebody else?" I tried to sound disappointed. "Did he get a Dodge Ram pickup like he was looking at?"

She gave me a look I couldn't decipher and, with a gliding move, turned her back to me. She placed her hands on her knees and went into what the rappers call a tip drill, rocking her butt side to side to the rhythm of the music. I watched for a moment like watching a tennis volley. When I looked up, she was staring around her shoulder at me.

"What's your name, honey?" she asked.

If I was going to shake Carl Hood's tree, I had to start somewhere. "John David Bragg," I said. "What's yours?"

"Crystal," she said, her eyes suddenly less vacant.

"So, did he get the truck or not?" I asked.

She stepped down off the table, took the five-dollar bill from her garter, and tossed it next to my beer.

"Carl wouldn't be caught dead in a fucking pickup truck," she said as she gathered her costume and walked away.

Kelly greeted me with an expectant look when I came out. "Well?" she said.

"No Carl Hood. But I did talk to his girlfriend."

"I'll bet that was a treat."

"It was different."

"You're blushing," she said, laughing. "What did she say?"

"I think she said Hood doesn't drive a white Dodge Ram pickup. But she tipped to my bullshit, so I'm unsure whether to believe her."

"She knew who you were?"

I thought about the look she gave me when I said my name. "I don't know. Maybe. Or maybe she just realized I was pulling her chain, and she didn't like it."

“It looks like we struck out,” I said, “so how about we stop for something to eat before we head back? It’s early enough to get in almost anywhere.”

“Thai food?” she asked and smiled. “I love it and haven’t found a Thai restaurant I like since Charlotte.”

“Then I’ve got just the right place,” I said

CHAPTER THIRTY-TWO

I drove to Cheshire Bridge Road and Little Bangkok, a hole in the wall at first glance, but actually, in my opinion, one of the best Thai restaurants in Atlanta. I got the feeling that Kelly wasn't looking for show; she was looking for substance. If that was the case, this was the place.

It felt like we were on a date, and I found myself liking the feeling. We were early enough to find a rare parking spot out front. Inside, we found the entire wait staff waiting for us like a hospitality line at a wedding reception. I caught Kelly surveying the empty dining room behind them with suspicion. I assured her that the lack of business was due to the early hour, not the quality of the food.

It didn't take long to prove me right as the small place began to fill up. We sat and studied our menus over a glass of Thai tea, and finally ordered the Tom Kha (coconut soup to me) and Pad Thai, and then experimented with a couple of specialties, resulting in a table laden with more food than we could ever eat. But it wasn't for lack of trying. For someone so thin, Kelly attacked the food like a lumberjack, her face morphing into various expressions of pure joy as she sampled each dish. I sat drinking in the sight of her. We ate leisurely and never ran out of things to talk about, although we avoided the subject of Grandfather's death, Carl Hood, or any other unpleasant recent event. She even kept her promise and didn't try to sell me on the *Clarion* buy-in offer.

Finally, I reluctantly said, "It's getting late, and we need to hit the road."

She looked at me for a moment, her face expressionless. "We *could* go back in the morning," she said.

"Well . . . yeah, we *could* do that," I said, wondering if I was succeeding at all in covering up the fact that she was causing my shameless imagination to run amok.

"I can pile up on your sofa if you don't have room," she said. "If you have a sofa, and I can find a toothbrush somewhere."

"Are you sure?"

"Positive," she said. Looking me dead in the eye. What I saw there made me giddy. I caught the attention of our waiter and signaled for the check. When I turned back, she was grinning at me.

"What's so funny?" I asked.

"You."

"I'm happy to amuse you."

"I would never have expected it."

"Expected what?"

"You're a gentleman."

"I think you have mistaken me for someone else."

"I think not," she said, still smiling.

"And what leads you to this revelation?"

"You blushed when I suggested I stay over. I almost expected you to offer to put me up in a hotel."

"How do you know I wasn't blushing at my disgustingly obscene thoughts?"

"I didn't say you were a saint. I said you were a gentleman."

"Don't go creating expectations I'll fail to live up to."

"Well, we've got the rest of the night to see, don't we?" she said, fluttering her eyelids at me.

She gathered up her purse and left me to pay the check. I couldn't get the credit card out of my wallet fast enough.

She came into my arms before I could close my apartment door. I kicked it shut behind me and, without speaking, led her to my bed. We unbuttoned, unzipped, and unpeeled, throwing off clothes in all directions until flesh pressed against flesh, the touch of her silky skin hot against mine.

She suddenly chuckled, and I rose up on my elbows and looked at her.

"Gentleman J.D.," she said, giggling.

"You're not going to laugh all through this, are you?" I said. "Because if you are, it won't be real good for my ego."

"I just might. I'm having a lot of fun," she said, pulled me down, and kissed me.

I began exploring her with my hands and lips, losing myself in the lushness of her. She moaned and arched her back, her fingers in my hair. She wrapped her legs around me, placed her hands on the small of my back, and guided me inside her. We made love with urgency and desperation as she thrust her hips against me with a fury that I responded to with equal vigor. I climaxed almost immediately.

"I stand corrected," she whispered hoarsely into my ear. "You are *not* a gentleman."

I barely found the breath to talk. "Consider it just sticking a toe in the water, so to speak."

We made love again, this time slowly and deliciously, like swimming in molasses. Afterward, we lay clinched together, perspiration cooling on our bodies, our hearts settling to a normal beat.

"You're forgiven," she said, soft and purring.

Outside, the rain was falling again as thunder rumbled somewhere over the earth's curve. Water tumbled down a drain spout near the window, creating a soothing, comfortable background. The words to an old Dylan song about "Shelter from the Storm" played through my head. Kelly rolled into the crook of my arm, breathing deeply. Her presence there felt alarmingly natural.

"If I smoked, I'd have a cigarette about now," I said.

"Too cliché," she offered.

"That was so incredibly . . . stupendous," I said, "I have the urge to do something cliché to help me get back to the normal world."

She kissed me in the hollow of my neck. "Oh, we can do better," she said, sliding a warm hand over my stomach, her fingers touching me lightly.

As impossible as I thought it might be, I felt myself stir again.

CHAPTER THIRTY-THREE

Later, while Kelly slept, I crawled out of bed on weary legs, went into the living room, sat naked in the dark, and called Eloise to tell her I wouldn't be home tonight. I didn't tell her that due to pleasant mitigating circumstances, the opportunity to call earlier didn't present itself. She probably already guessed as much, but I knew she would still worry. When I got her on the line, she was almost too forgiving at the late hour of the call, and I heard a trace of humor in her voice as she said she hoped Kelly and I were "getting to know" one another.

The phone rang in my hand the second I placed it in the cradle. I picked it back up quickly, hoping it didn't wake Kelly.

A male voice said, "We need to talk."

"Who is this? I asked.

"Carl Hood. I'm outside. Come on out, and let's chew the fat awhile."

I walked over and cracked the blinds. The rain had diminished to a mist, and through it, I could see a late-model Cadillac Esplanade parked directly in front of my apartment. Cigarette smoke curled through the crack of a driver's side window and trailed off into the damp night. The interior lights came on to show Carl Hood behind the wheel, bathed in the glow of the overhead dome as if he'd spotlighted himself for me to see.

I made sure Kelly was still asleep, put on my clothes, and went outside.

His window slid down with a low motorized hum as I approached him. He looked out at me as if nothing untoward was happening.

"Get in," he said.

"I'm fine right here. What do you want?"

"We need to talk. I told you that."

"Great, call me tomorrow."

"I came to tell you what a big disappointment you are. I was hoping you'd be better at your job."

"I have no idea what you mean by that," I said.

"The newspaper called you an investigative reporter. I think they need to do a retraction."

"I'll say good night to you, Mr. Hood," I said and took a step back toward my apartment.

"I had high hopes for you when you came snooping around Daddy's place."

I stopped and turned around. "What the hell are you talking about?"

"I'll tell you, but you need to get in the car. I'm getting a fuckin' crick in my neck looking up at you, we're both getting wet, and it's a long story."

"Then make it a short story," I said, standing where I was.

"I'm no threat to you, Mr. Bragg," he said, losing the grin. "And I haven't done what you think I have. But if you don't want to hear my side of the story, then go fuck yourself."

With an invitation like that, how could I refuse? I walked around the car and got in. The interior smelled of new leather, cigarette smoke, and lime aftershave.

"Have you had a nice day, Mr. Bragg?" he said.

"Say what you've got to say, Hood, and let me get back to bed."

"My day hasn't been so hot," he went on. "I spent it trying to prove to some cops that I was back in Atlanta from Thursday night on—and that I certainly wasn't down on the South Carolina coast killing a woman I only met at the closing of my daddy's property. Thankfully, I've got an alibi sworn to by a half-dozen people— otherwise, I'd be in a lock-up right now talking to a new cellmate. So, I decided it was time you and me had a talk."

I realized that if Hood's alibi was solid, he wasn't the one who shot through the window at Still Hollow, either.

"I was hoping you'd be my bird dog," he said, "But the only trail you seem to be on is mine."

"Your bird dog? What the hell are you talking about?"

"I figured you'd be better than me at finding out who killed my daddy," he said.

"Meaning it wasn't you?"

"I ain't killed nobody," he said, smiling a bitter smile. "Not lately, anyway."

I couldn't think of an appropriate comment for that.

He thumped his cigarette into the darkness, the butt trailing a shower of red sparks. "You're just like your granddaddy," he said. "He thought I killed my old man too. He called out of the blue and practically accused me of it. Not in so many words, but it was there between the lines. And it got me thinking."

"About what?" I said. "How to stop him from telling anyone else?"

Hood gave me an aggravated look.

"He got me thinking about how fuckin' convenient everything was," he said and stared out the window as if what he wanted to say next was out there somewhere—his grip on the wheel was raising little white circles on his knuckles.

He turned to me with an expression so intense I flinched.

"I guess I done enough in my life to have killed my daddy several times over," he said, his voice low and guttural. "And I'll have to answer for that. But what I can't and *won't* live with is thinking that somebody was so cock-sure I'd sell daddy's land, they killed him to put it in my hands. If they done that, it's like they made me a party to it. And I will not let them get away with that."

I heard the guilt beneath his anger and tried hard not to draw parallels to my own life, but I couldn't avoid it.

"So I guess you could say I have myself a conundrum," he continued and cocked his head at me. "That's a word I looked up in a dictionary when I didn't have much else to do but look up words in a dictionary. I need to find out who killed my daddy, Mr. Bragg, and my problem is, even if I could convince the authorities that his death wasn't an accident, which I can't, they wouldn't look any farther than me for who did it. You certainly haven't. I'm an ex-con. A murderer. I got no alibi for daddy's time of death—at least not one anybody would believe if they took a mind not to—and being his sole heir gives me the motive."

He gazed around the new car's interior as if he were looking at it for the first time. "You're sitting in a chunk of it right now," he said.

Despite myself, I was beginning to believe the guy.

"You know that old song that goes, 'You got the right string baby, but the wrong yo-yo?" he asked. "That was your granddaddy. I believe he had the right idea; he just had the wrong guy. When he got killed, maybe he finally found the right guy, repeated what he said to me, and was killed for it."

Hood sounded like me talking, I thought. "There's a sheriff in Pickens County that would disagree with you," I said. "He's convinced it's a case of happenstance. A simple robbery-murder."

"But you don't believe that," Hood said. "If you did, you wouldn't have given the cops my name for the Raines girl's murder."

"So what?" I said. "It's all supposition. I don't have any proof, and it sounds like you don't, either. Neither of us has anything real to back it up."

"Real?" he said. "What's real is that even though I begged Daddy to sell the place, I didn't do it for me. It was for him. He was too damn old to be working that farm like he did. He needed to start taking it easier, find somewhere to retire, and put his feet up. But he wouldn't hear of it. He said he was born there and he would die there."

He paused a long moment, then said, "And that's exactly what happened, ain't it? That's pretty damn real if you ask me." Hood fell silent, his eyes searching my face as if looking for empathy.

He didn't know how much I had pondered the implications of his old man's prophetic words since Eloise first told me about them.

"Who was your dad dealing with?" I asked.

"As far as I know, the same people I dealt with when I sold the place. The actual buyer on the contract is a company named Red Hills Developments. A lawyer named Arthur Pitt and this dead Raines woman, a real estate agent or something, were at the closing."

"What was it with you and this Raines woman anyway?" he asked. "What were you doing at the beach where she died— when you put the cops on me?"

I told him why I was looking for her and how I enlisted Grandfather's help to find her.

After hearing me out, he asked, "Then why didn't you assume that Barry Beal killed her instead of me? He had a reason to shut her up. I didn't."

"He also had an alibi, but I told the police about him too, which got me fired today. So, you aren't the only one who's had a bad day."

"Beal could have hired someone to kill her," Hood said.

"He could have," I admitted. "But I think she had other things to tell than what an asshole Beal was—maybe things about your daddy and my grandfather. She may have suspected, or even known, who killed them."

"What's all this about a pickup truck?" Hood asked. "Crystal said while you were staring at her snatch, you were laying down a long line of bullshit about some truck I was going to buy."

"I'm being followed by someone in a white Dodge Ram pickup," I said. "I thought it was you. If I'm wrong, I'm back to square one."

"Then you're back to square one," he said. "I don't know anything about that."

"What else do you know about this Red Hills Developments?" asked.

He thought about it for a minute. "Barry Beal's a part of it, obviously," he said. "Pitt introduced me to him here in Atlanta—I was supposed to be impressed. And there's at least one other partner, but I don't know who he is."

"Couldn't it be the lawyer, Arthur Pitt?" I said.

"No. I know it wasn't him; it's somebody local—Pickens County or nearby."

"How do you know that?"

"Something the Raines woman said at the closing. There was a question about a document, and she asked Pitt if they shouldn't at least get the local partner to review it. Pitt seemed annoyed that she brought it up and brushed her off, and we got on with the closing."

I sat quietly for a moment, digesting what he said. "Do you know a guy named Bobby Paige?" I asked. He's about my age. Looks a lot like a bulldog."

"I don't think so," he said. "But if he's involved, I'd sure *like* to know him."

There was a chilling tone to his words, and when I thought of him calling me his bird dog, I wondered if the hunt was all he was interested in. Or did he want to be in on the kill as well? I probably needed to get as far away from this guy as possible.

"I guess I've got plenty to look into," I said, reaching for the door handle.

"So, you believe me?" he asked.

"Why not," I said.

Bragg?" he said.

I looked back at him.

"Don't expect me to keep doing your job."

I let the comment lay and got out of the car.

"I'll be in touch," he said, and with something that passed for a grin, he drove away.

Kelly was still asleep when I went back in. I didn't wake her as I crawled into bed.

CHAPTER THIRTY-FOUR

I awoke before Kelly and lay there watching her sleep. Not even the harsh morning sunlight that raked her face from a crack in the blinds could diminish her beauty. Her skin was as flawless as fine china.

She stirred slightly, and a feeling of dread swept across me. What was I going to say to her? Something glib? I didn't feel glib. Something sappy? Not my style…or hers. As I lay there fishing the depths of my emotions for the truth of how I really felt about her, she opened her eyes and looked at me. Something she saw in my expression killed the beginning of a smile, and she rolled away quickly and started to get up.

I grabbed her by the shoulders. "Whatever you're thinking, stop it," I said.

Her cheeks colored. "What am I supposed to think? That was one of those 'I knew I'd hate myself in the morning and I do, looks.'"

"It was nothing of the sort."

"Leave me alone," she said and tried to pull away.

I grabbed her by her shoulders again, forcing her to look at me. "Maybe that was just the look of somebody struggling to find words to describe how great last night was."

I reached up and wiped a sprig of hair from her eyes. "You'd better tell me you feel the same way, or I'll open a vein."

I pulled her closer and buried my face in her hair. I felt the tension slowly leave her. There was a fragility about her I hadn't seen. Someone had hurt this woman. I pressed her down on the pillow and put my arms around her. We were still in bed an hour later, lying together like spoons in a drawer.

"Carl Hood paid us a visit last night," I said.

She pulled away and sat back. "What are you talking about? Here? He came here?"

I told her about it.

"And you believe him?"

"Yes, I do. He's pretty convincing. By the way, he drives a Cadillac Esplanade, not a pickup truck." I told her about Hood saying there was a local partner in with Beal on the development and that after thinking about it, I had a candidate. Bailey McDaniel, Bucky Streeter's father-in-law. He was interested in getting in on the development boom in the area; Bucky had said so, and he certainly had the money to do it. And I could tie him to Bobby Paige, who was, as Bucky put it, McDaniel's "go-to" guy. If that were the case, he might do anything for McDaniel, including trying to scare me back to Atlanta at gunpoint—perhaps even worse things like murder.

Kelly sat quietly for a moment, considering what I just said as if she were trying to decide whether there was anything to my new suspicions or if, as she had said on the way down, I was a delusional, paranoid, wacko. She finally said, "So, what do we do now?"

"The first thing is to get up and get going."

"Maybe breakfast somewhere first?" she said. "I seem to have worked up an appetite for some reason."

"I'm feeling a bit peckish myself," I said. "And probably for the same reason."

"Good," she said. "You need to keep up your strength if you're going to come over to my house tonight and prove that this wasn't a one-night stand."

"Then get your pretty butt up before I have to prove it to you again—which could very well put me in traction."

After a quick IHOP breakfast we were on the road back to South Carolina, discussing our next steps, the objective being to prove Bailey McDaniel was Barry Beal's local partner in Red Hills Developments. But even if he were, we would still have no proof tying him to any murders. We would cross that bridge when we came to it, I decided. First, we had to connect him to Barry Beal and the development.

So, we split up the duties. I would ask my old friend Bucky Streeter to help gather dirt on his father-in-law, which, from what I knew of their relationship, he'd probably do, and Kelly would try to break through the corporation firewall of Red Hills Developments and find out if McDaniel's name appeared there.

The only other decision we made was to have dinner together. I was to call her later for the time and place. I dropped her off at her house, an impressive native rock and redwood ranch on Club Drive near the Pickens Country Club. Eloise said Kelly had money; the place looked expensive. Kelly said she was leasing it, but the lease payments couldn't have been all that cheap, at least for someone at my pay grade.

Eloise and Mackenzie were making grilled cheese sandwiches for lunch when I arrived. They added another one for me. Mackenzie was staying home from school another week, a deal Eloise made with her if she kept up with her homework. She had a book open at one end of the kitchen table and was doing just that. None of us spoke about my night in Atlanta, but both kept swapping looks and grinning at each other when they thought I wasn't looking.

There was a knock on the front door, and Eloise went to answer it. A moment later, she called out to me. The two SLED agents from Georgetown stood inside the door, waiting for me.

They introduced themselves as Detectives Green and Snyder, which was good because I didn't remember their names.

"What, you guys change your mind, and you're here to arrest me?" I asked. Green almost smiled. That was more emotion than I'd seen out of him in Georgetown.

"Nothing like that, Mr. Bragg," he said. "We're hoping you can answer a couple more questions for us. Sheriff Bagwell told us where to find you."

"Fire away," I said and then held up my hands. "Wait, I didn't mean that," I quickly added.

Neither smiled. My cop humor wasn't working with these guys or with Eloise. She was looking embarrassed for me.

"The Raines girl appears to have had a boyfriend up here," Snyder said. "Would you know who that might be?"

"I don't know anything about her personal life," I said. "You might try her next-door neighbor. She and Raines seemed close."

"We've already talked to the neighbor," he said. The neighbor says Ms. Raines was seeing someone but didn't know who he was. All she knows is that he drives a pickup truck."

"So, the boyfriend's a suspect?" I asked. "I thought you guys were leaning toward a stranger and rape."

"The hotel maid saw her hurrying down to the beach around midnight, and her cell phone shows that she had received a call shortly before that, which may suggest she met someone on the beach by prearrangement. Her cell phone records show a number of calls made to and from the same number, going back for months, with the last call shortly before the maid saw Raines heading for the beach. Unfortunately, the number was from one of those pre-paid phones, or 'burners,' as they're called. So, the caller can't be traced. But the phone company's cell tower records can at least trace the calls to the general area—which was from this part of the state. They tried sending an electronic pulse or 'pinging' to locate the phone, but that didn't work. Evidently, the phone has been destroyed. But that last call was made from Litchfield beach right before the Raines woman went down to the beach."

"The caller was there when she was killed," I said.

They both nodded. "That and what the neighbor told us is why we're looking for a boyfriend," Green said. "But if there is one, they kept it on the 'down low,' as they say. We haven't been able to find him."

A question suddenly came to me. "The pickup truck," I said. "Did the neighbor say what color it was?"

"White," Snyder said. "Didn't know the make."

Well, knock me down with a feather, I almost said.

CHAPTER THIRTY-FIVE

After Green and Snyder left, a man named Hendricks called from Grandfather's bank. He first offered his sympathies for Grandfather's death, then said he had learned from lawyer Ellis Hagood III that I was now the owner of the *Clarion* and, therefore, the owner of Grandfather's bank notes. Hendricks said he would like to speak to me about them. He didn't sound happy when he said it.

I went right away. Bad news wouldn't get any better by postponing it. The bank was in Pickens, naturally, and Mr. Hendricks, a solemn little man in a grey suit, wasted no time telling me that one of the loans was presently due. The payoff came to over three hundred thousand dollars. It might as well have been three hundred million.

Hendricks went on to say that even if refinancing could be arranged—something in his tone suggested was about as likely as naming me to the bank's board of directors—they couldn't offer me the same terms and rates that they had given to Grandfather. His was a special relationship in deference to his standing in the community. Obviously, I held no similar cards by birthright.

I told him my plans to sell the *Clarion* and use the proceeds to pay off the notes. Hendricks expressed little faith in my ability to quickly find a buyer for the paper or keep it successfully running until I did. I guess he was worried that it wouldn't be worth anything when they got around to repossessing it.

However, to show that he was not completely insensitive to my plight, he offered—with great theatricality—to allow me to roll the note over for another ninety days. But I'd need to pay the interest immediately—an amount of three thousand, eight hundred and forty-one dollars and eighty cents.

I promised to get back to him within forty-eight hours. He looked uneasy with the delay but agreed. I'd learned that there was enough money in Grandfather's checking and savings accounts to pay that, but if the loans were called in before we could sell the paper, we were toast. The Bragg clan was in lousy shape, financially speaking.

"Then there's the other loan," Hendricks said. "We might need a new appraisal on the collateral to consider renewing that one."

"What other loan?" I asked.

"The one with the lien on Still Hollow."

Still Hollow? I couldn't believe what I was hearing. I could understand Grandfather using the paper as collateral for a loan— but *never* Still Hollow. He would have lost the *Clarion* before risking one blade of grass of the property that had been in our family since George Washington was president.

"Grandfather wouldn't mortgage Still Hollow for a *Clarion* loan," I said, "regardless of what equipment the paper needed. If he did, now I *know* the old man had become senile."

Hendricks gave me an even stranger look. "This one wasn't for capital improvements," he said. "Some years ago, he put Still Hollow up as collateral for a rather sizable loan of a personal nature—a hundred thousand dollars. I assumed you knew about it." He looked as if the subject made him uncomfortable.

"Well, I don't. How would I? Grandfather didn't share his finances with me."

"I just thought that since you were the reason he borrowed the money . . ."

I couldn't hide my surprise. "I was the reason? What are you talking about?"

He looked even more uncomfortable if that was possible. "Well . . . it's down on the loan agreement that it was for your college education."

"That can't be," I said. "I was on full scholarship. All I ever got from him was spending money every blue moon, and believe me, he didn't need to take out a loan for that."

"Mr. Bragg, I really shouldn't be talking about this . . ."

"If you're still our family bank, yes, you should."

Hendricks pursed his lips and looked at me for a second before speaking. "You have to understand," he said. "Garnet and I were very good and old friends, and I agreed to keep the real reason for the loan off the books. As I understand it, the money was to extricate you from some sort of trouble you were in."

If the bank's roof had dropped on my head, I couldn't have been hit any harder. How dumb was I? How naïve? Now I knew why the point-shaving thing went away so easily and why I was never contacted again by my blackmailer. Grandfather *bought* me out of it, and I knew it cost him more than just money. Mortgaging Still Hollow would have damn near killed him.

"I never knew," I said weakly and fell into a stunned silence.

Why didn't Grandfather tell me? That almost made me angrier than thinking he had turned his back on me. Was this another of his moral lessons that I was just not getting? He *didn't* turn his back on me, I realized. And I needed to adjust to that. Christ, who was I going to be mad at now? I'd lived so long with the anger boiling just beneath the surface that I didn't think I could feel normal without it. It was like I had nothing solid to hang onto anymore, no handle in the ground to keep me from falling off the side of the earth. I told Hendricks I'd be in touch, shook his hand, and left.

I drove to Melissa Raines' place and parked in front of her neighbor's house. I sat in the Jeep, still thinking about what I'd learned of Grandfather's loan to buy me out of trouble. Ten years had gone by, and I never even suspected it. What an idiot I was. Why did he keep it from me? I'd probably never know, now. I needed to place all of this in some back compartment in my mind to examine later. If I kept thinking about it now, I'd get nothing else done. And I had a murderer to find.

I walked up on the neighbor's porch again and found her peering at me through the screen door. This time she wasn't holding a screaming baby.

"How's the baby?" I asked her.

"Asleep," she said. "What do you want?"

Her reaction to me was one of suspicion and perhaps a little fear.

"I told the police about you," she said. "I gave them your description and told them you came here looking for her just a couple of days before she . . ."

"And what did they say?"

"They said you didn't do it. But how do I know they're right?"

Something in her tone told me that the screen door was probably locked, and there was a can of mace, or a gun, in the pocket she had her hand in.

“I’m terribly sorry about what happened to her,” I said, “but I didn’t do it. I was just at the scene when she was found. I’m here to ask you about the boyfriend you told the police about.”

“I told them all I know,” she said. “Melissa was seeing someone, but she never told me his name. I had the feeling he might be a married man. And he spent money on her. She was always wearing a new piece of jewelry or new clothes that didn’t come from Walmart.”

“And you never saw him?”

“I saw him down there, but it was always at night, and I never got a good look at him. He’d stay late sometimes, but his truck would always be gone in the morning. I don’t think he ever spent the night. He also came to get her sometimes, mostly on weekends, but he would pull up in front and honk the horn.”

“The cops told me you said he drove a white pickup truck. Do you know the make?

“I don’t know things like that,” she said. “It had a grill in front shaped like a cross. That’s all I can tell you.”

That sounded like a Dodge Ram to me. “Can you think of anything else about him? Was he young, old?”

“Well, from what I could see from his body shape and movement in the dark, he was a big man, but I couldn’t say how old he was.”

She seemed to have another thought. “He has a lake house,” she said.

“How do you know that?” I asked.

“Melissa always had a nice tan, and I was curious about it. When I asked, she said it helped to have a boyfriend with a house on the lake.”

I called Kelly from the car and caught her heading to the Registrar of Deeds Office to look further into Red Hills Development. She said she had spent the day so far on the computer and had made several calls to knowledgeable sources but had struck-out all around.

I gave her another job to do. I wanted her to find out if Bailey McDaniel owned a lake house and explained my reason. We made plans to meet at a Ruby Tuesday in the neighboring town of Easley for drinks and dinner. She said it wasn’t exactly *très chic,* but the drinks and food were okay, and it was usually a quiet place to talk.

I tried to call Bucky Streeter, but the call went straight to his voicemail. I left a message asking him to call me back. If Bailey McDaniel was Barry Beal's partner in the Eastatoe Valley development, Bucky would be the best source for that information. The question was, how far was he willing to go to help? Would he ask his father-in-law outright? Or covertly search his office files at the mill? Bucky couldn't hide his ill feelings toward his father-in-law or the subservient position he found himself in. And if I knew Bucky, that wasn't something he could live with for very long. My guess was that he'd do whatever it took to help me.

CHAPTER THIRTY-SIX

Before I knew it, it was nearly seven P.M. I went to meet Kelly in the town of Easley, eight miles south of Pickens. The astonishing news that Grandfather bailed me out of my troubles back in college kept invading my thoughts, but thinking about Kelly helped push it into the background—at least for now.

Ruby Tuesday's was out on Calhoun Memorial Highway, or "the bypass," as the locals called it, and I found it easily. Kelly was waiting at the bar for me when I arrived.

We ordered cocktails, and I saw she was no sissy drinker. She asked for a bourbon and branch water like a veteran. I ordered a Macallan on the rocks, which they surprisingly had, and listened as she went right into her efforts to uncover more about Red Hills Developments.

"I found out very little," she said with a disappointed look. "It's a shell company with invisible owners and no way to tell who they are or who controls it. But I found out that the account's signatory is Arthur Pitt. That connects it to Barry Beal, at least. A woman at the Registrar of Deeds Office told me that the county was way behind in filing transactions, so no recent sales within Eastatoe Valley have yet been recorded. I asked her if I could see any of the unrecorded documents, but she said she couldn't do that. It's against regulations, and she wouldn't budge. My guess is, for a golf course and residential development like I think this one is, the better part of the valley has been sold."

"I agree," I said, asking what she found out about Bailey McDaniel.

"He owns a lot of Pickens County real estate. He has that huge estate up near the Dacusville community in the northwestern part of the county where he lives, along with a sizable lake House on Lake Keowee near Crow Creek Road.

All the rest is commercial property, but nothing in his name in Eastatoe Valley. However, if he's a partner in Red Hills Developments, as we think, then his name probably won't appear, even when the transactions are officially recorded. It will all be under the company name.

I knew the Crow Creek area. It was a beautiful and expensive part of the large man-made lake. The lake house and Melissa Raines' comment about how she kept her tan were at least circumstantial evidence for an affair with a man like McDaniel. The part about him driving a white pickup truck—possibly a Dodge Ram—was still a mystery. I couldn't picture McDaniel driving a pickup truck, much less tailing me.

Nevertheless, it would help to find out if he had access to a truck like that. My next step should be to find Bucky Streeter and see what he could tell me about his father-in-law. He should know about the pickup truck, too.

Kelly and I discussed everything a bit longer; the conversation then drifted to her and Eloise's plans for the *Clarion*. Other than the fact that she could make an everyday business dress look like a top designer frock, she was no slacker when it came to business acumen. She had new but sensible ideas and the grit to make them happen. The more she talked, the less I worried about Eloise and Mackenzie's future.

I told her again that the next step should be seeking counsel from Ellis Hagood and turned that task over to her. She seemed pleased that while I didn't exactly agree to anything, I didn't disagree, either.

My stomach suddenly growled loudly enough to interrupt the conversation. Kelly laughed and clapped her hand over her mouth.

"Are we hungry?" she asked with a broad smile.

"Now that you mention it, I could eat the northbound end of a southbound mule right about now," I said. "How about you?"

"I'm fresh out of mule," she said, the smile still trained on me, "but I do have a couple of steaks in the fridge and a good bottle of Pinot Noir just waiting to be opened. Let me make you dinner at my place."

I paid the drink check and followed her home.

After dinner, we sat on her sofa, working on a second bottle of Pinot Noir.

"Will you promise not to get mad if I ask you a question?" I said.

She looked at me for a moment as if anticipating the worst.

"Ask, and we'll see," she said.

"Why are you here? Working at the *Clarion*? Eloise said you came from the *Charlotte Observer*. That's pretty high cotton in the newspaper world. You don't seem desperate for a paycheck because the *Clarion* can't pay you anything close to what you made in Charlotte."

"Oh," she said and sipped her wine for a moment, seemingly looking inward at, from the pained look she suddenly wore, was quite unpleasant. "I guess I came here to escape something," she finally said. "I admit that it began as a temporary place to hide out until I got my life together again, but I came to love what I was doing here. It may be small-time, but it's noble. It's back to the basics of newspapering—simple and worthwhile journalism. Providing real value to the people in the community. And then, there was your grandfather. I learned to respect and adore him. So, I stayed. As you said, money isn't the object."

"What were you getting away from?" I asked.

"Not *what*," she said. "*Who*. I was a fool in Charlotte."

"I can't see you being a fool about anything."

"You weren't there."

I remembered my suspicion that she may have left Charlotte for personal reasons.

"I was involved with my editor for almost a year," she said bitterly, "thinking he was separated from his wife and going through a divorce. Believing he loved me. Then I found out that not only was he not divorcing his wife, but he was taking her to a fertility clinic so they could have another child. I seemed to be the only person at the paper who didn't know that. I'd love to hear your definition if that doesn't make me a fool."

"You got fooled," I said. "That doesn't make you a fool."

"But, it left me with some pretty heavy baggage in the trust department. Relationships scare me now."

"Is that what Tuesday morning in Atlanta was all about?" I said. "You woke up thinking we were just a one-night stand?" I reached over and placed my hand over hers. "You're special to me, Kelly," I said. "Atlanta was special to me. You want to talk about fear of relationships; you're looking at a gold medal winner. I've managed to screw up every relationship I ever had. But I'm willing to give this one a chance if you are."

She looked at me a moment longer, smiled seductively, and said, "Then let the chances begin."

We were in her bed without clothes in less than two minutes, replaying our time in Atlanta and adding a few improvements, which I didn't think was possible.

Afterward, she slept, and I lay awake thinking about my history of relationships. I once dated a psychiatrist, and we almost had a serious thing going until I managed to screw it up, just like all my other relationships that came before. My hesitancy to go the extra step became apparent, and she broke up with me.

As a parting gift, she gave me a bit of professional analysis. I didn't want it, but I listened. She said I had a self-fulfilling prophecy, an uncontrollable thing within me that always made me leave someone before they could leave me. She told me that my difficulties stemmed from abandonment issues. Once abandoned, I was afraid of reoccurring incidences. She said it probably started with my parents' accidental death, which was a form of abandonment, especially in the mind of an orphaned child who begged the question, "Why did they go away and leave me like that?" Maybe she was right; who's to say?

I felt a similar abandonment when my grandfather turned his back on me. But now that I knew better, would it change me? Would this relationship with the woman sleeping beside me last? Somehow, that question didn't seem so fearsome anymore. Had Grandfather finally taught his most challenging student a lesson?

I watched Kelly sleep for a few minutes longer, then got up, got dressed, and went back to Still Hollow. I left a note on Kelly's kitchen table saying I thought it best not to leave my car in her driveway all night, and ruining her reputation with her neighbors, and would call her in the AM.

Eloise and Mackenzie were in their bedrooms behind closed doors when I returned, but the porch light was left on for me. I doubted if my new-found relationship with Kelly Mayfield was much of a secret to either of them.

CHAPTER THIRTY-SEVEN

Early Tuesday morning, I looked out the window to see Sheriff Arlen Bagwell in the driveway getting out of his patrol car. I went down to let him in, but Eloise had beat me to it. She was waiting by the open front door, wearing a look of expectance.

"We've arrested two suspects," Bagwell said, as he came in.

"Oh my," Eloise quietly said and sat down.

"Who are they?" I asked.

"They're pretty much who I said they'd be. A couple of meth- head bikers."

Looking at his face, I couldn't help but think of the cat that ate the canary.

"Real Einstein's, he continued. "They tried to sell your granddad's camera to somebody at a West Greenville beer joint, not three hours after they shot him. Somebody there finally put two and two together and called us yesterday. A search warrant of a house trailer these guys shared in the woods up near the North Carolina line turned up Garnet's camera and a .357 magnum revolver, recently fired. We also found a meth lab on the premises. We may not be able to match the weapon to your granddad without the spent bullet, but it's about the right caliber. We think we have a solid case here."

"You didn't mention the watch or wallet," I said. "Or the phone. Did you find those?"

"No sign of them," Bagwell said. "Maybe they found a buyer for the watch, threw the wallet away, and sold or traded the credit cards for dope. The cards haven't been used according to the card companies, but when they are, they'll show up. We're keeping an eye on that as well. Both suspects have a history of drugs and minor theft. I guess they finally worked up to the big time. That meth will sure put a snake in your soup."

"Can you tell me their names?" I asked.

Bagwell pulled a paper out of a shirt pocket and read from it. "A Randall Wayne Alexander, Age 32, and Mark Lee Wilson age 27. White males, both born in Pickens County."

I grabbed a pen and wrote down their names. I didn't know them and told Bagwell so. Neither did Eloise.

"I don't suppose they've confessed, have they?" I asked.

"They owned up to the camera theft right away," Bagwell said, "probably because we caught them red-handed with it. But they claim they didn't kill anybody and don't know anything about that. But what else would you expect? They said they found the car deserted by the side of the road, the doors unlocked, and the camera bag lying on the floorboard in the back. Said they just snatched it and took off—in and out. They didn't see anybody else around, dead or alive. Now they're lawyered up and aren't saying anything. I expect they'll probably try to cut a deal of some kind as things progress. This one could carry the death penalty."

"What if they're telling the truth?" I said, the urge to be contrary overpowering the good sense to keep my mouth shut. "What if it was two separate crimes?"

My words seemed to take Bagwell by surprise. But I couldn't figure out whether it was because I raised an issue he'd yet to think of or because he thought I was brazenly questioning his professional abilities.

"We've got the guys who killed your granddad, Mr. Bragg," he said, his tone suggesting that I had indeed insulted him. "All the evidence proves it. But if you know something of substance that I don't, please tell me. It doesn't mean I've quit working because these guys are in jail. That's my promise to the people of Pickens County and you and Eloise, personally."

I thought about unloading my theories on him: Cecil Hood's death and how that could have impacted not only my grandfather's murder but Melissa Raines' as well. But I still had no proof, and his capture of the two suspects would now make my conjectures even less likely. So, I kept my mouth shut.

Eloise sat quietly, listening to everything that was said; several times, she looked like she had a question but remained silent. Either that, or the questions were for me alone, and she was waiting for Bagwell to leave before asking them.

"I almost forgot," Bagwell said, looking at her. "We'll need to keep Garnet's camera as evidence, maybe even until the trial's over, but I thought you might like a copy of the pictures he took on it."

He removed a USB flash drive from his shirt pocket and handed it to her. "They're all of mountains and waterfalls and such, like these," he said, looking around the walls at Grandfather's landscape photography examples. "I figured you would like to have them."

Eloise took the thumb drive from him and thanked him for delivering the news about the arrests in person. We stood in the doorway and watched him drive away.

"That thing about there being two crimes," she said. "Do you really believe that?"

"Part of me does," I said. "And part of me just wants to give him a hard time."

"You *were* being a little hard on him, John David. He's a proud man."

"I know he is. That's what I'm counting on. He's a guy who needs to be right, and regardless of what he says, I don't think he's comfortable with what he's got here. So I will keep pushing until he broadens his horizons a bit.

"Broad enough to see that everything that's happened is connected somehow?" she asked.

I didn't answer, but she knew that's what I meant. Bagwell had his two suspects. I had Melissa Raines' death, a white Dodge Ram pickup, Bailey McDaniel, Bobby Paige, and a lot of loose ends. And I wasn't quitting until I tied them up.

After Bagwell left, I plugged the thumb drive he brought over into Grandfather's computer and examined it. On it was a file entitled "Bragg photos," and inside was a row of JPEGs numbered 1 through 12. I opened them all, one by one, and they appeared to be what Bagwell said they were, photos of the Carolina countryside. I scanned through them, admiring Grandfather's talent for composition and his ability to capture a fresh view of what was prominent and frequently photographed local landmarks. The first few were of Chimney Rock over in North Carolina—I recognized the familiar rock spire. Several more were of Caesar's Head, just inside the state line in Greenville County, a mountain promontory that someone in the colonial era thought bore a striking likeness to Julius Caesar. How they would have known that I hadn't a clue. Then there was one each of Table Rock Mountain and Whitewater Falls—also well-known scenic landmarks in the area.

The last one was no less artfully composed but wasn't a well-known landmark. This one showed a typical scenic stretch of a mountain highway, found almost anywhere in the general area, the road angling away into the distance and disappearing around a wooded curve. The long afternoon shadows from a row of tall pines along the road made this photograph special. Not any recognizable landmark. They fell across the highway at even intervals like railroad ties, creating a design of diminishing horizontal stripes, which made an artful composition. In the foreground on the left-hand side of the road was a rusty sign that read, "Jesus is coming." I suddenly realized it was like the sign across from Grady Morton's garage. This could be the last picture Grandfather ever took.

The only flaw in the shot was the vehicle parked along the shoulder in the distance. It didn't fit the timelessness of the photo. But I suppose it could easily be retouched out, which may have been Grandfather's plan if he decided this one was a "keeper." Then I looked closer. It was a white pickup truck bearing the crossbar grille of a Dodge Ram. A single occupant sat behind the wheel. I zoomed in even closer. The face was just a silhouette with no features other than a vague distinction that it was probably a man and not a woman. I studied the photograph in more detail. There were no houses, mailboxes, driveways, or anything else along that barren stretch of highway to suggest why anyone would park there. *Was my tail also tailing grandfather?*

I ejected the thumb drive, stuck it in my pocket, and called Kelly to fill her in on everything that had happened. She listened to the news of Bagwell's arrests, my "two-crime" theory, and my description of Grandfather's last photograph. She didn't question my conclusions—which made me fonder of her more than ever—and agreed with my plan to push ahead with what we were doing.

I called Bucky Streeter again, wanting to find out what else he could tell me about his father-in-law and the likelihood of him driving a white Dodge Ram pickup, but the call went to his voicemail again. I started to call him at work but decided I'd go see him instead.

CHAPTER THIRTY-EIGHT

The headquarters of McDaniel Mills was housed in an unassuming red brick building adjacent to one of his remaining textile plants, located just north of Easley. McDaniel Industries was a major employer in the county for almost a century, and there was a time when this mill, and all the other cotton mills in the area, ran around the clock, three shifts a day, seven days a week. Those days were gone. The McDaniel's' wealth now came from numerous other sources, which, if I were right, included real estate development.

I parked in a visitor's space out front and entered the mill offices. A receptionist pointed me down a hall to Bucky's office, where a young woman, not at all unattractive, sat behind a desk by his door and looked up at me as I approached.

"Is Bucky in?" I asked, with a nod toward the closed door.

"Did you have an appointment with him?" she said, frowning as she glanced at an open appointment book on her desk. "I thought I called everyone."

"I don't have an appointment," I said. "I'm an old friend from out of town and thought I'd stop by to say hello."

"I'm sorry, Mr. Streeter is out sick today. I think he's got this bug that's going around."

"Oh, sorry to hear that," I said, told her to tell him I stopped by, and made for the exit. As I left, I heard footsteps behind me and turned to see her disappearing into a small room down the hall. A moment later, I heard the sound of a copy machine go to work. A large well-appointed office stood open and vacant on my right. A small brass nameplate by the door read Bailey McDaniel. The copier was still whirring and clicking, and I quickly stepped inside.

I really didn't expect to find anything helpful, but I did. One of the many photographs that decorated a wall caught my attention. Two men stood on the steps of a building somewhere, smiling into the lens. One of them was Bailey McDaniel. The other was Barry Beal. I didn't know why or when the photograph was taken or if Beal and McDaniel were in business together. But at least I could tie them together. Another step forward.

Outside, I noticed a large fenced-in area beyond the mill offices that appeared to be a storage compound for construction materials, equipment, and trucks. I walked over and peered through the fence. A white Dodge Ram pickup sat nose-out against the back fence. A man came out of a trailer office and bounded down the wooden steps into the lot. He wore a hard hat and carried a clipboard. Under the hat, I recognized the face of Bobby Paige's sidekick from the bar, Nick.

I walked down the fence line toward a large rolling gate, finding it open. A guard shack sat to one side, but no one was manning it. I entered the lot and headed for Nick. He saw me coming and began to back-peddle until I had him against a wall of stacked lumber, a handful of his shirtfront in my fist. He'd dropped the clipboard and was holding and put his hands up, palms out.

"Whoa," he said. "Wait a damn minute. I ain't done nothin' to you. That was all Bobby."

"Where is he?" I said.

"He didn't come in today."

"Where is he?" I asked him again.

"Hell, I don't know. He's the boss. He don't report to me."

"That truck over there, who drives it?" I asked.

"I don't see what the fuck . . ."

I cut him off. "Nick? Don't go pissing me off again."

"Okay, okay. All of us in building and maintenance do," he said. "We got three of them.

They're company trucks."

"Just alike? White Dodge Rams?"

"Yeah. So what?"

"So. Bobby Paige has the use of one?"

"Of course."

"Where are the other two?"

"Bobby's got one right now. The other one pretty much stays at the big man's house. Mr. McDaniel's yard Mexican uses it."

Nick looked over my shoulder, and I turned to see an older man in a guard uniform approaching. I let go of Nick's shirt.

"What's going on here, Nick?" the man asked. "Who's this feller?"

"We were just horsing around, Claude. He's a friend of mine."

The guard looked at me and then at Nick.

"You know he ain't supposed to be in here if he ain't signed in," he said. "You gonna' get us both in trouble."

"Sorry about breaking the rules," I offered. "But the gate was wide open, and no one was in the guard house. I thought it was okay to come on in." I let the fact that he was not at his post sink in and gave him my best smile. "I just need a few minutes with old Nicky here, then I'll be gone. It would be like I was never here."

The man studied me for a moment. "Next time, you check in with me," he said, walking away.

I waited for him to get halfway to the guard shack before I turned back to Nick.

"Where does Paige live?" I asked.

Nick began shaking his head right away. "Nothing you can do to me would be worse than what he'll do to me if I tell you that."

"I won't tell him. And then you won't get hurt by either of us," I said. He gave me Paige's address, and I wrote it down. On the way out, I gave the guard, now at his post in the guardhouse, a snappy salute. He returned a pained look.

CHAPTER THIRTY-NINE

I sat in my Jeep in the parking lot trying to decide what to do next. I knew the location of Bailey McDaniel's house was nearby, as did everybody else in Pickens County. The hilltop mansion near the small community of Dacusville was a little smaller than Versailles and had been a local attraction for years. I was curious to see if I could spot the white pickup somewhere on the sizable grounds. Maybe I could read the number on the tail gate. So, I drove over there.

I found it easily and parked on the country road out front. I didn't spot a white pickup through the bars of the tall wrought iron fence that protected the well-tended grounds, but with a four-car attached garage, it didn't mean there wasn't one there. I couldn't think of a way to look closer without getting arrested.

A Hispanic man pushing a wheelbarrow loaded with flats of impatiens came around the corner of the house and headed down the drive toward me. He wore a gray work shirt, jeans with soiled knees, and a lacquered-straw cowboy hat. I got out of the Jeep and walked over to a spot across the fence from several bags of potting soil, and waited for him.

"Excuse me," I said. "Might I have a word with you?"

He looked at me suspiciously. "Si?" he said, adding something in Spanish I didn't understand.

"I'm looking for someone to do some landscape work," I said. "Would you be interested, or do you only work for Mr. McDaniel?"

"Si. I work for Señor McDaniel.

"Yes, but do you work for other people too? Do you hire out?"

His expression showed we had a language problem, but it probably didn't matter since I didn't know where to go with this anyway.

"But you'd need a truck," I rambled on. "Do you have a truck you can use?"

I made a motion with my hands on an imaginary steering wheel. A tiny spark of comprehension glowed in his eyes.

"Si, truck," he said and gave me a nervous smile. He obviously thought I was several beans short of a burrito.

I was trying to think of some clever way to find out if McDaniel ever drove the company truck himself when the gate on the driveway made a buzzing sound and began to open. Behind me, a Black Mercedes S-Class turned into the drive and stopped short of the gate. Both the passenger and driver-side windows slid down, and the driver leaned across the seat and looked out at his gardener from the passenger side. I recognized Bailey McDaniel III from newspaper photographs. He looked young for someone with a married daughter. An easy life sometimes did that to people.

"Hector," he said, "I don't see how you can get those flowers planted before our dinner guests arrive by standing around talking."

Hector didn't seem to have any problem understanding *that,* I noticed, and began unloading the flats from the wheelbarrow.

McDaniel then turned to me, letting his eyes linger on me for a moment.

"What is your business here, sir?" he said, with the same emotionless tone he'd used with Hector.

I walked over to the window. "My name is John David Bragg, Mr. McDaniel. One of your company pickup trucks is checked out to your yard man over there, and I'm trying to find out who, in addition to him, has access to it."

He seemed to look at me anew. "You're Garnet Bragg's grandson."

"Yes, I am."

"You have my condolences. He was a credit to the community. Is there some problem with the truck?" he asked.

"Not with the truck. Just with whoever was driving it."

He studied me briefly, then said, "Whatever this is about, Mr. Bragg, I can't help you with it. If it involves an accident, I suggest you call your insurance company. They can contact someone in our general office."

"Mr. McDaniel, do you own a company called Red Hills Developments?" I asked.

He looked at me for a moment, then rolled the window up, and drove through the gate. It closed behind him with the same buzzing sound that opened it.

I sat in the Jeep outside the gate thinking. You didn't have to be a Sherlock Holmes to read the clues. Both Bailey McDaniel and Bobby Paige had access to a white Dodge Ram pickup. So, *one* of them had been following me—*and* my grandfather before me. And one of them was Melissia Raines' boyfriend. That had to be McDaniel, what with the lake house and connection to Red Hill's Development. But while I couldn't see someone with his wealth, power, and stature spending time trailing me around, I could see him having it done. If Bobby Paige was indeed McDaniel's go-to guy, as Bucky had said, it was probably him. And reporting back to McDaniel.

Paige could also be McDaniel's beard, I thought, chauffeuring Raines to clandestine meetings with McDaniel at his lake house. And, with his penchant for violence, Paige could handle the more serious dirty work, disposing of anyone who threatened Baily McDaniel's plans. Like Cecil Hood, Melissa Raines . . . *and* my grandfather.

So, the question was, what could I do about it? I had no real proof. But Bobby Paige would be the weakest link in this chain. He hadn't McDaniel's wealth or stature. So, I decided to do what I'd always done as a quarterback. When trapped behind the line with nowhere else to go, you tuck the ball, lower your head, grit your teeth, and charge the likeliest opening in the line. I would go confront Bobby Paige head on. But first, I wanted to see what else my old friend Bucky could tell me about his father-in-law and get his take on my thinking.

CHAPTER FORTY

I called the number Bucky had entered into my iPhone contacts, but it went straight to voicemail. He had also written down his address, and rather than leave a message, I decided to go see him. If he was under the weather, maybe he'd turned off his phone to get a little rest. But what I had regarding his father-in-law to couldn't wait. I googled his address and headed for it.

He lived in the same neighborhood as Kelly, near the Pickens County Country Club. When I arrived, I found a large brick colonial, more impressive even than the house Kelly was leasing. Not bad for a guy whose dad spent his life hanging onto the end of a worn-out hoe.

I parked in the circular drive, walked to the door, and rang the bell. A petite brunette with a deep-water tan opened the door and stared at me. She was wearing shorts, a wild patterned sleeveless top, sandals, and sunglasses atop her head.

"Yes?" she said, giving me a look that said if I was selling something, don't even bother.

"Is Bucky home?" I asked.

"May I ask who you are?"

She spoke with that aloof nasal quality that sometimes afflicts those who spend a lifetime looking down their noses at the rest of us.

"John David Bragg," I said. "I'm an old friend of your husband's."

"Yes, I've heard of you," she said. "You're the one whose grandfather . . ."

"Yes," I said.

She didn't offer her sympathies, which after all the gushing condolences of late would have been refreshing—if her face hadn't shown that she really didn't give a rat's ass one way or the other.

"I heard he was out sick. If he isn't too contagious, I'd like to see the old boy."

"You think he's ill," she said. It wasn't really a question.

"That's what they told me at his office," I said.

"Well Bucky isn't here, and I don't know where he is. If he's sick, it's of me—and the feeling is mutual." She gave me a look that could chill wine and added, "And to quote Clark Gable, "frankly my dear, I don't give a damn."

Then she closed the door in my face.

As a couple, they obviously weren't Ozzie and Harriet, I thought. I felt sorry for my old friend.

From there I decided to track down Bobby Paige and see what vehicle he was driving today. With the address his sidekick Nick had given me, I found his street with little effort. The problem was getting to his house. It was cordoned off by yellow police tape and surrounded by police cars. I parked as close as possible and went to the police barrier. Sheriff Arlen Bagwell stood in front of the tape talking to Snyder and Green, the SLED agents who questioned me earlier. Bagwell saw me and motioned me over.

"What are you doing here?" he asked.

The SLED agents looked at me like they wanted to know the same thing.

"I was just in the neighborhood and saw all the commotion. What's going on?"

"You're not trying to tell me you don't know who lives here, are you?" Bagwell asked.

"Whatever happened here, I wasn't part of it," I said, looking at them.

Snyder and Green were staring openly at me.

I watched a uniformed cop come out of the house carrying a cardboard box, duck under the tape, and head toward a county Crime Scene van.

"What *did* happen here? I asked.

"Paige blew out the back of his head with a shotgun sometime last night," Bagwell said.

"Suicide?" I said, taken back. The white Dodge pickup sat in the driveway, I noticed, but I was having a hard time wrapping my mind around a guy like Paige committing suicide.

"Why would he do that?" I asked.

"Remorse, it looks like," Sheriff Bagwell answered.

"He killed the Raines woman, Green said. "Left a suicide note on his computer that said so. This Paige and Raines were obviously in a relationship that went wrong. We have love notes she wrote to him and a calendar with notations that show the days and times they met over the past few months. We also found her phone numbers— cell and home—along with the address of her hotel at Litchfield Beach."

"The love notes were actually addressed to Paige?" I asked.

"They weren't addressed to anyone," Snyder said, "but they were signed by her, and we found them on the nightstand by his bed. Who else would they be for?"

A good question, I thought. I was having almost as much trouble imagining anyone writing love letters to Bobby Paige as I was of him committing suicide over killing someone. But then, perhaps I was prejudiced.

Bagwell dipped his chin at me, and he and the SLED agents went under the tape and back into the house. I turned to go, my path taking me right by the crime scene van. The rear doors were standing open, and the cardboard box I saw the cop bring from the house was sitting just inside. I looked at it as I passed and noticed that it held what appeared to be the contents of a file cabinet or a desk drawer. Envelopes and papers and things, now sealed in clear plastic evidence bags. Something I saw there caused me to stop.

One bag, in plain view, contained copies of employment checks, the kind a company sends you when your paycheck is deposited electronically to your bank. These were Bobby Paige's paychecks from McDaniel Mills, and something written on them caused an old memory from my boyhood to bloom in my head like a flower filmed in time-lapse. Love letters with no names, houses on the lake, company pickup trucks. And finally, the *"WS"* in Grandfather's notes. The answer was there all along that I just didn't want to see. I stood and stared at the checks a moment longer, then headed for my jeep.

CHAPTER FORTY-ONE

I let my memory guide me to the Marina on Lake Keowee. The sun was well over the horizon, and the lake was dark when I arrived. The marina's name was new, and the place was larger, but I had been there before. I skirted the entrance, drove along the fence line on a small gravel road to the end of the marina property, doused the headlights, and crossed over a steep wooded rise into a narrow cove.

The house was still there, nestled into the trees below me, near the water's edge. It was small by Keowee lake-house standards but nicer now than I remembered, obviously the result of some recent remodeling. A bigger deck now spread across the back of the house, with a stepped path that led down to the dock. Moored there was a cabin cruiser of considerable length. The dock lights were ablaze, and I could see a man on the gangway by the boat working over a smoking barbeque grill. It was my old pal, Bucky Streeter.

I left the Jeep where it was and went down the hill, walking around the house on a driveway that led to the back. I picked up the scent of fresh redwood. The deck was new, and two vehicles were parked underneath it in a carport: Bucky's silver sedan and a white Dodge Ram pickup.

I was almost to the dock before Bucky saw me. He didn't seem surprised. He was smiling when I walked up to him. He held a drink in one hand and a grilling fork in the other.

"You're just in time, old bud," he said. "I've got a steak on the grill big enough for both of us."

A couple days of stubble darkened his jaw, and his jeans and shirt had a sleep-in look, the shirt bearing a smear of something mustard-colored on the front.

When I got near him, I smelled a rank sourness like old sweat underneath the smell of booze.

"I thought you sold this place," I said.

"I sold the marina, not the cabin," he said with a weak smile. "Too much sentimental value."

"It's a bit more than a cabin now," I said.

He stopped what he was doing and gazed up at the house. "Yeah," he said. "Done some work on it over the years."

"Nice boat, too," I added.

He turned and looked at the boat.

"She's the one girl I'm going to miss," he said.

I gave him a puzzled look.

"Casey's divorcing me, and the boat belongs to the company. Tax advantages and all that. So. No marriage, no job. No job, no boat."

He took a long pull of his drink, turned the steak on the grill, and smiled an empty smile. "That shit about easy come, easy go?" he said. "It ain't true. Nothing comes easy. And it's even harder when it goes."

He caught me looking at the back of his boat. The name *Good Times* was painted on it in blue and gold script.

"Guess you could say I was overly optimistic when I named her," he said.

"Grandfather called you, didn't he, *Wendell*?" I said.

He stopped what he was doing and turned to me. "Did you just call me Wendell?" he said.

"Grandfather called you on the day he died. I saw your initials on a notepad by his phone. WS. Wendell Streeter. I'd forgotten that was your given name until I saw it signed on a paycheck for McDaniel Mills. Only two people ever called you that. Your dad—when he was really pissed off at you. And Grandfather. Because he disliked calling anyone by a nickname, another of his irritating eccentricities. Did he say something to you that touched a nerve? Did he insinuate that you killed old man Cecil Hood?"

"What the fuck are you talking about?" Bucky said and laughed. But in his eyes, there was no laughter.

"What have you done, Bucky? I asked.

He studied me for a moment, then leaned over and raised the lid to a locker on the dock.

"Bucky . . ." I said, and he stepped over and hit me above the ear with something hard. I took one faulty step toward him and, with a strange sense of removal, watched as he raised his arm—a large wrench in his hand—and struck me again. The world turned a brilliant white, then went as black as midnight.

CHAPTER FORTY-TWO

I wasn't sure how long I'd been out, but as my faculties limped back, I realized I was lying on a bunk in Bucky's boat, rolled up like a burrito from chin to feet in a gasoline-soaked bed sheet. It was a discovery that did not portend happy times ahead.

Bucky entered the cabin with a five-gallon fuel can and began dousing gasoline over the walls, the carpet, the curtains, and me again. He went at his work without expression, silent and deliberate, like a man carrying out a routine, tedious chore.

"Bucky," I said quietly. "Whatever it is you're doing, don't."

He stopped and looked at me momentarily, then studied a scuff on his knuckles. The hull rocked beneath us, the chop of the water suggesting we were no longer tied to the dock.

"Explain this to me, Bucky. You owe me that," I said.

He sat on the bunk across from me, placed the gas can on his lap, and rested his arms on it. "Things just got out of hand, John David. *Waaay* the fuck out of hand."

He looked suddenly older, deflated, like somebody had let the air out of him. He refocused his eyes on me.

"Developing Eastatoe Valley was my idea," he began. "My vision. My plan. I set it all up. Lined up all the options and went after Barry Beal and sold him on it. It was the payday I've been working for my whole life. And I was so fucking close. Then . . ." He shook his head at a bitter thought.

"Cecil Hood's death wasn't an accident, was it?"

"Depends on how you define accident," he said. "I didn't go out there to kill him if that's what you mean. I was only trying to talk some sense into the stubborn old son of a bitch. He'd been offered twice what his place was worth and still wouldn't sell it. I guess I just lost it. I shoved him, and he went sailing out of the barn loft before I could grab him."

I lay silent. The revelation of his words was as big of a blow as hitting me on the head.

He set the can between his feet and wiped his hands on his pants legs. "Who would ever have thought that old fool would turn down that much money? First, he was going to sell, then he changes his mind. He was fucking everything up."

Bucky seemed to want to explain things to me as if he thought it could help justify his actions. His voice was pleading, as if he were the victim here.

"Beal was threatening to pull the plug," he said. "Cut his losses and move on. But I had my whole life in this thing."

I felt my teeth grinding and said, "I guess it was just lucky for you that Carl Hood inherited the place and was so eager to sell, huh?"

"What do you think he would do with it? Move in and start growing taters and beans? He *wanted* his old man to sell."

"And that wasn't in your thoughts when you pushed his daddy out of the barn? Sell this somewhere else, Bucky. I'm not buying."

"Fuck you. I told you I didn't mean to do it."

"What about Grandfather? Was that an accident too?"

Bucky glared at me. "You're right," he said. "He called me. He knew I was the one trying to get old man Hood to sell. I guess Cecil Hood told him that. And he was looking for Melissa Raines. I didn't know then that he was trying to find her for you. I thought he was after me. I couldn't let him talk to her; she knew too much. She was a sweetheart, but she wasn't all that bright. I don't know what she would have said if Garnet started grilling her. She was already a basket case for what Beal did to her, the stupid prick."

Bucky sighed and gave me a remorseful look. "I had to do something," he said. "I was following Garnet, and when he pulled in that turnout to take a leak, it was just too good of an opportunity to pass up. I had to manage the risks."

"Manage the risks," I repeated and stared across at my old friend. Somewhere along the trail of years, he had become a frightening doppelganger of the guy I grew up with. I tried to gauge my chances of rolling out of the tightly bound sheet and through the open door, or hatch, or whatever it was called before he could stop me. I came up with some very long odds. It seemed my only course was to try to keep him talking and hope for a better chance.

"So, what happened with Melissa Raines?" I asked. "You and Beal tire of paying her to keep her mouth shut?"

He sat watching drops of gasoline slide down the cabin wall and puddle onto the floor.

"Nobody had to pay her to keep quiet," he said. "Beal wanted to, but I told him it wasn't necessary. I mean, I gave her money to go stay at the beach, but it wasn't a payoff."

"So why did she keep quiet about what Beal did to her?"

He looked at me with something he must have thought was a smile, but it came off as a grimace. "Little thing called love," John David. "She kept her mouth shut for *me*. She wanted Beal's ass fried for what he did to her, but I talked her out of it. It's not like he raped her, for God's sake. He just slapped her around a bit when he realized she wasn't going to put out. But she knew if she tried to hurt him, she would hurt me too."

"So why make crab bait out of her?"

"Ask yourself that question, old buddy. You get to share the blame for that one."

I saw that he was serious. It was as if his psychopathy made it impossible to admit fault for anything.

"You had to call her and rile her up. Christ, John David, talking to you would have been worse than talking to your granddad. I couldn't have that."

More risk management, I thought. Or was it damage control this time? I was losing track of all of Bucky's reasons for killing people. "You know the cops have Bobby Paige for it?" I said.

"I hope the hell so. I worked hard enough to set it up to look that way. And Bobby can't exactly say different now, can he?"

"Sooner or later, they'll discover it wasn't a suicide, Bucky. There are bound to be signs. Bobby Paige couldn't have gone quietly."

"It was easy. Bobby never thought I'd do something like that to him. He trusted me. Remember when I told you Bobby had this special thing with my father-in-law? I lied. Bobby Paige was my 'go-to guy,' not his."

"And you put him on me."

"He knew about the development. I promised him a part in it as a building contractor. He also knew about me and Melissa and what Beal did to her. I told him you were looking for her to expose Beal for it, and if you did, the publicity would ruin everything. I told him we needed to scare you back to Atlanta, but I should have known it wouldn't work. All it did was light your fire. As to the cops figuring out that his death isn't a suicide, it's hard to detect blunt force trauma to the back of the head when there is no 'back of the head."

Bucky went quiet, lost in some thought he was having. "I guess I ought to be asking you who else knows about this," he finally said. "But you wouldn't tell me, would you?"

I knew where this was going and didn't like it. "I've kept Eloise out of it, Bucky. She doesn't know anything."

"What about the Mayfield woman? And don't try to tell me you ain't screwing that."

"Then you ought to know we don't spend our time together talking about you."

He studied me for a moment, his eyes, now expressionless, probing mine. "When I have time," he said, "I'll have to give that some more thought."

I suddenly feared for Kelly and Eloise both. "What about Barry Beal?" I asked. "What does he know?" I had to keep him talking. It was all I could think to do was try to postpone what looked like the inevitable.

"Beal's like a fucking ostrich," he said. "Only his head ain't stuck in the sand; it's up his own ass. All he gives a shit about is getting what he wants without getting his hands dirty. He don't ask questions about things he don't want to know about."

"The shot through my window?"

Bucky sighed. "Yeah. I was going to kill you, you know. It was either you or Melissa."

"You shot my image in the mirror, not me."

Bucky gave me a sheepish look. "I'm amazed you figured that out. Imagine how dumb I felt when I saw that mirror shatter. Then you turned the lights out, and all I could do was get the hell out of there.

He exhaled deeply and said, "Enough of the chit-chat, John David." It ain't gonna change anything." He went over to the galley and did something to the stove. I heard a hissing sound and smelled the rotten-egg odor of propane fuel mingling with the other gas. He then returned to splashing gasoline over the cabin, the fumes rising up and around me, invading my nostrils and making my eyes water.

"You've been stupid, Bucky," I said. "They're going to catch you."

"I don't think so. But whatever happens, you won't be around to help them. Let's see, a houseguest taking the boat out alone, a leak in the fuel lines, a malfunction in the safety mechanism of the butane stove, a cigar . . . and kaboom. If I'd been with you, I might have been able to prevent such a tragic accident from happening to my best buddy."

He took out a large folding pocket-knife, punched holes in the empty gas can, then took it out and threw it overboard. I wondered if the knife was the one he used to cut Melissa Raines' throat. When he returned, he said, "How have I been stupid?" as if he'd been thinking about it all the time he was outside.

"You're the only one who's tipped to any of this, and you had to get lucky to do it. Hood was an accident; meth-heads killed your granddad, Bobby killed Melissa, and his death is a suicide. Tell me where I made a mistake."

"The mistake was you didn't need to kill any of them. Grandfather, Melissa Raines, *or* Bobby Paige," I said. "You could have had everything you wanted without that. Now all you'll get is a table down in Columbia with a needle in your arm. Or does South Carolina still use the electric chair? I forget."

At least I had him listening. "So what if Melissa Raines did talk?" I added. "She didn't know anything, did she? What could she really say? That Barry Beal beat the crap out of her? Jesus Bucky, these days, football stars get charged with murder and go to the Pro Bowl the next year. Okay, so Beal would have taken a body shot to the reputation, but as much as I hate to admit it, he would have survived along with the development project. That's why God made public relations people. And Grandfather couldn't have hurt you. He had no proof, regardless of what he may have believed."

"I wish you knew what the fuck you were talking about, John David," Bucky said. "I really do."

"Then enlighten me. You just said yourself that the whole world is convinced that Hood's death was an accident. You'd gotten away with it, Bucky. You didn't need to kill anybody else."

He shook his head slowly. "Melissa knew all about the development. I couldn't let her go public with that."

"Why on earth would that matter? How could that hurt you or Beal?"

"Because I took money from McDaniel Mills to fund my stake in the development, goddammit. I needed seed money to secure the property with options and money for start-up operating expenses."

He gazed at me as if I should understand and even approve.

"So, you embezzled it," I said.

"I borrowed it. I just didn't let anybody know. The second the banks release the major financing—which will come any day now— I'll replace every cent, and nobody will *ever* know. But I can't risk anything coming out before that. I'm done if anybody shines a light on me before I'm ready. Bailey McDaniel would wonder where I got the money, and he ain't the forgiving sort. He'd be overjoyed to see me as a permanent resident of a gray-bar hotel somewhere."

He seemed to reflect on his words for a minute, then opened a locker beneath the bunk and took out a flare gun. It was a safe bet that he didn't plan to use it to signal for help.

"Bucky, how did you come to this?" I asked. "You've killed four people and are about to make it five. Did you totally lose your fucking mind?"

"If you had to live on what some rich bitch and her old man doled out like a fucking allowance, and kiss ass every day of your life, maybe you'd lose your fucking mind too," he said. "This was my chance to get out from under all that—and finally wash the goddamn red clay off my heels. Nothing that's happened was part of the plan."

There was something new in his voice—or maybe I was just now hearing it. Greed alone wasn't driving my old friend, or insanity, although he had to be insane to do what he'd done. Another motivator was present, and it was desperation. Desperation that wasn't born of the present events but of the past, beginning with the mother who deserted a towheaded kid when he was not yet three years old and a father whose highest goal in life was just to make ends meet.

He held the flare gun up and examined it. "Think I can shoot this through an open hatch from fifty yards out?" he said.

"They'll figure it out, Bucky," I said. "Forensics is quite the science these days."

"You've been watching too much TV, old buddy. These yokels around here ain't all that smart. Besides, I doubt they'll look into it that far. I'm counting on that sheet burning off, but even if it doesn't, it'll just look like you were tangled up in them and laying in the bunk when it happened . . . if they can find enough to even work that out."

He turned a flat gaze on me, his eyes like opaque marbles. "Guess it wouldn't matter if I said I was sorry, would it?" he said. He held the gaze a moment longer, then walked through the hatch, pushing it open as far as it would go.

I heard a short, indecipherable word, the boat rocked, and there was a splash. Bucky had apparently dived into the lake. I tried to roll off the bunk, but I was bound to either end of it with strips of torn sheet, leaving me hopelessly immobile. I tried shifting my body feet-first, extending my legs toward the open hatch, trying to close it. Shaquille O'Neil might have reached it, but I came up two feet short.

The first wave of panic rolled over me, and I struggled against my restraints with everything I had, pushing the muscles in my shoulders and arms to the snapping point. I tried to gain leverage with my legs against the braces of the bunk to break them, but nothing gave.

I stared at the open hatch and tried to guess how long it would take Bucky to swim far enough out to shoot a flare back through it without frying in the firestorm himself. Five minutes? Less? Was that all the life I had left?

I tore at the top of the sheet with my teeth, flinging my head from side to side like a feeding shark, the taste of gasoline flooding my mouth and burning down my throat.

Then Carl Hood stepped through the hatch.

CHAPTER FORTY-THREE

"Need a little help?" Carl Hood asked and grinned. He was dressed in black jeans and a black t-shirt and dripped water from his ponytail to his bare feet. He took out a pocketknife and began sawing away the strips of sheet that fastened me to the bunk.

"Where's Bucky?" I asked him.

"If you're referring to the gentleman who put you here, I don't know," he said. "I hit him pretty good, and he went overboard. I lost sight of him in the water."

The thought of Bucky drawing a bead on the open hatch with his flare gun sent shivers up my spine and frightened me more than I'd been all night. Maybe it was the thought of dying so close to freedom.

"Close the hatch!" I shouted.

Carl Hood looked at me as if I'd lost my mind.

"Gas! Flare gun! Bucky!" I shouted in shorthand. Understanding swept across his face as he looked at the gas-soaked sheet. He cocked his head toward the open hatch, sprang up, and slammed it shut.

"Guess it wouldn't be a good time to have a smoke, would it?" he said and finished cutting the bindings away. He rolled me out of the sheet like someone laying a rug. I hit the cabin floor on all fours, slid the hatch open again, and scrambled up on deck with Hood right behind me. We dove into the water and began putting as much distance between the boat and us as we could. The shoreline was invisible, the night pitch-black. For all I knew, we were headed toward the middle of the lake. I didn't care. I'd worry about drowning later. Right now, my only thoughts were not getting blown to bits.

Suddenly Carl Hood was no longer swimming beside me, and I turned to find him treading water behind, looking back at the boat. Bucky Streeter was standing on the deck watching us, the light from the cabin behind casting him in silhouette. I stopped and treaded water, too, ready to dive under if I suddenly found he'd traded the flare gun for a weapon that dispensed something other than a ball of flaming chemicals.

I watched him pick something off the deck and turn his back to us. He stood there for a moment; shoulders slumped, head bowed, the figure of a man who knows with finality that the game is lost, and the season is over. Slowly, he stretched out his arm and pointed at the hatch I'd left open when we escaped. A streak of red light shot into the cabin, followed by a more brilliant flash of orange and yellow that lit up the night sky and sent a rolling ball of fire and thunder across the water to upend me and knock me under. I surfaced a moment later, breathless from the explosion's impact, coughing, sputtering, and blowing water out of my nose. All around me, pieces of debris fell burning and smoking into the water, much of it no larger than my hand. I looked back to where the boat had been and saw only a burning shell.

From twenty feet away, Carl Hood shouted at me and pointed over my shoulder toward the shore. I began to swim, forgetting how tired I was, re-energized by a new awareness of simply being alive.

Flat on my back on the muddy bank, I lay staring up at the stars and trying to catch my breath in open-mouthed gulps. Carl Hood lay beside me but didn't seem nearly as winded.

When I could speak I said, "I guess I need to thank you for saving my life."

He grunted, brushing it off as lightly as if I'd thanked him for the use of a ballpoint pen.

"What are you doing here?" I asked. "Don't get me wrong, I'm glad you are, but how did you just show up in the nick of time and save the day like something out of a B-movie?"

"I was following you. I have been all day. I watched from the trees when he hit you with that pipe wrench."

"Pipe wrench. So that's what it was."

"But before I could reach the dock, he pulled you aboard, cast off the lines, and motored off. I followed around the shoreline keeping the boat in sight until he finally anchored. Then I swam out."

Hood stopped talking and stared at me across the darkness. "This guy was a friend of yours?" He finally asked.

"Lifelong," I said.

He stared at me a moment longer as if trying hard to understand my criteria for friends.

Then he asked, "He kill my daddy?"

I returned his look. "He killed them all."

Hood's gaze turned to the lake, the embers of Bucky's boat fading and blinking out as the water finally engulfed them.

"I don't suppose you'd leave me out of this?" he said. "Like I was never here?"

"But why?" I asked. "I'd be soggy toast now if not for you. You're a hero, for Christ's sake. They ought to give you a parade."

He turned back to me, unsmiling. "I got what I want." He said.

"I don't see how I can get away with this. How would I explain it?"

He stood up and looked down at me. Our eyes locked. "You're a writer," he said. "Make something up."

"I thought I was an investigative reporter," I said.

"That too," he said. "And not a bad one, either."

A compliment from Carl Hood? Who'd a thunk it? "Get the hell out of here," I said.

He gave me a short parting nod and disappeared through the trees. I went back to Bucky's lake house and called 911. My cell phone, which Bucky took from me, was probably blown to bits or at the bottom of the lake.

A week after the firestorm aboard Bucky's boat, things began to calm down. Sheriff Bagwell and other law enforcement officials grilled me long and hard, and I talked myself hoarse, telling them the story. But the discovery of Bucky's theft from McDaniel Mills did more than anything to make them believe me. After that, everything Bucky did fell into place like tumblers on a combination lock.

They ruled Bucky's death a suicide and closed the books on the murders of Cecil Hood, Grandfather, Melissa Raines, and Bobby Paige. But I didn't tell them the whole story. I kept my promise to Carl Hood and omitted the part where he came to the rescue at the last minute. I didn't even tell Eloise or Kelly about that. I spun a tale that portrayed me as inconsequential to the outcome of the events, saying that all I did was pick an opportune moment to roll out of the sheet, jump in the lake, and swim away like a man with hungry crocodiles snapping at his heels. If you removed Carl Hood and the crocodiles from the picture, that was basically what I did. Carl Hood's part would forever remain a secret between Carl and me. And I would forever remain in his debt.

I spent much time thinking about Bucky and probably always would. There was a sickness in my old friend that I didn't see, something magma-like that lay beneath the surface and bubbled and boiled until it finally erupted. It made me wonder if I really knew anyone.

The two meth-head bikers, still in jail, pled to grand larceny and a dope charge. A well-meaning but insensitive member of the District Attorney's Office told us cheerily that we'd get Grandfather's camera back in a few days. It was a thoroughly underwhelming consolation for all that had happened.

Unfortunately, I couldn't add Barry Beal's assault on Melissa Raines to the tally of crimes solved. Without her, proving it was impossible. And without Bucky, no one could say how much or how little Beal knew about things. He managed to skirt justice entirely, and I could do little about it. Beal might not have been directly responsible for anything Bucky did, but he was a catalyst for it. He set things in motion and then turned his back on them without the slightest display of guilt or responsibility. He must have known something. He couldn't have been oblivious to everything that transpired. He was also an abuser of women and, in general, a foul and disingenuous human being. Maybe he wouldn't go to jail for any of that, but I wanted desperately to believe that justice was waiting for him if in no other form than exposure someday of the man he is. At least, that was my naïve hope.

The Jeep was in the driveway, packed and ready to roll back to Atlanta. I sat on the front steps waiting for Eloise and Mackenzie to come out so we could say our goodbyes. They were still out back feeding the animals, which in this household took precedence over my leaving.

Bucky's madness was no longer front-page news, but I knew people would continue to talk about the bloody wake he left for years to come. It was a sordid and sensational story of embezzlement and murder involving the wealthiest family in the county, a beautiful valley made vacant with houses crumbling and fields and pastures giving way to weeds and erosion—but still, a valuable chunk of real estate awaiting a developer's next steps.

The good news, at least for me, was that whoever would eventually develop Eastatoe Valley—which was inevitable—wouldn't be Barry Beal. Amidst unsettled legal complexities concerning the ownership and division of properties, Beale had turned his share over to Arthur Pitt to sell. Under the flood of bad publicity and unanswered questions, Beal dropped out of the remaining PGA schedule and went to his native South Africa to play a few tournaments.

Kelly and I have spent much of our waking (and sleeping) time together. Without either of us speaking of it, we have mutually concluded that anything significant may not come of it unless one of us pulls up stakes and moves. She knows not to ask me to stay, and I know she wouldn't give up the *Clarion* to come to Atlanta. So, are we realistic enough to see that we are on divergent paths that may never merge? Time will answer that question. All I know is that I won't be the one to break it off. I'll settle for a long-distance relationship before I do that. It's the new me.

Kelly and I are also joined professionally. We'll soon be partners in the *Clarion*, albeit my role will be strictly hands-off. She and Eloise will run the paper. I agreed to sell her forty- nine percent of the company. In a miraculous act of feminine fortitude, she and Eloise descended upon the bank with plans, projections, and Kelly's new cash infusion and convinced them to renew all loans. They managed to save both the paper and Still Hollow without my help at all.

However, the *Clarion* was their dream, not mine. The need for employment took me back to Atlanta; I had a couple of job interviews set for the following week.

As to Bucky, no matter how much I try, I can't make myself hate him. I knew that he was not always an evil person. The memory I choose to carry of him is from our youth when neither of us would ever believe it possible to become a monster one day. But I can't forgive him, either. Somewhere along the way, he stepped over a line. Maybe he didn't see it or didn't even think about it. Maybe he didn't realize how hard it would be to get back once crossed; or that most paths on that side of the line lead in only one direction—into the abyss. The choice was his and no one else's.

Bucky obviously believed that what he wanted was more important than what he had to do to get it. I've come to realize that the sanctity of that *line* was Grandfather's philosophy and religion, and he, its evangelist. He tried to teach me that the choices we make chart the course of our lives and that there are lines that shouldn't be crossed, which determine whether we become worthy citizens of the human tribe or vile predators who roam the darkness beyond the cook-fires. As a boy, I could only see his antiquated dogma as that of a harsh, judgmental old man.

Now, I know that all he ever wanted was for me to recognize the fatefulness of my choices, view them with clarity, and understand the treacherous landscape that may lie on the other side of the lines we cross. And he did it because he cared for me.

Eloise and Mackenzie came out and sat down on either side of me. Eloise was holding something that looked like a hatbox wrapped in tinfoil. I suspected it was one of her gargantuan pound cakes she'd baked for me as a going-home gift.

"It's going to be lonesome around here without you, little brother," she said.

"You'll be so busy with the paper you won't miss me."

"I'm going to work there too," Mackenzie chimed in, a wide, excited smile on her face. "Kelly said I could be a reporter and cover high school stuff and youth activities—part-time, of course. I'm even thinking I might major in journalism when I go to college. What do you think, Uncle J.D.?"

"I think you have plenty of time to decide, and working on the paper will help you make that decision. But if you choose to do that, I know you'll be good at it. It's in your genes."

"Eloise," I said, "I've been thinking. I want the Cadillac if it's all right with you. I'll be back in a couple of weeks to get it." She looked at me in pure amazement. "I thought you said you didn't want it because it reminded you too much of Granddad."

"Would that be such a bad thing?" I asked.

Eloise smiled from ear to ear and handed me the cake.

EPILOGUE

Atlanta, a few months later.

On a nice, crisp Autumn day, I sat in my car at the Varsity drive-in near Georgia Tech, eating a second chili dog with onions and reading the newspaper.

"Golfer Found Dead in South African Hotel," the headline read. The story said that world-famous pro-golfer, Barry Beal, was found dead in a Johannesburg hotel, a cheese knife from a room service tray plunged in his neck. A young woman with swollen eye and clothes in disarray was seen leaving his room earlier, her name or whereabouts unknown.

An elderly curb hop came over, took my tray from the car window, scooped up the tip, and dropped the refuse into a waste can below the large metal hanging menu.

"Nice ride," he said to me.

"Thanks," I said, "I get that a lot."

I backed out and slowly drove my recently inherited vintage 1959 black Cadillac Eldorado onto North Avenue, then immediately turned right on Spring Street toward the offices of *SportsWord* magazine and a job I recently reacquired—hired by my old friend and editor, now the new Publisher, Joe Dennis. As I drove, I tried my damnedest not to smile. And failed.

"Cheese knife," I said to myself. "Who says Lady Justice doesn't have a sense of humor?"

Thank you for reading *CADILLAC TRACKS.* I hope you enjoyed it. As an independently published author, I rely on you, the reader, to spread the word. One day I may be able to spend the money to advertise like the big New York Publishers, but until then, I must count on the honest reviews of my books to help bring them to the attention of other readers. So if you enjoyed the book, please tell your friends, and if it isn't too much trouble, I would appreciate a brief review on Amazon. Thanks again. All the best, and happy reading.

-Ron

ABOUT THE AUTHOR

Ron Fisher has been a creative director and writer for several of the top advertising agencies in the country, including his own, and has won numerous awards including a Gold Lion at Cannes. Originally from South Carolina, he's lived in San Francisco, Dallas, and now Atlanta, where he can be found happily writing more J.D. Bragg mysteries.

Coming soon,
J.D. Bragg mysteries 2 and 3.

Some people would kill to be rich.
Some kill *because* they're rich.

A teenage stable boy goes missing in the uber-wealthy horse country of Upstate South Carolina. Most believe he's on the run for killing his employer's million-dollar stud horse. But the boy's brother, a bedbound paraplegic, suspects something entirely different. He asks J.D. Bragg, an old friend and ex-college football teammate, to find his brother and prove the boy's innocence. It's a request J.D. can't refuse—he's the reason his college buddy will never walk again.

You can get mad.

Or you can get even.

A young female journalist is savagely beaten and left in a coma. The police are on it. And so is J.D. Bragg. To the cops, solving the crime is just a job. But to J.D., it's personal. The journalist is the woman he loves.

Learn more about Ron & his books here.
www.ronfisherwriter.com

www.ingramcontent.com/pod-product-compliance
Lightning Source LLC
Chambersburg PA
CBHW030428310726
48979CB00009B/1670/J

* 9 7 8 1 9 4 9 0 7 3 0 2 7 *